THE WOMAN IN BLACK

Also by Erik Tarloff

Face-Time

The Man Who Wrote the Book

All Our Yesterdays

ERIK TARLOFF

THE WOMAN IN BLACK

A Vireo Book, Rare Bird Book
Los Angeles, Calif.

This is a Genuine Vireo Book

A Vireo Book | Rare Bird Books
453 South Spring Street, Suite 302
Los Angeles, CA 90013
rarebirdbooks.com

For more information, address:
A Vireo Book | Rare Bird Books Subsidiary Rights Department,
453 South Spring Street, Suite 302,
Los Angeles, CA 90013.

Set in Dante
Printed in the United States

10 9 8 7 6 5 4 3 2 1

Publisher's Cataloging-in-Publication Data
Names: Tarloff, Erik, author.
Title: The Woman in Black / Erik Tarloff.
Description: First Hardcover Original Edition | A Genuine Vireo Book |
New York, NY; Los Angeles, CA: Rare Bird Books, 2019.
Identifiers: ISBN 9781947856974
Subjects: LCSH Actors and actresses—Fiction. | Motion picture industry—
History—Fiction. | Los Angeles (Calif.—Fiction. | Hollywood (Los Angeles,
Calif.)—Fiction. | Homosexuality—Fiction. | Satire. |
BISAC FICTION / General
Classification: LCC PS3570.A626 W69 2019 | DDC 813.54--dc23

For Julie and Geoff Owen

By Way of Introduction

Gordon Frost (producer, film historian)

A S EDITOR OF THIS book, in deference to its "oral history" nature and to keep it consistent throughout, I'm speaking my few words of prologue into a recording device rather than writing anything down. And I solemnly promise not to correct any grammatical solecisms I might commit as I do so. This goes against the grain for someone like me—my students sometimes refer to me as a grammar Nazi, and I don't think they mean it affectionately—but it wouldn't be cricket to accord myself a privilege denied the others who were so generous with their time contributing to these pages. Although, to be fair, the others weren't talking in an otherwise empty room, they were always talking to me. Doing this solo does make it that much more awkward.

But, regardless! Almost every word in this volume will have been delivered orally, without notes, let alone a script. Occasionally, in the course of conducting the interviews, I've asked a question to prompt the speaker or clarify a point, and my questions do not appear in the text (although in context it's usually apparent this was the case). But the words themselves haven't been edited or altered in any way, except for the excision of a few repetitions and the occasional "er" or "uh."

Okay. I trust we've got that straight.

Many years ago, in one of my early books, I wrote that Chance Hardwick was the best actor of his generation. And of course, in the years since, I've come to regret such a stupid, such a ridiculously categorical statement. Even my students give me a hard time for it on occasion, the ones who bother to read my old books. Which, by the way, is something they *ought* to do before they sign up for my class, both as sensible preparation and as a gesture of respect. But most of them don't. Most of them don't read *anything* anymore. They think the world started the day they were born, that nothing of value happened before they came to consciousness. In the old days, at least *some* of them read, and the ones who didn't read at least knew classic films. Good God, it was a *film history* course, you'd think they might at least have some passing familiarity with movies. But they frequently come in as ignorant as stumps. Hitchcock who? Where's this Kurosawa guy from, he sounds like a foreigner? Hey, I thought Renoir was a painter. And they probably don't even know *that*.

I guess they think it can all happen in the classroom while they sit there with their mouths agape. They expect everything to be handed to them. They're used to being spoon-fed. And they no doubt think watching a movie is a lot more fun—by which I gather they mean *easier*—than reading a book, although they'd also probably prefer to watch funny clips of playful kittens on YouTube rather than a full-length film. But we don't offer YouTube courses yet, thank God. We haven't fallen that far. It's only a matter of time, though. I just hope I'm not here to see it.

But anyway, I was talking about Chance Hardwick as the best actor his generation, and my embarrassment about having asserted as much. My heavens, that was such an *extraordinary* generation, even restricting ourselves to men, and to American men at that, because those Brits always could give us a good solid run for our money, and the French came into their own after the war, Constantine and Belmondo and Delon and blah blah blah. But if we're just talking about American actors, well, most people would say Brando, of course, he's the obvious choice, and honestly, who can argue? He was astonishing. Maybe unique. But there was Monty Clift, too, and James Dean and Dennis Hopper and so many others, so many others. Including the glamor boys—no reason to be snobbish and exclude them. There were some terrific actors among them, underrated in many cases. Underrated for being so pretty, probably. As if sex appeal and talent can't coincide. Like Paul Newman and Steve McQueen, and Jack Nicholson once he got noticed, after those American International horrors...I guess it was *Easy Rider* that finally did it for him. Respect definitely took its own sweet time with Jack. Probably *self*-respect too. But I mean, gosh, the list is just endless. It was a veritable acting Renaissance. The Method investment in the '30s and '40s, those lessons everyone took with Lee Strasberg and Harold Clurman and Stella Adler and so on—commies all, incidentally—finally started paying off handsomely.

But still, Chance Hardwick was an incandescent talent. No denying that. I can't imagine there'd be too many dissenting voices. Such promise. Not *just* promise, of course. He gave us magnificent performances, and we have some magical celluloid moments. But he was just getting started when he was taken from us, and damn it, I do still believe that had he lived, he might be remembered as the greatest of them all. Which is what prompted the fatuous sentiment I began with. The promise. He was like Schubert, plucked from us way too early. If Beethoven had died at the age Schubert died, we'd think of him as a relatively minor composer with enormous potential. It's a sobering thought, no?

And of course Chance was a *movie star* as well. That might have come second in *his* mind, but stars do have some special quality that ordinary actors, even ordinary *great* actors, lack. Call it star quality, call it charisma, call it magic. Whatever it is, the great ones, the ones who become legends have it. Even if they aren't actually great actors. Take Monroe, for example. Compared to some of her contemporaries, you would hardly call her a master of her craft. But she didn't need to be. The camera loved her. She was luminous. She was a *star*. And that's the thing about stars. You can't take your eyes off them, and you somehow feel you have a personal relationship with them. You *fall in love with them*.

Chance had that magic in spades. If you want proof, just look at the fan clubs that still exist, still are thriving more than half a century after his death. Or the posters you can still find in college dorms all over the country. In Europe, too; Hardwick paraphernalia remains a minor industry in France. You can buy bad portraits of him in Montmartre, not just the entrance to Central Park. His face is on T-shirts and cigarette lighters and coffee cups and God knows what other tacky crap. Probably mostly purchased by American tourists, but still. Or consider that old lady, that mysterious old lady dressed all in black, who still lays flowers on his grave every year on the anniversary of his drowning. I don't know if she was a fan or a woman who had some sort of personal relationship with him, but she's been devoted to his memory for over fifty years. That's not a casual attachment.

Now, in case I'm leaving a false impression, let me stress that I never actually met the man. My students think I'm ancient, but I'm not *that* ancient. I was ten or so when he drowned. Unlike the people whose interviews you'll find herein, my familiarity with him comes from watching his movies. Watching them closely and repeatedly and analytically. Literally frame by frame in many cases. And from talking to so many people who *did* know him, which of course is how this book has come about, indeed what it entirely consists of. So I can't talk personally about what he was like as a human being. Plenty of others can and will do that. It's the reason I conducted those interviews and assembled this book.

It's the fruit of several decades' work. I started these interviews in the late 1980s. At first simply to satisfy my own curiosity, I wanted to talk to the people who knew Chance Hardwick and gather their impressions before they passed from the scene. I began by talking with the people a generation older than he, folks who'd known him as a boy and young man, along with those who had already reached their middle years when they had dealings with him. This may have been a macabre calculation on my part, but it seemed an actuarially sound strategy, and one which has been vindicated by time: Most of those people left us ages ago. I've spent many years since, in the intervals between teaching and writing—and a relatively brief few years producing several independent films of my own, quite unsuccessfully, I regret to say—hunting down people who'd played a role in Hardwick's adult years. Some remain prominent and were easy to find. Others required a fair amount of digging. At a certain point, it struck me that I was no longer doing this only out of casual interest; I was aware it was turning into a book. My third book about Chance Hardwick. [laughs] Did someone say "obsession?"

In my own defense, Hardwick continues to arouse fascination and enthusiasm among movie lovers the world over. As a student of cinema—and dare I say it, as a *fan*, because after all these years of study I remain a fan above all else, certainly above being a film scholar—the most I can do is attest to his artistry, and say wholeheartedly that if any actor has ever deserved an oral history, which is, I suppose, a kind of thespian beatification, it would be Chance Hardwick.

The boy could do *anything*. He disappeared into whatever role he was playing. You forgot he was acting. He just *became* the character. Vocally, physically, every way. And he was *so* beautiful. A Greek god. More mesmerizing than Brando, cooler than Paul Newman. He was already a star when he died, as I've said, but he was going to be gigantic. The biggest. And then...well, you know...it all got to be too much for him. A soul as delicate as that, he just couldn't handle the bullshit that came with fame.

The fan clubs, the paparazzi, the autograph seekers, the movie magazines, the gossip columns, the impossibility of leading a normal life or enjoying an anonymous minute...it simply overwhelmed him. He was by all accounts a simple soul in many ways, not with regard to his artistry, never that, but in his private life. And fame complicated that life beyond his ability to handle it. Now, make no mistake, he wanted fame, he hungered for it, he didn't go to Hollywood in order to be a nobody. Ambition was a key element of his character. Everyone who knew him seems to agree on that. But you can't prepare for the actual experience of fame. You can't begin to know what it's going to be like until it happens to you. And with Chance, it hit him like an oncoming tractor-trailer.

So yes, he was a star. But the important thing to remember, the thing always to bear in mind, is that Chance Hardwick was an artist. He was an artist before he was a star. The stardom was almost incidental. He lived to act. He was like an acting votary. And possibly the purest talent I've ever seen. And along with it, as a natural concomitant, the most sensitive personality. A naked, scintillating ganglion. No insulation, no protection. That receptivity is what made his acting so powerful, and of course it's also what destroyed him.

The Witnesses (in order of appearance)

Gordon Frost (producer, film historian)

Mary Bennett (aunt)

Caitlin Kelly (elementary school classmate)

Anne Thayer (teacher)

Ned Fitzgerald (elementary school classmate)

Joel Weingott (boyhood friend)

Dorothy Goren Mckenzie (sister)

Helen Campbell (junior high school drama coach)

Haley Jackson (junior high school classmate)

Derek Stephens (actor in Downtown Players)

Amy McCandless (actor in Downtown Players)

Terri Howe (high school classmate)

Morton Brock (high school guidance counselor)

Wilson Denny (college roommate)

George Berlin (English professor)

Nancy Hawkins (girlfriend)

Leon Shriver (actor)

Michael Strachan (writer)

Ellie Greenfield Lerner (girlfriend)

Don Barlow (director)

Kendell Fowler (actress)

Robert Bluestone (actor)

David Bayer (acquaintance)

Eppy Bronstein (widow of agent)

Gil Fraser (roommate)

Irma Gold (agent)

Matthew Devon (actor)

Gerhard Fuchs (musician)

James Sterling (acting teacher)

Sir Trevor Bliss (director)

Mike Shore (stand-in)

Kathy Brennan (first president, Chance Hardwick Fan Club)

Briel Charpentier (girlfriend)

Hector Mennen (acquaintance)

Dennis O'Neill (detective, LAPD Vice Squad, Retired)

David Osborne (director)

Buddy Moore (actor)

Alison McAllister (actress)

Benny Ludlow (comedian)

Charles Cox (director)

Dolores Murray (actress)

Bruce Powers (actor)

Mark Cernovic (producer)

Jerome Goldhagen, MD (psychiatrist)

Martha Davis (reporter, Variety)

Heather Brooke (neighbor)

Bernice Franklin (secretary)

Ward Paulsen (Memorial Park groundskeeper)

THE EARLY YEARS

Mary Bennett (aunt)

He was the cutest baby you ever saw. Not that all babies aren't cute, of course. Don't you think? Just the sweetest little things. But still, I truly believe if my sister had wanted it and if we lived where those kinda things happen, Chance could've been a professional baby model, like that darling drawing on the Gerber's jar. That's how adorable he was. Everybody said so. A little angel. Strangers would stop us on the street to coo.

[Starts to cry] Sorry...It's been so many years, I ought to be used to it by now, but when I start to think about him...I mostly try not to, you know, but you're here, you're asking about him, and... it was such a tragedy...such a loss...I loved that boy like he was my own child. Give me a second, okay?

[Deep breath] Okay, I'm gonna start again. Sorry. Please forgive a silly old lady.

Now let me say this about his name. I know some people believe it was those Hollywood types, those movie moguls, who gave him the name "Chance," that Chance was some kind of actor name, like, I don't know, "Rock" or "Tab." Well, that just ain't true. Now, it's a fact he was *christened* Wendell, that much is so, but I don't recollect anyone ever calling him that, except maybe *me* once or twice when he was being really naughty, giving me some sass, and maybe a couple of teachers in grade school at the beginning of the school year when they didn't know any better, just reading off the roll call. But from the start, well...you can't talk to a baby and use the name Wendell, can you? No way a name like that's gonna fit a darling little bundle of sweetness.

See, Wendell was his dad's name and Wendell Sr. insisted his son be a Jr. Typical. He was a real conceited person, Wendell Sr.

was. Everything had to be about him. So naturally his son had to have his name. He basically forced the name on him—on all of us, come to that. Sally and I didn't like it. Sally was my little sister, Chance's mom. We argued with ol' Wendell, but he was kind of bullheaded, and also kind of a bully, and he put his foot down and that was that. He wasn't the kind of fella who'd brook any insubordination, especially not from women folk. And so Chance was christened Wendell Jr., it was a done deal, it's right there on the birth certificate. And wouldn't you know it, soon after that his dad just upped and skedaddled. Insisted on a rule change and right away quit the game. So long, Wendell, it's been good to know you. Don't let the door hit your fanny on the way out.

Good riddance to bad rubbish, I say. Although I'm not sure Sally saw it exactly that way. Not at the time, anyhow. I told her so, lotsa times, but she always acted like she didn't wanna hear it. Even got a little snippy with me, something she didn't usually do. "You just stop that talk, Mary. No one asked you for your two cents." I guess I can understand why. She was still a young gal, Big Wendell kind of swept her off her feet when she was fresh out of high school, and besides, everyone knows love makes you stupid. And listen, Sally, God rest her soul, always was a wild one, she didn't consider consequences when she wanted something. Left it to the rest of us to pick up the pieces. And by the rest of us, I guess I mean *me*, her big sister. And Big Wendell was something she thought she wanted. At least at first. Maybe always. I'm not sure she ever got over him, although the good Lord knows she tried.

He left so soon after Chance came along I thought we maybe ought to just rechristen Chance as something else. Mike or Tom or anything normal. But Sally couldn't be bothered. That was Sally for you. She'd go to a lot of trouble to avoid a little bit of trouble.

So like I was saying, *little* Wendell was always so active and lively and mischievous, so full of ginger and energy and zest, seemed so heedless of danger, always going right up to the edge of things, that we took to calling him Chance. From early on. From the time he could move on his own, darn near. He was always taking chances, didn't even seem to know they *were* chances. So that was no Hollywood name. The boy was always in a dither, grabbing at electric cords, grabbing at pots and pans, climbing up rickety structures, so that's why he was called Chance. And the name stuck. He was always Chance. From the get-go.

Matter of fact, he told me once that those Hollywood boys wanted him to change it. Probably to Rock or Tab. But he wouldn't do it. He'd got to liking the name Chance. Insisted on keeping it.

Caitlin Kelly (elementary school classmate)

SURE, I REMEMBER CHANCE. I'd've remembered him anyhow, I'm blessed with that kind of recall. But once, you know, he became famous, everybody started talking about how we all went to school with him and how amazing it was that we'd grown up with someone the whole world knew about. It became a badge of distinction. As a rule, famous people don't come from these parts. I can't think of a single one besides Chance Hardwick. But like I say, I would've remembered him anyhow.

Partly because he was the cutest boy in our class. That likely wouldn't have registered in the early grades, but by the fifth or sixth, all us girls were starting to look at boys in that different way, we were all beginning to find boys, you know, attractive. We used the word "cute" back then, it was safer than "attractive," I guess, or maybe being attracted to somebody was still too new an idea for us to get our heads around. I mean, our bodies were sending us messages we weren't ready to deal with yet.

But Chance was real cute. Quiet, though. Shy. I don't think he knew how cute he was, or maybe knowing it just made him uncomfortable. Some guys are like that. Being handsome makes it harder to be invisible. He didn't speak up much in class, either. I don't reckon he was an especially good student or anything. Seems now like we all underestimated him. But in fact, I remember once, I think this was in the sixth grade before we all went on to junior high, they gave us some sort of IQ test or achievement test or something of that nature, and apparently Chance did better than anyone else in class, like way off the charts, and everybody who knew him was shocked. The principal, our teachers, all us kids. Because he never made much of an impression that way at all.

When the results came back, we had some sort of assembly, and our sixth grade teacher, Miss Thayer, said, "Chance Hardwick! Where have you been hiding all these years?" And we all laughed. Everybody but Chance. He just blushed this deep, deep red. He was so embarrassed. I honestly think he would've deliberately done badly on the test if he'd known he was gonna get all that attention.

It's funny he became a movie star, huh? Someone in the public eye, someone everybody stared at. You don't imagine a really shy kid's gonna be famous, unless he's maybe a scientist or a computer inventor or Stephen King or something. Doing something you do in private. In a way, even though he was so cute, he was like the last person you'd expect.

Anne Thayer (teacher)

OH YES, CHANCE WAS deep. We used to give the kids this standardized achievement test in the sixth grade—the TBS, it's called. It was supposed to measure a student's mastery of the basics, and Chance tested through the roof. It wasn't an IQ test, strictly speaking, but still, his scores were so amazing you'd have to say he was genius level. A lot of people were surprised at how well he did. I wasn't. See, I'd graded his math tests, I'd seen his little essays and things. We didn't assign a lot of writing back then, though we did try to get the kids proficient at verbal expression before they went on to junior high. And not only could Chance write beautifully, he expressed very profound thoughts. I won't say I knew he would go far, because you never can be sure about that kind of thing, but I definitely was aware he was special.

Mary Bennett

WHEN SALLY MARRIED STEVE—THAT was her second husband, Steve Goren—things changed a lot. In a way, it was good she met Steve, 'cause she'd had a couple of wild years. I'm not going to tell you about them, you'll just have to take my word for it. That's how wild they were. I'm not even going to tell you how she met Steve. Some things decent folk don't talk about.

I never much liked Steve myself, and I didn't like what happened after at *all*, but I can't deny he was good for Sally in some ways. I don't know she ever really *loved* Steve, not like how she felt about Wendell anyways, but he was a pretty good dancer, he could do man-type things like change the tire if you had a flat or fix the plumbing, and he turned out to be steady in ways I wouldn't have guessed. I mean, given the way they met and all, you might have expected he'd be another good-for-nothing, like Wendell. That was Sally's type, anyway, the good-for-nothings. She liked the bad boys. Probably thought Steve *was* a bad boy, probably was disappointed to learn he was a solid, upstanding citizen. But by then it was too late. She was already pregnant with Dot and she wasn't going to let herself be single again. Not without a struggle, anyway.

Ned Fitzgerald (elementary school classmate)

CHANCE AND I HAD a fistfight in the fifth grade, one afternoon after school. I don't remember exactly what it was about. We weren't friends, we weren't enemies, we weren't much of anything, even though we'd known each other since we were six. He was just part of the ecosystem for me, is how I remember it, and I can't imagine I was more than that for him. So it's hard for me to even guess what could have set us off.

But if I'm being honest, I'd have to surmise it was my doing much more than his. Chance was a quiet guy, a shy guy. He kept to himself, so I can't really picture him initiating hostilities. It wouldn't just have been out of character, it's almost literally unimaginable. I must have started picking on him. Not for any reason, just to do it. I was a shitty kid back then, to be completely honest with you. A bully. A crappy home life can do that to you. I'm not at all like that now, and it still gives me a twinge to recall some of my behavior, but back then...I mean, I was a good athlete, I was big for my age, I was kind of an alpha dog. Even had my own posse, a group of guys who hung out with me, and I was more or less the ringleader of whatever we got up to.

Just considering the possibilities now, Chance's being good-looking might have been enough to set me off. Plain old jealous resentment, even at age ten. Or his being so shy and quiet. That can be like a red flag in front of a bull to some people, especially if they imagine the shy and quiet kid is observing and judging them. You want a reaction, you want a hint of what they're thinking. You're afraid they're registering more than you want them to see. And I had plenty of issues of my own, of course. My home life was... well, this is about Chance Hardwick, not about me, but I'm just trying to indicate I was more troubled than I would have admitted to anyone. Took me years to understand myself.

But the bottom line is, it's hard to say what's going to enrage a kid with unresolved anger issues when the hormones are starting to roil. Maybe—and this is the worst possibility, but I'm trying to level with you—maybe he struck me as so vulnerable, such an easy, inviting target, I just couldn't resist. Throw my weight around, make my dominance that much clearer. And I probably intuitively thought, given his vulnerability, and the unlikelihood of his being able to fight back, that not only would he be an easy mark but the other kids would side with me. That's how kids are…no, it's how we *primates* are…we side with the aggressor more often than not, regardless of who's in the right. It isn't a pretty picture. We aren't a pretty species. Believe me, I know what I'm talking about.

Anyway, I think I started goading him in some way. Maybe I called him "faggot," although I wouldn't have even known what that meant. But that wouldn't have stopped me. I would have had some instinct the accusation would draw blood one way or another. Or maybe I said something about his mom. She had a bit of a reputation in town, and news of it might have reached my ears. Again, without my knowing what it even meant, or what "having a reputation" *is*, but I might have had an instinct it was a profitable wound to probe. And, you know, I could tell it had something to do with sex, and at that age sex has a unique sort of power, since you don't really know anything about it but you can already feel its stirrings. Which are, let's face it, unruly, both scary and enticing at the same time. And clearly taboo. In any case, I swear I can't recall now what got us fighting.

But I can picture it. By which I mean, I can still see the setting in my mind's eye. We were in this empty undeveloped lot a block or two from the school, just dirt and weeds, and a whole bunch of kids had followed us there to watch the show. Because that's what Homo sapiens are like. It's why boxing is popular, and even pro football. The violence. If they brought back gladiatorial games, you can bet they'd be the most popular thing going. So the other kids formed a circle around us, and as I indicated, I believe they were rooting for me to give him a really sound thrashing. They would have made up a reason to explain why it was justified, even though there was absolutely no justification. "He had it coming," that sort of bullshit. "He had it coming because yadda yadda yadda." But it wasn't really justice they were after, it was spectacle.

So we were in the center of this throng, in the middle of this overgrown vacant lot, and we were kind of circling each other, scoping each other out. I was mainly trying to figure out where to start on him. I figured I could call the shots. And then, suddenly, without any warning, Chance came at me. Just flew right at me. Amazingly fast. And the point is, contrary to my expectations, I got my ass handed to me. Chance was a slight kid, a skinny kid as I've indicated, and like I said, at least in those days a recessive personality. Completely unthreatening in the aspect he presented. I figured that after I threw the first punch he'd roll himself up into a little ball and cower on the ground while I rained blows down on him and everybody jeered.

Well, that isn't how it worked.

He was a fricking firecracker. Fast, fierce, fearless. Wiry, with that kind of tensile strength that isn't necessarily visible to the naked eye. And full of wrath…there was a lot of anger hidden in the guy, a lot of rage roiling around inside him. I could *feel* it all of a sudden. He seemed so placid normally, but you just can't ever tell what's going on with those quiet types. His rage, once he let it out, it was like coiled fire, there was a…an *exultant* quality to the way he went at me. Hit me in the face before I knew what was happening, then in the stomach, really hard, knocking the wind out of me, then, when I doubled over, gasping for breath, another blow to the face. After that it was effectively over. I went down. I was on my knees, and I made a move to get up—mostly because I still couldn't believe what was happening—and he hit me in the face again, and that was totally that. I wasn't unconscious, but I couldn't make my body do what I told it to do. Not that I was in any mood to get up anyway.

And the crowd cheered him—their loyalties had turned on a dime, it's the way of the world—and he immediately strode off without uttering a syllable. No victory dance, no snarling insults, no gloating. Just *vamoose*. I saw a couple of kids clap him on the back as he left, but he sort of shrugged them off. And from my rather special vantage point I could see he was crying. Silently. I'm not sure how many others noticed, because he just quick-stepped out of there. And I stayed down for a while, partly because I was hurting but mostly because I was too humiliated to get up and face everybody.

I was pretty banged up. When I got home, my parents wanted me to go the hospital, but I refused. I just wanted to hide out in my room. And then my dad forced me to go to school the next day. He was that kind of guy. I think it was punishment for losing the fight. He thought losers lose because they deserve to lose. Of course, I didn't want to show my face in school. In addition to what everybody would have heard about my humiliating defeat, I had a black eye and what we used to call "a fat lip." I was a walking PSA against bullying. But I had to face the music, and in the event it was just about as bad as I imagined it would be. There was a lot of mockery. My alpha dog status had evidently evanesced over night.

Mary Bennett

CHANCE AND STEVE NEVER got along. I don't know how hard either of them tried, maybe not very, but if they did, it just never took. When Sally urged Chance to call Steve "Dad," he said, "No way, Mom. Not gonna happen." And when Steve suggested Chance take his last name, become a Goren, the boy just laughed in his face and said something about hell freezing over, pardon my French. And the good Lord knows it wasn't out of loyalty to old Wendell, who he never really knew. It was about Steve's own self.

Now, I say it was about Steve, but it could be Chance wasn't going to cotton to anyone his mom married no matter what. He had her all to himself—to the extent anyone had Sally—and now he had to share her. A boy's going to resent that intrusion.

But there was also something about Steve in particular, he really rubbed Chance the wrong way. He was loud, he was in-your-face, he told bad jokes, he crowded you. It was like he had a personality especially designed to drive Chance bananas.

And make no mistake, Steve returned the favor. At first he tried to pretend he liked the kid, tried to josh him, brought him a few pieces of athletic equipment, as if Chance would care about athletic equipment, took him fishing on a couple of Saturdays, but it felt phony all along, and it didn't last. Steve just found Chance a pest. An annoyance. Him and Sally had just gotten hitched, she was expecting, he didn't want a souvenir from her previous marriage in his hair all the time. He wanted to go out and have fun, he wanted to make whoopee at home.

And then Dorothy came along, and that was the final nail in the coffin. Steve was nuts about Dot. I'm not sure he was thrilled when Sally got in the family way, I don't think that was part of his game plan when they started spending time together, but once she brought Dot home, he just fell head over heels in love. And of course Chance could see that, and feel hurt by it. And Steve no longer wanted to give Chance the time of day. He had a kid of his own now, not somebody else's he was saddled with. He was short with Chance, took the belt to him more than once, complained to Sally about him. "Your kid" is how he'd refer to him. "What's the matter with your kid? Why's he so soft? How come he don't like sports? Why's he so rude to me?" That kind of thing. Poor Sally didn't know how to handle it. She was well and truly caught. And what with Dot in the picture...well, you can imagine who's going to come up tails in that kind of predicament. A husband and baby daughter on one side, a kind of sullen, resentful growing boy on the other. Sally did her best, but her best was none too good.

Which is why Chance finally came to live with Earl and me. I don't guess anyone was too happy with the arrangement, not at first anyway, but things were coming to a head and something had to give. And we were childless and we had an extra room. So me and Earl, we talked it over, and I have to say Earl was good about it. Chance was no blood kin of Earl's, and not an easy kid to get along with, but Earl said, "Hey, it's the Christian thing to do." Earl was like that when he had to talk himself into doing the right thing, he had to bring up Jesus. Add Jesus's voice to the discussion, give Him an opportunity to weigh in. But that's fine. Whatever it took. At least he did what was right more often than not. And whether he liked it or not.

Joel Weingott (boyhood friend)

CHANCE AND ME, WE became friends the summer we were at camp together. No way we could have met anywhere else. We came from totally different worlds. Different universes. We were thirteen or fourteen at the time. I had my fourteenth birthday that summer, in fact. At camp. Not much of a celebration. The previous one had been a big deal, though—big ritual, big party, lots of presents, more horah than you can shake a stick at, so I guess I shouldn't complain.

The camp was a dude ranch type thing out in Wyoming. I was a New York kid, my background was about as far from a dude ranch as you can get. I guess my parents thought hanging out in the country would be good for me. Or maybe…see, I have this weird notion that what gave them the idea was that I was a big fan of cowboy movies when I was younger. There were a lot of them back then. Singing cowboys like Gene Autry and Roy Rogers, tough guy cowboys like Johnny Mack Brown and John Wayne, and also real actors, serious dramatic actors, who occasionally took cowboy roles, like Henry Fonda and James Stewart. And I liked them all. Well, not the singing cowboys so much, even then they struck me as kind of ridiculous, but most of the others. My mom used to drop me off at those Saturday matinées, you'd be there all day, there would often be two full-length feature films and a dopey newsreel and a cartoon and a serial, all for a dime, what a deal, but I only wanted to go if they were showing at least one western. And so, in addition to probably thinking a radical change of scene would be good for me, just on general principle, getting out of the city into a whole new environment, fresh air and allergens, my folks must have also thought, because I liked movies about cowboys and horses and the open prairie so much, I'd enjoy the reality too.

Ha!

Of course I hated it from the start. Jesus, I was a city kid. Manhattan was my natural habitat. I could navigate New York with ease, buses and subways held no terrors for me, but anywhere else I was a lost soul. Central Park was a breeze, but mountains and valleys were hostile territory. Horses were nice to look at, but we had nothing to say to one another. Plus I hated sharing a bunkhouse with all these boys I didn't know. Most of them farm kids from other parts of the country who sneered at the whole idea of New York, and therefore sneered at *me*. They mostly seemed to have a hick sense of humor, too, which was off-putting; joking around was what made kids like me friends with other kids. It could be the entire basis of a friendship, finding the same things funny. Well, no chance of that. A lot of them had notions about Jews, too. Most of them had never met a member of the tribe before, but that didn't slow them down. They had their prejudices and they were convinced these were fact-based. I don't mean to suggest it was like *Hitlerjugend* or anything, it wasn't some sort of hate-fest, but I definitely felt isolated and disregarded and casually disliked. Tolerated at best. The butt of mean jokes at worst. There were a lot of mean jokes. A lot of feeling around my head trying to find my horns, that sort of stuff.

Or maybe they weren't even kidding.

And the thing is, Chance hated the place too. That was what first brought us together. That was our initial bond. He later told me his stepfather had arranged for him to go. "He wanted to get me out of his hair for a while," is how he put it. And then he added, "And he doesn't even have any!" That made me laugh. But he was obviously pissed about the whole thing. He said his stepdad wanted to send him to boarding school too. That's where his mom drew the line. But she didn't put up a fuss about summer camp since it was supposed to be a treat for him. She could pretend they were doing him a favor. And even though he told her he didn't want to go, that carried no weight whatsoever. Boy, did I recognize *that* particular dynamic. Accents aside, it was identical to the conversation I had with my mom. Chance's mom just blithely assured him he was wrong, he really *did* want to go—typical parent bullshit—and anyway, once he got there, he'd love it.

Ha!

Now, to be clear, Chance was...well, he wasn't exactly a farm kid, but he did come from a rural area, from a small town surrounded by farmland. A lot of the kids he went to school with were farmers' kids. So he wasn't as obviously out of his element as me. But camp life definitely was not his cup of tea. Like me, he disliked the regimentation, he disliked the chores, and he really *hated* the communality. He hated that aspect even more than I did, possibly. He was a loner by temperament. A private person. I think he liked the horses a lot, that's one way we differed, he seemed to have a real feeling for them, but he didn't want to be told when he could ride and when he couldn't. And he didn't want to be in a group when he did it, he wanted a personal communion between himself and the horse. He'd sometimes sneak into the stables and just hang out. He let me come with him a couple of times, a meaningful gesture coming from someone like Chance, and it was almost uncanny, the emotional way he connected with those animals.

See, the essence of his personality, at least as I understood it, was his need for privacy. He wanted to be able to go off by himself when he felt like it, just go for a walk or sit under a tree and daydream. And they wouldn't let him do that. Everything had to be done according to a set schedule and as part of a group. Maybe it was because of their insurance policy, maybe they had to have the kids under their charge at all times, or maybe they were just those kind of people. But it sure didn't sit well with Chance.

And then, toward the end of the first week, Chance and I were both given KP duty. That's work in the kitchen if you don't know. It was punishment. KP was supposed to be punishment because it was considered girlie. As far as I was concerned, other chores, like mucking out the stables, were much worse, but mine was a minority view. And speaking of minority views, that's how come Chance and I were being punished. Every night after supper there was a camp meeting where we sung those dumb camp songs like "Bill Hogan's Goat," and then there'd be a little lecture by the head counselor, one Mr. Monty MacBride, whose official title was "Foreman." Of course it was. And then there'd be a prayer to Jesus, which got all the other kids to stare at me and see what I'd do at the "Amen" part. I kept my head down and my mouth shut. Some battles just aren't worth fighting, although I think if my parents knew about that part they'd have been outraged. Might have even pulled me out of camp. Hey, maybe I should have told them! But it's funny, because I bet I knew more about the New Testament than those kids who were lording it over me. [laughs] *Lording it over me!* I didn't mean it that way. Anyhow, to them it was just a matter of rooting for the home team, their captain was Jesus, and it didn't matter so much what He stood for, they rooted for their team and their captain and wanted the other teams to lose and that was that.

But we also got that regularly scheduled sermon from the Foreman, and it was usually obnoxious and ill-informed. And one night it was about…jeez, it's hard to remember whether this was the warning about the mortal dangers of masturbation or the heads-up about Communism, but it was something deeply stupid, and Chance and I both laughed at the same moment. That was apparently a big no-no. So we were punished by being assigned KP for the next week. Now, I didn't mind nearly as much as I was supposed to, although I acted upset so Monty wouldn't change his mind. KP was about as close to solitude as you could get in that hellhole. It was almost a relief.

I'd been vaguely aware of Chance already because he was so quiet. That probably sounds like a paradox, but it was a really raucous group of boys there at the camp, so someone who hung back, who didn't holler and laugh really loud at things that weren't funny, he kind of attracted my attention. But I didn't know anything about him, and certainly didn't feel particularly drawn to him. There was nothing inviting about him. His whole manner seemed to say, "Keep your distance." And the other guys *did* keep their distance. Unlike me, he didn't have anything obvious to pick on, so they just left him alone, by and large.

But this one morning we were in the kitchen together washing the breakfast dishes. The camp didn't have a dishwasher, God forbid there should be any modern conveniences, that would have violated the whole camp aesthetic. He was washing and I was drying and stacking and we weren't saying anything, just each doing the chore and sulking in silence. Which wasn't my usual way, sulking out loud was how I generally handled it, but I'd come to realize this was a place where I'd be better off keeping my trap shut, no one wanted to hear from me, and they certainly didn't want to hear any complaints from me. I'd been confronted with the phrase "whiney Jew" more than once already. So I'd learned that lesson.

And then, out of the blue, as he handed me a wet plate, Chance said, "Tell me something, Joel. Do you hate this place as much as I do?"

It was downright startling. He'd barely said a word up to then. I needed a second to process the question, and then I said, "At least."

Chance nodded and granted me that small twisted smile I came to know well. And a few years later, the whole world came to know it just as well, a sort of Chance Hardwick trademark, a significant aspect of what was said to make him such an icon of cool. A wordless, mordantly amused acknowledgment of the world's crappiness. He was quiet for a few seconds after that, and then he said, "All the other guys seem to love it. Is there something wrong with us, do you reckon?"

"Uh huh," I said. "There absolutely is. It's a serious problem. We're not idiots."

Which got a rare laugh out of him. "Do you ever wish you were?"

"An idiot? Can't say I do."

"No? I do. All the time. Well, maybe not an idiot, but I wish I could fit in better. Not just here. Everywhere."

"You don't fit in at home either? "

"Hell no." He snorted his incredulity at the notion. Then he extended his wet hand and introduced himself. We shook. As Rick Blaine would say, it was the beginning of a beautiful friendship.

Dorothy Goren Mckenzie (sister)

I DIDN'T SEE THAT much of Chance growing up. He was living with Uncle Earl and Aunt Mary, and he'd come by once a week or so for dinner and he'd babysit me now and then or take me to a movie matinée on a Saturday afternoon, or sometimes let me come to one of his play rehearsals if I promised to be quiet. I mean, he was nice enough to me, but he acted more like an uncle than a brother, maybe. 'Cause of the age difference, I guess. And because we weren't living in the same house.

But he didn't treat me like an enemy, which I guess he could've, seeing as how my dad and him were usually fighting like cats and dogs. I hated that, by the way. It was always tense when those two were together. And listen, it's not like anyone ever made me choose sides or anything, but I felt like I was caught in the middle all the same. Looking back, I can't honestly tell you who was right and who was wrong. Probably both were right and both were wrong. But at the time, I looked up to my dad, as little girls do, and I also looked up to my big brother, which is also what little girls do. So I hated that they were always fighting when they were together. It made me sick to my stomach. Literally sick to my stomach. It must've had the same effect on my mom, although she didn't say so. Not to me, anyway. And you know, when I was little, like I said, I looked up to my dad, but later, when I was a teenager, we had lots of problems, him and me. Lots. Finally we were like almost completely estranged. We barely spoke at all after a certain point, and it pretty much stayed like that till the day he died. I'm not saying he was a bad man, exactly, but he wasn't an *easy* person. And he probably wasn't what you'd call a *good* man either. He could be awful mean. This wasn't something I felt I could talk to my mom about. She had her own problems.

I would have loved to have been able to confide in Chance during my high school years, he's the one I would have naturally turned to, and I have no doubt he would've been sympathetic, would've understood better than anyone else. But he was already gone. We were in touch in one way and another, and he definitely was aware I was having problems at home, but he was in college and then he was living in New York and then LA, and long-distance phone calls were kind of a production, so I can't say he was really there for me. He was sympathetic, he was willing to listen when he was within range, but it wasn't possible for him to be some sort of mainstay. I had to deal with my dad on my own.

Anyway, what I'm trying to say is, the fact that Steve Goren was my dad—my biological dad—could have been enough to make Chance dislike me when we were growing up, but it didn't. Plus he could have resented how I'd kind of taken his place in our mom's affections, or even pushed him out of the house. You know, new husband, new baby, there wasn't as much time for him as there used to be. And my dad made no secret of who he cared about more. Chance became a kind of afterthought at best. If he thought about him at all. But Chance didn't seem to blame any of that on me. He was even affectionate in his own way. I wouldn't say he was *good at it* or anything—[laughs]—but he made an effort. He did more than he had to. It's my impression he cared about me all along, and cared *for* me. In his own way.

And I adored him. My beautiful big brother. He was a total mystery to me, same way I guess he was to practically everybody, but I idolized him.

We became something like friends later, but even when he was kind of a distant figure to me, I worshiped him. From the start.

Helen Campbell (junior high school drama coach)

CHANCE SIGNED UP FOR the Drama Club in the ninth grade. He later—much later, when he was back in town visiting his mom and his aunt for Christmas—he told me he did it only because it was offered as an alternative to Phys Ed. In the seventh and eighth grades all the kids had to go to gym, but their last year they had a choice. Not many boys took advantage—they all loved sports, or thought they had to pretend to love 'em to prove they weren't, you know, sissies. Effeminate. But Chance didn't care about that stuff, and he really detested competitive games. He had no burning interest in theater, I don't believe, not at the time. He just wanted to avoid playing sports. Which is interesting, since he was actually a terrific natural athlete. And he moved beautifully on stage. He just didn't like all the macho stuff, the braggadocio and the physical violence that seem an unavoidable aspect of adolescent athletics.

But that put him in a pretty good position in terms of casting. When it came to good male roles, he didn't have a heck of a lot of competition. A handful of doughy nerds and one Greek god. I mean, who would *you* cast?

Still, before he was admitted into the class, he had to audition. We used to make *all* the kids audition. The audition was more an initiation ritual than a *real* audition, of course. I can't remember ever turning anyone down, even when they were awful. But we pretended it was a test, and the kids sometimes got a little nervous about having to perform. Partly because they apparently believed their participation might really hang in the balance, but also because performing in front of a group of people is always intimidating. I used to ask the kids to do a little wordless mime. Of their own devising. They could choose what it would consist of.

Chance didn't seem at all nervous before he did *his* little bit. Maybe he was too confident to be worried, or more likely he just didn't care that much. He rarely seemed to care much about anything. That shrugging teenage disengagement was part of his affect no matter what was really going on inside him. Anyway, when it was his turn, he chose to do something very simple. Just pretended to eat a dish of ice cream. That's all. He sat at an empty table at the front of the classroom and mimed eating a dish of ice cream. And it was totally riveting. We could all see the dish, his left hand steadying it. We could all see the ice cream. We could feel its icy resistance to his imaginary spoon. We could feel how cold it was when it went into his mouth, hurting his teeth, and then taste how delicious it was. His use of sense memory was completely intuitive and technically perfect. So it was obvious to me from the start that this kid had astonishing talent.

I'm no pro, I don't pretend to be, but I'd done a lot of community theater, and I'd worked with kids in theater classes for years, and I'd never before seen anything to compare with this. It was as if Marcel Marceau had accidentally wandered into my classroom.

At first, I was a little concerned that, no matter how amazing he was at mime, maybe he wouldn't be so good verbally. He was so shy, and apparently so inarticulate—a mumbler—that my worries weren't based on nothing. But another thing I did, I always had the kids recite poetry at our first class meeting. Again, mostly just to get them used to declaiming in front of other people. And once again, he simply blew me away. He read "My Last Duchess." That Browning thing? It was his choice, by the way…I didn't know he was a reader, but apparently he was. A secret reader. And it was a revelation. He was shattering. The speaker of the poem became this vivid, self-deluding monster oblivious to his own malevolence. It was hair-raising. And exhilarating. For me, it was almost like what people say it was like to see Brando in *I Remember Mama*.

Haley Jackson (junior high school classmate)

I WAS IN CHANCE's first play. You might say I got his career off to its start, ha ha. It was a little one-act, a two-hander as they say. Just Chance and me. We performed it at a school assembly one afternoon.

I honestly can't remember much about the play itself. Not the title, not the author, not the plot. But I do remember Chance and I had to kiss in it. That was a big deal in those days. Kissing wasn't something kids took lightly. Lots of embarrassed giggling when we read the play and realized what it would entail, as you might imagine. Actual kissing! In front of people! And with permission! My gosh! And to do it with Chance Hardwick! What an opportunity! It was like a dream come true. When I was chosen for the girl part, all the other girls were really envious, I can tell you that. Giggly, as I said, and kind of scandalized, but just oozing jealousy. We all had a crush on Chance, you know. None of us had paid him much notice in the early grades, he was so quiet and retiring. But after we'd started to develop, it suddenly hit us he had everything a teenage girl might want in a boy: He was incredibly good-looking, he was painfully shy, he was kind of mysterious, he was a little sullen without being really mean. And no acne! He was perfect.

I always half-hoped that our rehearsals—not the ones in front of Miss Campbell, of course, but when we rehearsed just the two of us, after school, at my house, which we did several times—I always half-hoped they would turn into make-out sessions. Because we had to practice the kiss so as not to bump noses or whatever, and it seemed possible that once that got started...well, you know. And it sort of did happen, once. We got a little carried away. I mean, we didn't *do it* or anything, that possibility never entered my mind and maybe never entered Chance's mind either. In those days, at least in our school, girls *didn't* do it. Or even imagine doing it. We thought we were gonna save it for when we got married. Of course, when most of us got to college we abandoned that plan, but we kept to it through most of our teens. But anyway, Chance and I did do some heavy petting that one afternoon. Well, heavy*ish* petting. I was too shy to hold up my end, if you get what I'm saying. But it was heaven all the same. Until my mom came home and found us. She wasn't too happy about it.

I'd hoped there would be a repeat, but there never was. I don't know why. Maybe because my mom scared Chance so bad he was afraid to risk it.

For the rest of my life, though, I've been able to brag that I starred in a play with Chance Hardwick, and that he and I made out one afternoon on my parents' couch. So you could say my life hasn't been completely wasted. [laughs]

Helen Campbell

AT THE END OF the school year, we put on a real play. I mean, a week-long run, performances at night, parents came, kids came, even some locals who were just curious. We did *Our Town*. Not an especially original or interesting choice, I realize. But, heck, it's a nice, simple play with nice, simple emotions, and everyone can relate to it, and back then it wasn't quite the cliché it's become. And anyway, it was hard to find plays we could cast. Basically we had to dragoon boys into our productions. They really didn't want to participate, most of 'em. It wasn't just that they preferred sports—our big end-of-school-year productions didn't conflict, they were extracurricular—it was just, I don't know, it wasn't anything they were interested in. And they found performing like that embarrassing. It was amazing how these cocky, strutting boys would become awkward and shy and mumbly when they had to get up on stage, but that's how it was. Still, we somehow managed to get the thing populated. We always did in the end. I think word may have gotten out that it was a good, unpressured way to spend time with girls. By age fourteen, that was becoming an issue for them.

I cast Chance in the role of stage manager, which was kind of a no-brainer. He had the presence, he had the charisma, he had the chops. And he was so good, I did something I'd never done before and have never done since. See, I was in a community theater group, we did amateur theatricals, it was a lot of fun even though our work wasn't anything to write home about. Some of us believed we were better than we actually were, but we weren't. Anyway, I went to the guy in charge of the thing—a fellow with the glorified title of "company manager"—and told him he ought to include Chance in our company. It was all grown-ups, so this was sort of unprecedented, but I had no doubt he would be a great addition. He'd probably be the best actor in our group from day one.

I had to pester the guy before he gave in. He wasn't inclined to pay me any heed, even though I taught theater and should have been expected to know *something* about it. Which I did, by the way. I'd wanted to be an actress as a girl, and it was tough to realize I just didn't have the talent. But along the way I'd done my share of studying and reading, I knew a lot of plays, I knew a lot about acting theory. And I could damn well recognize talent when I saw it.

When I mentioned the possibility to Chance, he pretty much jumped at it. I'm sure there are people around here who'll tell you how shy he was, what a loner he was, how closed off and private he was. Well, it's a bunch of malarkey. If you met him halfway, he was as open and voluble as any teenager you might want to meet. He had a great laugh, and he was even willing to confide some of his feelings in you. More than many teenagers in that regard, in fact. At a certain point I thought of him as being as much a friend as a student.

Well, Dick finally let Chance audition, and while his age made it difficult for him to be part of our company—he couldn't play our contemporaries, for goodness sake, the age difference was too obvious, so we could only use him when the play called for an adolescent—but Dick had to admit the kid was really good. He didn't want to admit *how* good, because then he would have lost face, he would have had to concede I was right. I think he always felt competitive with me, so disagreements like this often became little power struggles. But he admitted Chance was good enough to act with us.

And then...well, I'm a little reluctant to talk about this. Aside from being embarrassing to some people who are still alive, there might even be legal jeopardy involved. But, well, you can imagine, this beautiful boy, all these grown-ups around. Grown-ups who looked at him and responded with pure appetite. Some of the men as well as some of the women, I'm sorry to report. And I'm not going to say much more than that on this particular subject, but suffice it to say I believe Chance lost his virginity the summer he joined our repertory company.

And you know, I know about his fan clubs, and I read about that woman in black who's always laying flowers on his grave, and I think about how, even before he was famous, before he was even grown up, the level of lust he inspired in people, and I have a sense of what they mean by the phrase "animal magnetism." Chance had it. He simply had it. In addition to his good looks. It was something else, something extra. And completely involuntary. It wasn't something he *exercised*. I don't believe he was even aware of it back then. And looking back, I suppose I wasn't immune to it either, although I certainly wouldn't have dreamed of acting on it. I was his teacher, after all. You don't do that kind of thing.

Derek Stephens (actor in Downtown Players)

CHANCE WAS A BIT of a disturbing element in our little theater troupe. So young and so beautiful. When he joined, it was like an injection of pure energy.

See, up to then, we were just a group of hobbyists, basically. I mean, it was like a club more than a professional company. Everyone had a day job, or no job at all. I was manager at the bank, Helen taught school, Dick Dolphy owned one of the cafés downtown, Amy McCandless was a waitress there, and so on. We had fun putting on plays, and because there wasn't any real theater in the area, people came to see us. No serious competition except for the one movie theater. For live performance, we were the only game in town. So we obviously didn't have to set our sights very high. I don't mean to suggest we were *bad*, just that we weren't especially slick.

All right, all right, we were pretty bad, I admit it. But it was also a case of...see, we'd been in operation for six or seven years by this time, and a certain, I guess you might call it lethargy was starting to take over. A certain routine. A kind of "who cares?" attitude. Our audiences weren't particularly discerning. They seemed to prefer the non-adventurous fare. Safe stuff. Whenever we tried something modern or modestly experimental, we tended to have a hard time filling the house. Ditto with Shakespeare, by the way. So it was becoming a challenge to take ourselves at all seriously. And now, all of a sudden, having this beautiful young boy join us and then discovering how talented he was, well, it just made all of us try to up our game. It was like a shot of pure adrenaline.

By the way, I don't believe Chance was entirely unaware of the effect he was having on everybody. He was a bit of a minx, truth be told. Looking at you with those deep, soulful eyes of his. And not everybody shared my scruples. My lips are sealed otherwise. I'm just saying the poor boy was plunged into a sexual maelstrom. He may have had some minimal notion of what was happening—he knew and he didn't know is how I'd describe the situation—but I doubt he had the tools to navigate it. He was still a child, and his sense of his own erotic power was doubtless rather inchoate. I'm sure he enjoyed the effect he was having, and was willing to use it—he could be a seductive little rascal—but I don't think he had the vaguest idea how destabilizing it could prove to be in the grown-up world. Not at first at least.

I'm thinking especially of the period during our production of *Tea and Sympathy*, the first play we did after he'd been added to the company. We chose the play specifically to make use of his being in the group, we figured we might as well find a piece with a good solid part for someone that age. But you can probably see how fraught the situation might become with a play like that. Especially if the actors take their work home with them, as the old saying goes. Well, one thing led to another. Beyond that, I'm not uttering a word. Least said, soonest mended, as another old saying goes.

Amy McCandless *(actor in* Downtown Players*)*

I PLAYED LAURA REYNOLDS in our production of *Tea and Sympathy.*
Chance was Tom.

Have you talked to Derek? I know he loves to gossip. I don't
know what he's told you, but I'm sure it was tawdry. That's Derek
for you. Behind that refined exterior, that gentleman banker
manner, there's a mean little snake. Besides, I think he was jealous
of my relationship with Chance. I don't mean to imply anything
unnatural by the way. Everyone in the company was crazy about
Chance, everyone wanted to be his friend. He had that kind of
charisma. Just drew you right in.

But the thing is, there *was* gossip about Chance and me,
even at the time, and I'm not saying Derek started it because
I don't know that, but I have no doubt he was happy to pass it
along to all and sundry. And it's utter nonsense. Chance and
I grew very close during the rehearsals and the run of the play.
I don't deny it. If anything I'm proud of it. I think I played an
important role in his life at that time. He needed a grown-up
he could talk to. But there was never anything...*improper* about
it, or *carnal*. He was just a kid. Fourteen years old. A beautiful
boy, of course, a Caravaggio youth, but it would have been
impossible for me to think about him *that way*. Chance and
I, we had a friendship for sure, and I guess it was a friendship
that kind of mirrored or reflected the relationship in the play
in some ways. But goodness gracious, not what happens at the
final curtain! That would never have occurred to me. Or if it
ever did, I would have dismissed it from my mind immediately.
He confided in me, and I did care about him deeply, and I felt
a responsibility for him because he *needed* someone to feel a
responsibility for him. His mom was kind of an absent figure in
his life, and his aunt cared deeply about him—I think she adored

him—but she wasn't the sort of person who could fathom what was going on inside such a beautiful, delicate soul.

He was a terrific listener too, by the way. When you talked to him, you felt the totality of his being was paying close attention to the totality of yours. It was a two-way street, this friendship between him and me. Not some act of emotional charity on my part. That's what I'm trying to convey.

He was such a sensitive child, such a troubled child, with such a complicated situation at home, and of course he had an extraordinary talent, which is a burden as well as a blessing. He had a hard time connecting with his peers. His talent—his whole artistic temperament—was deeply isolating. Maybe that's always the case, I don't know.

Of course, we all noticed the talent right away. From the first rehearsal. He blew us all off the stage. Just doing a scene with him—and this is a fourteen year old boy we're talking about!— just being on stage with him was an education in the art of acting. We all learned a lot simply by watching him work. It's as if he'd somehow *intuited* Stanislavski without ever having been taught. I'm pretty sure he hadn't read *An Actor Prepares* yet. The technical stuff came later. He just kind of made up the Method on his own.

And to give you some idea of how incredible his talent was, how able he was to utterly transform himself, he and I once did a scene from *Richard III*. Just as an exercise. The company never did any Shakespeare, we knew there was no audience for it around here, our people would have stayed away in droves. But Chance was eager to give it a try. He thought it was important to have some familiarity with the classics, to be comfortable with the verse and the diction and the artifice. So we picked the scene where Richard woos Lady Anne. And here's the thing: *He made himself look ugly!* I don't just mean he contorted his body, although he did that too. I mean his features became grotesque.

I can't to this day explain to you how he managed that. It wasn't make-up or anything. We were in my apartment, it was all very informal, he wasn't wearing any makeup. He just...he worked from the inside out, always. That was his way. And somehow he found something inside himself that turned this beautiful boy into a monster. It was almost scary.

And he loved being in our little troupe. He didn't have many friends his own age, but we all more or less adopted him as part of our little theater family. He was a great sport about being a member. When there were props to be moved, sets to be built or painted, lighting to be adjusted, anything like that, you could count on him to help out, to do whatever was required. There was no hierarchy in the Downtown Players. We all pitched in. And Chance pitched in more than anyone.

When I read about his death however many years later it was, I was heartbroken. I hadn't seen him for several years, but I always felt connected. We exchanged letters from time to time, and he always sent me cards for Christmas and presents on my birthday. We never lost touch completely. So it came as a complete shock. I was devastated.

Tell me, do you think it was, like they sort of hint, a suicide? Or was it a plain old everyday drowning accident? Do you have any idea? I guess in those situations, one never knows for sure. Not unless there's a note or something, and I gather there wasn't.

Joel Weingott

AFTER THAT SUMMER AT camp, it was a challenge to keep the friendship going. We lived over a thousand miles away from each other, and at that age, a lot is happening to you. You're changing on a daily basis, so there's a real danger of growing apart just in the ordinary course of events. But we did keep up a correspondence.

People find it hard to believe that Chance was much of a letter writer, since he had a reputation for being, you know, sullen, or taciturn. And incommunicative too, barely articulate. Maybe he was like that with other people, but he was never that way with me. And he was terrific in terms of holding up his share of the correspondence. Always answered my letters promptly, and he wrote great letters himself. Funny and wry and personal. Full of sardonic observations about the people around him and the shit he was going through at school and at home and so on. Can I say "shit?" Well, feel free to substitute the word "stuff" if you need to.

The summer after the summer we were both at camp, he invited me to come visit him for a couple of weeks. And maybe I was a little apprehensive about it, because God only knows what I'd be getting myself into, but I missed spending time with him, so I said yes. He was living with his aunt and uncle at the time. I guess there were tensions with his stepfather or something, so he wasn't living at home, but the Bennetts were very welcoming, or tried to be. At least his aunt was. His uncle Earl wasn't *mean*, I don't mean to suggest that, but he didn't seem to know what to make of me, so he pretty much kept his distance. Grunt a good morning and a hello and a good night and that was about it. I'd sometimes catch him sort of staring at me like I was some sort of alien life form. Same kind of shit I used to get from the guys at camp. His aunt Mary, she didn't know what to make of me either, but she made more of an effort. Sometimes it was sort of laughable, like she bought frozen bagels for my breakfast to make me feel at home, that sort of thing. But it was well-intentioned. And when I laughed about it, she laughed too. She understood that she'd been flailing about and that I could see she'd been flailing about. And she understood I appreciated the attempt. So the laughter broke the tension.

Chance and I got along just fine those couple of weeks, but it wasn't the same as the summer before. So much of that closeness came from our feeling so alienated from all the other guys there, it was a real bond. Plus trying to wriggle out of the camp activities as much as possible. On his home turf, things were a little different. Not that he didn't feel alienated on his home turf, by the way. Chance was a guy who lived in a state of perpetual alienation. It's part of what made him so attractive to people.

But the major difference between the two summers is that in between he'd caught the acting bug. His letters to me had mentioned it, so I was aware it had become a big interest on his part, but I wasn't really prepared for how obsessed he'd become. He was in that grown-up acting group, he was reading plays all the time and biographies of actors and directors and so on. And it's mostly what he talked about. I tried to keep up—I mean, it's not like it was uninteresting, so I was happy to try to understand what got him so engaged—but still, I felt a little left out. He invited me to attend rehearsals, and the grown-ups in the company were okay with my being there, not exactly warmly welcoming but not being shitty about it either...oops, there I go again, you can substitute "crappy" or "lousy" if you want. Anyhow, no matter how nice everybody was or wasn't, I did feel like an outsider or an intruder when we were at the theater. And I sometimes got a little bored talking about, oh, I don't know, Brando versus Olivier, stuff like that.

But I'll tell you a funny detail. Chance was less excited about those big stars, those legendary names, than he was about the character actors. Funny, no? I mean, considering what a big star he became himself? But he would enthuse about Lee J. Cobb, say, or Rod Steiger, or Martin Balsam, or Eli Wallach, or Nancy Walker, or Judith Anderson. "Just look at them!" he'd say. "No one pays much attention, and that's because their acting is completely invisible!" That was the highest praise he could offer a performance, you see. When the actor wasn't acting, or in any case you couldn't *see* him acting, he or she was just...I don't know, *behaving*.

We had dinner at his mom's one night. She apparently told him she wanted to meet his friend. Probably because he didn't have many friends. I don't think there was a single kid in his junior high class he considered a friend, or who considered him a friend. So she was curious, or wanted to encourage him, or God knows what. We went to her place for dinner, and I've got to tell you, it was tense. His mom was all right, just seemed sort of nervous and chirpy. But his step-father—not that Chance ever referred to him as a step-father, he just called him Steve—but Steve clearly detested Chance, and Chance clearly detested Steve. There was this icy chill between them, and that's at *best*, when they were on good behavior, when they didn't start arguing. A couple of times it got overtly nasty. Very uncomfortable to be around, I can tell you.

His little sister Dorothy was there too. Very quiet. I got the impression she adored Chance, but he seemed almost oblivious of her. I think he was too consumed with rage against Steve to notice much else, you know?

Terri Howe (high school classmate)

CHANCE WASN'T A STAR athlete, which was the main way to become a big shot in our high school. He was in school plays, so he was known for that, and he was sure enough the best looking boy in our class—in the whole high school—so he wasn't invisible. If someone passed him in the hall or on the stairs, they might say "Hi, Chance." Or they might not. He didn't have many people who didn't like him, I don't think, but I'm not sure he had many close friends either. He wasn't the kind of kid who would get elected to student council—not that I can imagine him running—or be chosen prom king or anything of that nature. The girls all thought he was cute, but also maybe a little weird. He wasn't like anyone else. We didn't know what to make of him.

I always liked him. His weirdness was part of his appeal to me. And maybe even his being so quiet. A lot of the boys, they'd talk your ear off, mostly in a sort of braggy way. Or they'd explain things to you that you already understood. Chance could sit quietly for long minutes at a time, and that might get awkward, like, should I say something to break the silence or just sit here and wait for him to do something? But it also was a relief if you'd been out with somebody on the football team or the basketball team. They'd just describe the games they'd played and tell you what the coach said about their throwing arm. Yawn!

I went to the senior prom with Chance. It would be an exaggeration to say he was my boyfriend, but we'd been out together a few times, and when he asked me it was a surprise but I was happy to say yes. I knew we made a cute couple, and that mattered to me back then probably more than it should have. And as I say, I liked him well enough. I was a little surprised he planned to go to the prom at all, though, since he seemed so—what's the word? *Detached.* Detached from all the school social stuff. Detached and sort of...superior. Not that he was braggy, not like those athlete guys, just indifferent to all of it. Like it didn't figure in his thoughts at all. Like he couldn't be bothered, and couldn't believe anyone else could be bothered either.

But we went, and we danced, and we even went to one of the post-prom parties. Where I mixed with everybody and he just hung back and watched. We both got drunk, though. Someone had got hold of some cheap gin and poured it in the punch.

Mary Bennett

THERE WAS STILL A draft back then, and that thing in Korea was underway, so of course we were all concerned about that. It was kind of hanging over the head of every boy growing up at that time,

Chance very much included. And I figured, based on his experience at that dude ranch when he was a kid, he'd have *hated* the Army. I mean *really* hated it. Not the physical demands so much, he could have handled that if he had to, but the fact he'd have no privacy. That's one thing. And even more, always being told what to do, and having to follow orders, and having to salute and say "Yes sir" to someone he didn't respect. He didn't do it with Steve and he might have had a hard time doing it with some officer he considered a darn fool. It might not have killed him, but believe me, it wouldn't have been a character-builder either. It just would have been two years of misery for him, would have taken something out of him he might never get back.

And if he'd had to go to Korea, the combat would have been awful for him too. Maybe that sounds obvious nowadays, but back then it was a different time, a lot of the boys he knew really looked forward to going to war. Like playing cowboys and Indians, but with real guns. A lot of 'em enlisted right out of high school. They were gung-ho, as the saying goes. But not Chance. He wasn't no coward, but the idea of shooting at strangers, I just don't think that would've set well with him. And *them* trying to kill *him* wouldn't've been to his liking neither.

But then he was classified 1Y. I never knew exactly why. I asked him, of course—I was so relieved, and he was so relieved, it was impossible not to be curious, even though I didn't want to seem nosy—and he said it was a health issue. But he didn't say anything more than that, and I could tell he didn't want me to press him on it. Earl, who didn't really approve of any American shirking his duty in wartime—Earl was an old-fashioned patriot, you don't ask questions, when your country calls you, you go—Earl asked him a few times, was even a little aggressive about it, but Chance's answers were always on the hazy side. He'd had some operations as a kid, so it might have been from that. But him being so hazy and all, I figured it was probably one of those male things. An undescended prosticle or something.

Morton Brock (high school guidance counselor)

WHEN IT CAME TIME for the seniors to start applying to college, I worked with them one-on-one. We were a small school, relatively speaking, so we could manage to give them that level of attention. Besides, not all of our kids applied to college—maybe that's obvious—so that made it even easier. You can probably guess that our school—our town—wasn't...isn't...exactly a hotbed of intellectual ferment [laughs]. More a placid, semi-rural, all-American kind of place. Football matters a lot more than academics. We have a pretty good-size 4-H Club chapter. And this may be less true now, but back in the fifties, the time you're asking me about, quite a number of the kids after they graduated stayed home to work on the family farm or to work in one of the local factories. And there was the army, of course. Still, probably more than half went on to college. We tried to encourage them to do that, and naturally we tried to direct them toward schools that both met their needs as well as where they'd have a reasonable chance of getting in.

Now, to be honest, when you first contacted me, I didn't remember much about Chance. Much? I didn't remember anything, not even his name, despite its being kind of memorable. Not many Chances crossed my threshold. I never made the connection between the famous movie star and the kid who came to me for guidance. Stupid, huh? I must be the only person in the entire school administration who didn't realize we'd graduated a celebrity. My guess is I knew him as Wendell, not Chance, so I never made the connection. And I'm not much of a moviegoer, I guess that's obvious. I might have recognized the face if I'd seen him in a picture. But the whole thing passed me right by. The only famous person ever to graduate from Monroe High and I was completely unaware of it.

Anyhow, fortunately, I keep careful notes, and I never throw 'em away. That habit started way back when because I was afraid of being sued by one of the kids for one reason or another—a college catastrophe that some shyster convinced them to blame on me—so I wanted to keep my records handy and in order just in case. And then, when I finally realized that I was being a little nuts, no one was going to do anything like that, it had already become automatic. It's sorta my personal collection, memoranda of all the kids who'd passed through my office. I kept the files at school until my retirement, but then, when it was time to go, I had a little crisis—throw them out or not?—and finally opted to take them home with me. I'm not much of packrat generally, but... well, anyway...

So after I got your email, I was a little confused, but I went through my files, and damn if I didn't find my notes on Wendell Hardwick's case. Wendell Castle Hardwick Jr., dontcha know? Sounds like an investment broker in one of those stuffy East Coast firms, doesn't it? So anyway, as you see, I can't help you much, 'cause as I say, I don't really remember the boy. But I have his file here, and I see I made some notations about his interests—all drama all the time, evidently—and about his grades—good but not great—and about his various achievement test scores—downright brilliant, which is another reason I'm surprised I can't remember him. Funny how some kids hide their light under a bushel like that, isn't it? Brilliant mind, mediocre grades. It almost seems like a choice, being an under-achiever. I can't fathom it.

I see here I recommended he apply to State, where I was reasonably sure he'd get in, and that was the obvious suggestion. But I also thought he should maybe take a flyer at Yale and NYU and UCLA, you know, because of their theater departments. His grades weren't really good enough for those places, but I thought the admissions people might find him to be an interesting enough candidate to be worth making an exception for.

But he apparently dismissed those ideas. I've got little X's in the margin next to 'em. They must have been out of the question financially, that's the only explanation I can think of. Otherwise, why wouldn't a kid like that want to head out to one of the coasts? But he just applied to State. And got in, I see. It must have been frustrating for him. State didn't have a Theater Arts department back then. I'm guessing he probably ended up as an English major. I have no idea whether he stayed for all four years or not. We didn't do follow-up.

Mary Bennett

WHEN CHANCE LEFT FOR college, I was heartbroken. I didn't realize how attached I'd gotten to the boy till he left. There was just this gigantic hole left in the house. It was like...it was like he was the son I never had. Now, I don't think Earl saw it that way. I think Earl was perfectly happy to see his rear end. "Don't slam the door on your way out" kind of deal. I don't mean to be harsh. Earl'd been a good sport about Chance living with us—there was some grumbling, but only to me, never to Chance, and it was usually mostly sort of humorous, you know, about how much food Chance was eating, how he was going to bankrupt us, how we had to go see all those lousy plays he was in—but I think down deep he figured, no kidding around, enough was enough.

And he might have been a little jealous too. Earl and me, we weren't much for talking to each other. Earl wasn't much for talking to anybody, really, except to say what had to be said, like "We're out of milk," or "I'm going down to the hardware store but I'll be back in time for supper." Just practical everyday stuff. But Chance and me, we could sit around jawing for hours. About all sorts of stuff, about movies and religion and people and the president and I don't know what. Just everything under the sun, except really personal matters, which he never opened up about. But everything else. And I don't think Earl liked that. I reckon he felt left out, even though he himself didn't want any part of it neither. He used to gripe to me, "The two of you natter away like a couple of old ladies." But the thing is, it showed him a side of me he didn't know was there, and I got the impression that made him uncomfortable. Like, why should Chance see that side of me and not him? Like, say you're not hungry for cake but you still feel somewhat p.o.'d—pardon my language—when someone else gets cake and you're not offered any.

So Earl wasn't too broken up when Chance left for college, is what I'm saying.

Chance wrote us letters—well, wrote me letters, but they were addressed to both of us—every couple of weeks or so. From college, I mean. He didn't phone much, but you know, long-distance calls were kind of a big deal then. Expensive. You had to go through an operator. That wasn't something you did just to say hello. You did it if someone was being born or dying, some big deal.

He wrote nice, chatty letters, but I can't say they were very informative. He always said school was going fine. Who knows what that really meant? He was kind of sparing with personal details, Chance was. Always had been, as I said. A private person. We didn't know who his friends were or whether he was keeping company with any special girl or anything like that.

Helen Campbell

JUST BEFORE HE LEFT for college, Chance wrote me the sweetest note. It said, "Dear Mrs. Campbell, you may not know it, but you saved my life. Without you and the world you opened up for me, I would have been lost. So I want to say thank you." It's funny because in some ways I never really felt I knew him. I liked him a lot, and admired his talent extravagantly, but I never felt I had a sense of who the real person was. And I definitely never appreciated that I'd played an important role in his life. So learning that was very gratifying.

Wilson Denny (college roommate)

FRESHMAN YEAR, THE SCHOOL assigned you to a dorm room and assigned you your roommate. You didn't have any choice. For sophomore year you could put in for a change or even live off-campus. I guess they figured by then you'd have made friends of your own. But for freshman year, they wanted to mix things up, take you out of your comfort zone, expose you to new things. Not that anyone said "comfort zone" back then. Those words came along later. But making people uncomfortable has always been with us.

Not that making *me* uncomfortable would have taken much. But I had some experience with that kind of discomfort, I was an old hand at being uncomfortable. See, I'd done my stint in the army for a couple of years. I'd been stationed in Germany. Being in the service in those days...well, it wasn't long after Truman had integrated the army, and let's just say things could get a little hairy for no particular reason. Not so much from the Germans, surprisingly enough. I think they'd had their fill of racism by then. They'd gotten royally drunk on it and were now experiencing the worst hangover ever. But some of my so-called buddies, my comrades-in-arms, were a different story.

Anyhow, Chance and me, we were thrown together by forces beyond our control—namely the college housing office. I have to say, I was a little apprehensive about pretty much everything before I got to State. I mean, apprehensive in addition to the usual apprehension any incoming student feels about being in a competitive, high-pressure academic environment, which is reason enough. Am I smart enough? Am I prepared? Can I cut it? Now, I guess "high pressure academic environment" might, looking back, seem like a funny way to describe a dinky state college, but compared to the dinky district high schools many of us were used to…plus, you know, being two years older than most of the other freshmen, you might think it conferred some sort of advantage, but the truth is it cut both ways. You might have some extra maturity— and in addition to my age, having spent a couple of years abroad had definitely broadened my vistas—but you're also, I don't know, you're *not one of them.* You know what I mean? At that age, things are changing so fast, what's in and what's out, and two years can be an eternity. You don't know if you're going to fit.

But what I'm saying is, in addition to that set of worries, I also…see, I understood it wasn't Arkansas or Mississippi, I didn't expect to be spat on or shouted at or threatened or something of that nature—I didn't expect it, although I didn't exactly discount the possibility either. There weren't a lot of people of color at State, or in *the state* for that matter, back then it was almost 100 percent white, and you just never could be sure how people were going to react to you. I mean *anywhere.* As a kid, just going into town to shop, or to get a burger or to see a movie, never mind really living among people, it could be eye-opening. Sometimes it was fine, sometimes not so much. People would stare. They might mutter something. A couple of times, although to be fair only a couple of times, my mom and me were actually refused service. It was still the fifties, a different world in lots of ways. Like you know that book that starts out saying the past is a different country? *America* was a different country back then. You couldn't even assume people knew it was a bad idea to admit they were racists. I'm not talking about *being* racists. Lots and lots of people are still racists, but they at least know better than to say so. Most people now, when they're about to say something really racist, they start by saying, "I'm the least racist person in the world, but…" and then they say something disgusting and racist. But copping to it is a social taboo nowadays. Back then, though, it was almost legitimate, one point of view among many. Maybe not *classy*, but not a big no-no. The major civil rights legislation hadn't been signed yet. Brown v. Board was still being litigated. The movement itself was barely underway. No one knew who Martin Luther King, Jr. was.

So you can see why, while I was really proud and excited to be going to college, to be the first person in my family to ever be going to college, you can see why I was also kind of scared shitless. I'd just spent two years doing my army stint, which is what made college possible. The GI Bill. But I'd spent the last two years in the army, and frankly, this was scarier. The orderliness in the army, the discipline, the structure, they suited me. Now, I hadn't been in a combat zone, I lucked out in that regard, I wasn't dodging bullets in Inchon or some other godforsaken Korean hellhole. Things were frankly pretty cushy in Trier. But still.

So of course college was an adventure, and obviously offered a big opportunity, but it was also terrifying. Like rock-climbing or whitewater rafting. For four years without interruption. I might be in for a really miserable stretch of time. The army wasn't so bad after basic training—I'm not saying I loved it, and God knows there were hassles from time to time, but the way it was regimented, the way the rules and the hierarchy were so clear, it had a kind of stability to it. This was going to be different, looser, much more free-form, and it was going to be my life and I had no idea what it was going to be like.

I got to campus pretty early. To face down the demons before they paralyzed me. You know what I mean? If I'd hesitated too long before making my move, I might have found myself heading straight back home instead of going through with it. So I forced myself to get there early, I registered right away, I got my room assignment, I went up to my dorm room. Unpacked, sat on the bed for a couple of minutes wondering what I'd gotten myself into—I felt like crying all of a sudden, but knew that would be a big mistake so I managed to get control of myself—and then started putting the linen they'd given me on the bed when I heard the door open behind me. I turned around just as Chance was coming through the door carrying a suitcase, a couple of boxes, and his bed linen. Kind of weighed down. For a second or two I stared at him and he stared at me, and his eyes widened—he seemed almost frozen—and then he said, "You're a colored guy!"

So…it was kind of hard to know how to take that. Was he just stating a fact—a fact he found surprising, but still, just a fact—or was there some kind of attitude behind it? It was a tricky situation, but I decided not to jump to any conclusions. Give him a little more rope, you know? See if he was going to hang himself. So I went over to help him unload his stuff, and as I took one of the boxes from him, I said, "You noticed." And then, "And you seem to be a white guy."

"It's just, I've never met a colored guy before," he said.

"Looks like your ship has finally come in."

And that made him laugh, which led me to think there might be hope. Then he set the rest of the stuff down on his bed and stuck his hand out and said, "Howdy. I'm Chance." Friendly, you know? Easy-going. Comfortable. That was encouraging too.

So I shook his hand and told him my name. And then I said, "Listen, are we going to have a problem? 'Cause if we are, let's take care of it now, before classes start."

"Problem?" he said. He gave me an odd look. "What kind of problem do you mean?"

And he wasn't being cute, you know. Or like one of those phonies who say, "I don't see color." Maybe because he'd never met any black people before, or because he came from a place where absolutely *everybody* was white, he simply hadn't been exposed to much racism. It may have been around, it *must* have been around, at least in people's hearts, but the subject just hadn't come up much. I mean, later, I learned that for example his uncle was pretty racist, but I think that came as news to Chance too. There'd been no reason for anyone to mention it. No occasion for it. So I guess what I'm saying is, it's not that Chance was enlightened, he was just innocent.

George Berlin (English professor)

CHANCE TOOK MY FRESHMAN English class. English 1A it was called. A requirement. Basically an introduction to writing. These kids would arrive from the boonies without knowing how to construct a sentence let alone write a coherent essay. Most of them hadn't read much either. So we had assigned reading each week—usually something not too challenging, but maybe a cut above what they might have encountered in high school—and then on Friday they had to write a paper in class about what they'd read. I'd put a question about the reading on the blackboard and they'd have to answer it within the allotted hour.

Chance could write. I mean quite well, better than most of the kids in the class. Well enough so that he didn't really need what amounted to a remedial writing class. But that's how he came to my attention, through his writing. At first, because it was a large class, I didn't even know he was the good-looking, quiet kid who usually sat way in the back of the room. I didn't put the face and the name together. But I noticed his essays. His written work was consistently good, invariably A or A-. And it wasn't just that he could write decently. He had some interesting ideas.

But he was mostly kind of invisible that semester. Didn't talk in class, didn't…on Mondays, I used to hand out mimeos of some the essays that had been handed in—without identifying who'd written them, of course—and have the kids critique them. Chance never uttered a peep. Never raised his hand. If I'd call on him anyway, as I sometimes did, he'd just mumble something. "I think it's pretty good," he might say, or something vaguely, meaninglessly positive. He didn't go in for specifics, and he seemed to make a point of not going in for criticism. Maybe he felt above it all, maybe it was a form of arrogance, but I swear it didn't come across that way. Maybe he was just being kind, didn't want to hurt anyone's feelings. If that was the case, it makes him almost unique. Those kids could be vicious!

But when it was one of *his* essays under discussion, he just looked down at his desk. It didn't matter if someone was praising it or criticizing it, he wouldn't take the bait. I don't think any of the kids would even have been aware the essay was his.

I only saw him really come to life in class once, and that was almost scary. The class had been assigned "The Lottery" that week, the Shirley Jackson story, and a couple of the kids were complaining about its being totally unbelievable. And Chance suddenly spoke up from his perch at the back of the room. He said, "Unbelievable? Everyone in this room would behave exactly like the people in the town!" A couple of the kids took it personally—maybe they were meant to—and started arguing with him. He stood his ground, and maybe, as things heated up, crossed a line or two in terms of civil discourse. Implying they were easily manipulated, hadn't ever learned to question things or think for themselves. Well, not implying it, *saying* it. *Implying* they were stupid.

I finally had to break things up. It was getting so intense I was afraid it might turn physical. But it was a surprise to see Chance show such fierce passion. He'd been so passive in class up to then, as I've indicated. I was even a little worried someone might jump him after class, but instead a bunch of the students gathered around him as he was leaving the room and started talking to him and arguing with him or agreeing with him. A couple of minutes later, when I happened to glance out the window while I was gathering up my notes and things, I saw them out there in the quad still talking. Lots of animation on display, but no fisticuffs, just clearly a very intense discussion. To my mind, that's what college is supposed to be about, so I was pleased with how things turned out. Despite a couple of anxious moments.

The next semester, Chance asked if he could take my Dramatic Literature seminar. It was supposed to be limited to upper-division English majors, but I made an exception for Chance. I figured he was sufficiently prepared for it and would be an asset to the class. I was right on both counts.

Wilson Denny

ONE OF THE THINGS I liked about Chance from the start...I mean, a lot of white liberals, they always want to talk to you about race. That's like *all* they want to talk to you about. And it's not that I'm saying their intentions are bad or that they're hypocrites—necessarily— it may just be a way of dealing with their own discomfort, or they may think that by praising Sammy Davis Jr. or Ray Charles or Sidney Poitier or whoever, it will bring up something they might have in common with me. And don't get me started about what it was like after Obama started running...sheesh!

But that stuff gets boring, you know? There are other things to talk about, other things to think about. I'm not saying it's possible for a brother or sister *not* to think about race a lot of the time, because life is always shoving it in your face, but still, it's not the only thing in the world. Grant us our humanity, okay? We have actual lives. We're not *just* our race and we're not *just* victims. Thinking that's the whole story is another kind of racism.

But Chance, either out of a natural sense of tact or simply because he'd never given the matter any thought, mostly didn't talk about it. Even to me. We talked all the time, we'd often be up past midnight talking, but we mostly talked about other stuff. We were young guys, young lusty guys, and there were other things that mattered to us. Movies and music and cars and our grades and our plans for the rest of our lives. I'd introduced him to jazz. I was into jazz in a big way and he didn't have much taste in music at all, he just listened to whatever popular music was on the radio, what his uncle and aunt liked to listen to, and he'd never paid it a lot of attention. So he sort of followed my lead there, and he got pretty enthusiastic once he started listening closely, because he'd had no idea music could *matter*, you know? Up till then he thought it was just pleasant background noise. So we talked about different players and how they changed jazz and what set them apart, and that was a pretty big topic between us for a while. And we talked about girls, of course. Girls took up a major portion of our conversation. And Chance being Chance, he went on at great length about acting. I had to put up with a lot of *that* shit. Sometimes I even wished he'd talk about race, just for a change of pace. Just to get him off, I don't know, someone like Paul Muni, who I'd never even heard of before I met Chance. He could spin epic prose poems about the genius of Paul Muni.

Now, don't get me wrong, the civil rights movement was gathering steam while Chance and I were roomies, so it's not like the subject never came up. We weren't *avoiding* it. We couldn't. It was unavoidable. And he was curious, humanly curious. He'd ask me about what it was like to be black, he asked me my opinion on various political developments. Which I appreciated, by the way, his asking rather than telling. 'Cause that's another thing white liberals often do, tell you stuff rather than ask you stuff. They're kind of anxious to establish their liberal bona fides, maybe. Want to lay their cards on the table before you can get a word in edgewise. And God knows it isn't just white liberals who do that. White conservatives are even quicker off the mark. And when they do it, they say "you people." At least most liberals know better than to do that.

In general, though, Chance just wasn't at all political in those years. Politics wasn't on his radar much. The red scare was still a pretty big deal in those days, but Chance was basically oblivious to it. Thought Communism was bad, I suppose, and maybe even believed domestic commies were a threat, since that what he'd been told, but I doubt he'd devoted more than five minutes' thought to the subject in his entire life. Political obliviousness is a luxury that comes with being privileged, I guess; you can afford not to pay attention and not to care. I'm pretty sure all his people at home voted Republican, and he probably thought he was a Republican too, insofar as he thought about the matter at all. But politics—race and the Cold War and Korea and the H-bomb and all the other shit that was in the news in those days—was probably of even less interest to him than sports, and he had zero interest in sports. Trust me, I tried to talk baseball with him once or twice. *Nada*. But if he had any kind of political awakening in college at all, and I don't think he had much of one, mind you, but if he had any, it would have come from having me as his roommate. I'm not saying I radicalized him, I wasn't especially radical myself and I wasn't a proselytizer in any case, but racial stuff hit close to home and it's possible I might have opened his eyes to it a fraction of an inch.

Come to think of it, talk about race and talk about jazz are kind of related, aren't they? They might, in a funny way, have opened his eyes to some of the same issues.

Nancy Hawkins (girlfriend)

WHEN CHANCE BECAME FAMOUS, I was like...I mean, like, holy cow! That was my boyfriend! The guy I used to go out with had become a movie star! It...this is probably silly, but it sort of makes you feel special. And besides—I mean, I always thought he was really great looking, don't get me wrong, my friends used to envy me and so on—but it was only when I saw him up on the screen, that's when I realized he wasn't just the cutest guy in our class, he was totally gorgeous. *Movie star* gorgeous, a whole different category. It was one thing to be hanging out with him on a day-to-day basis and taking it for granted, but something completely different to look at him through the eyes of...you know, just some person in the dark of a movie theater, or flipping through the pages of a movie magazine. It suddenly hit me, this guy I used to go out with was like a world-class babe.

My husband at the time—he's my ex now, we got divorced a long time ago—he wasn't too thrilled about it. When he found out, I mean. I think one of my friends must have mentioned it to him, because I sure as heck didn't. He got very...well, jealous, sure, but also, you know, competitive. Like, what's he got that I haven't got? I said, "Honey, calm down, it was a long time ago, I haven't spoken to Chance in years and years. And anyway, me and him, we just had a kind of college romance. You're the one I married." And he said, "Right, maybe, but then again, Hardwick never proposed to you, did he? If he had, you probably would have..." and here he made a pun, although he didn't mean to. He said, "You probably would have jumped at the chance."

Which was almost surely wrong, by the way. We were just kids, me and Chance. Some of my girlfriends *were* getting married while they were still in college, or right after graduation. Their families kind of expected it of them, I guess, or they had no career plans and no reason to put it off. Or they'd stayed virgins all through college, for religious reasons or whatever, and just couldn't stand to wait any longer. But none of that was true for me. No pressure from my folks, I'm proud to say, and I wasn't ready for anything so serious myself. And I'm darned sure it wouldn't have even *occurred* to Chance. He had dreams, you know? Ambitions. Neither of us ever so much as breathed a word about marriage while we were a couple.

We started spending time together toward the end of our freshman year. We met because we were in the same math class. Introduction to Calculus. There was a math requirement for everybody freshman year, and which class you were assigned to was based on how you did on the standardized tests you took in high school. I had done pretty good, I guess, so they put me in the intro-calc class, as we called it. And the same must have been true for Chance. And we were both totally at sea. I'd been pretty good at algebra and geometry, but once we got past that...holy cow, it was like a foreign language. Me and Chance were drowning. So one day as class was ending he suggested we might study together, see if we could put our heads together and try to figure out what the heck was going on.

It was completely out of the blue. I don't think we'd even said hello to each other before that. I guess he could see I was struggling, and he made no secret of his own confusion. And... well, even if I'd been totally on top of the material, I would have said yes. Here was this great-looking guy suggesting we spend time together. I didn't have a boyfriend at the time—well, there was my high school boyfriend back home, but that was already feeling like a fading memory, the official break-up was just a matter of time—and freshman year had so far been pretty lonely from that point of view—and…well, you can imagine. If he'd been funny-looking, I might have said yes anyway, because I needed the help. But because it was Chance…I mean, if he'd suggested we, I don't know, tour a sewage plant or something, I probably still would have said yes.

Wilson Denny

Do COLLEGES STILL HAVE parietal rules? Well, we damn sure had parietal rules at State. No member of the opposite sex could be in your dorm room at any time. Period. The administration took that *in loco parentis* thing really serious. And they just assumed your parents didn't want you to be getting any.

Me and Chance, we weren't going to let that stop us. Or at least stop us from trying. But it's tricky when you're sharing a room. So we worked out an arrangement. He'd read somewhere that guys in East Coast colleges, Ivy League schools, would hang a necktie on their doorknob to signal to their roommates they'd snuck a girl into the room so please keep out. Now, neither Chance or me owned a necktie between us, so that wasn't gonna work, but we were adaptable. We put a towel on the door knob to let the other guy know we weren't alone. It didn't prove we were scoring, of course—Richard Pryor once called the fifties "the great pussy drought," and while it wasn't really as bad as all that, it was definitely a lot scanter than the heyday that was to come a few years later—but the towel on the doorknob was a sign that one or the other of us was giving the project our best shot.

And oddly enough, for the first few months, I did a lot better than he did. Good-looking guy like Chance, you wouldn't think it, but he kept missing the bus. But me…when I first got there, I was kind of reconciled to not having any luck at all, I figured those white chicks would regard me like some sort of plague. You know, a lot of 'em must've been brought up to regard black folk as a lower species of humanity. But in fact it wasn't like that at all. It must have been the first time a lot of 'em had had any contact with a brother, no momma and daddy around to disapprove, and they were maybe a little curious, or maybe they mostly just wanted to prove to me and to themselves that they weren't prejudiced. Or, I don't know, the exotic and the unfamiliar always seems to appeal to girls, whether it's a black guy like me or some Italian exchange student with an accent or a guy just out of the military or whatever. A novelty. I'm not saying I had sex with all of those girls, or even most of them, 'cause I definitely didn't, but they did go on dates with me, and a few of them did take the risk of coming back to the room. A fair amount of foreplay, and the occasional completed pass.

Chance used to tease me about it. In a humorous way. Pretend to be furious I was getting action when he wasn't. Now, he wasn't exactly a monk, and girls were always attracted to him, that was clear from the start. But getting laid was a challenge back then. At least in our freshman year. Girls were still torn between their upbringing and the new reality of being on their own. Plus, in addition to their religion—most of 'em, maybe all of 'em, were Christers—the culture kind of kept premarital sex a secret. It didn't give them permission the way it would a few years later. Sex before marriage was treated like something exceptional, and something… if not downright sinful, then at least dangerous. In movies, if a girl and her boyfriend got carried away and did the deed, she also immediately got pregnant and a crisis resulted. Often ending in somebody dying. That would be the whole plot right there. So girls needed some internal adjustment before they realized they were actually free to take the plunge if they felt like it. Of course, this was before the pill. Important to bear that in mind. Taking the plunge *wasn't* always risk-free. Being cautious wasn't just about Jesus or prudishness.

But anyway, toward the end of that first year, Chance met Nancy. And they were an item for a while.

Nancy Hawkins

Was I surprised Chance's roommate was a colored guy? Nah, I'd seen them together around campus from the start. I mean, everybody had. By the time Chance and I started seeing each other, it was old news. An accepted fact of campus life. They were almost famous in a way. These two freshmen, both really good-looking, one a Negro and one a white guy, who were kind of inseparable that year. Having coffee together in the commissary, studying together in the library, hanging out all the time. No one had seen anything like it before. They were a feature of freshman year, this sort of odd couple. I don't mean it *bothered* anybody—well, I'm sure it must've bothered some people, but that wasn't the main impression; I think most kids thought it was pretty cool as a matter of fact, it was possible to be naïve and sentimental about racial issues in those days without thinking about them particularly deeply—but it was sort of novel and got your attention. When parents came to visit, their kids would point out Chance and Will if they happened to be crossing the campus at the time. Like, "That's the chapel," and "That's the chem lab," and "Oh yeah, that colored guy and that Caucasian guy, that's Chance and Will, they're best friends." Like they were a local point of interest.

Wilson Denny

It took Chance a couple of months to score with Nancy. He told me he was afraid his blue balls might actually turn into a chronic condition. He had this whole elaborate shtick about going to the college infirmary to tell the nurse his balls had turned a vivid shade of azure and days had gone by and they hadn't changed back to pink. Did a whole elaborate routine, with hobbling into the infirmary—he had incredible physical performance skills, you probably know that about him already, he could have given that French guy, what's his name, that mime guy, a run for his money, or later, Robin Williams—so he would do this awkward painful unbalanced walk and damn it, it was so vivid your *own* balls would start to ache—and he'd act out the probing examination by the nurse—filthy and outrageous and a complete riot—and the doctor giving him the ominous prognosis—[pompous voice] "I'm sorry, young fellow, but I'm not sure they can be saved"—and going through the ordeal of some crazy sci-fi experimental therapy, the whole works. Side-splittingly funny. Chance could be hilarious once he got going. A lot of people wouldn't believe that about him, all they knew was the tortured soul stuff, the legendary moodiness and the world-weary angst. But he could be a scream when he got into the groove. Like Lenny Bruce almost, building these elaborate crazy fantasies, one insane thought leading to the next, one daffy idea piled precariously on top of another. And look, I was pre-med, I knew blue balls was a myth, there is no such thing, I could've straightened him out on that score. But I sure as hell wasn't going to stop him when he was in full flight. Besides, I couldn't talk. I was laughing too hard.

But my point is, 'cause I've kind of lost the thread here, but my point is, that towel was on the doorknob a lot. I often had to find somewhere else to study, and sometimes even to sleep, and for a long time he would report to me later that Nancy was always drawing a line. The line wasn't fixed, it was moving, he was making progress, but she kept drawing it *somewhere*, and for the longest time. For months. I finally got fed up with him. With her *and* him.

I said to him, "Look, pal, if you're not going to screw her soon, I want to get back to my room. I'm not gonna wander the halls for hours like the fucking flying Dutchman just so you can get to second base."

George Berlin

THERE WAS SOME RESENTMENT about my letting Chance attend the Dramatic Literature seminar. I mean on the part of some of the other students. It was supposed to be restricted to upper division students, and I heard some grumbling. For one thing, it meant some other upper division student, some junior or senior who wanted to take the class couldn't because it was a seminar and there were a limited number of places available. So that was one complaint, that I was depriving one of their number, and I guess it had a certain validity. Another was that a freshman would just slow everything down, everyone else would have to sit silently through his puerile contributions when the older kids had something of actual value to say. You know what kids are like, especially when they've finally made it to the top of the heap: jealous of their prerogatives. Intent on preserving their sense of superiority.

And for the first couple of weeks, Chance was pretty quiet. It was a seminar, participation was sort of the point, but I'd have to prompt him with questions to get him to say anything. And while what he had to say was always sensible, it was usually brief, and rarely especially striking. I knew he could do better. I'd read his papers in 1A, I knew he had an original mind and a penetrating way with a text. So I was a little frustrated. It was important to me that he demonstrate his right to be there. I don't know if he was intimidated by his classmates—by which I mean by their age—or more likely just felt it would be tactful not to be too assertive. He was aware his presence was resented by some of the other students, he'd heard some of the complaints, some of them were directed his way. So he may have felt he was there on sufferance. Or on probation.

Now, sometimes in class I'd have the students read scenes from the plays we were studying. Read them out loud, I mean. A given student taking an assigned part. These weren't meant to be rehearsed performances, you understand, but rather...see, the point I was trying to make to them was, this isn't material written to be read silently in one's study, it's written to be performed, to be *sounded*. So it was important for the students to learn to read plays *as* plays, the way, say, a musician reads a score. To actually *hear the voices* in their heads, not just take in the meaning in some passive way. And so I figured these little ad hoc performances, no matter how rough or stumbling, might train the kids to approach their at-home reading differently.

And you probably can imagine that most of them didn't even try very hard to give anything resembling a performance. That might have entailed a loss of face, emoting in class like that, trying too hard. So they mostly just read the words flatly, without much expression. Playing it safe. And often they struggled just to get the words out. Even though this was an upper division class, some of the students still had trouble reading at college level. They sure as hell couldn't *write* at college level, many of them. We didn't get the cream of the crop at State.

Anyway, we were reading *King Lear*. I always restricted the class to only one Shakespeare play per semester, I didn't want to scare kids away. And even though Chance was a freshman and by rights shouldn't be in the class at all, I took a flyer and asked him to read Lear's scene on the heath. And I have to tell you, he just knocked it out of the park. He *became* this crazy old man, full of rage and pain and wild madness. It was heartbreaking, chilling, frightening. The essence of tragedy.

He made the hair stand up on the back of my neck. I swear to God, his interpretation wouldn't have been out of place in the Royal Shakespeare Company or the National Theater. And when he was done, there was total silence for a long few seconds, and then the whole class burst into applause. That had never happened before. A totally spontaneous ovation. They knew they'd just witnessed something incredible.

Nancy Hawkins

How WAS IT WITH Willy? [pause] You mean when Chance and I were together? With Willy being around all the time? Yeah, it was fine. Actually, better than fine. The three of us got along real well. Gangbusters. But you have to understand, by the time I was with Chance, he and Willy were kind of BMOCs at State. Not in the usual sense, not by being good athletes or whatever. But just by having this aura around them. This cool aura. Partly it was the exotic nature of their friendship, and partly it was how good-looking they both were, and of course because Willy was black, that added to it, and word of Chance's acting had gotten around, he was in a couple of drama club productions and had impressed everybody. So they were kind of the stars of our class, and they had this magic circle, a circle of two, and nobody could penetrate it. They had other friends, jointly and separately, they weren't especially stand-offish, but they also had a kind of bond that seemed to exclude everybody else. You could be their friend, but if you tried to get too close to one or the other of them, to worm your way into the charmed circle, there was this sudden sort of chill in the air, and you either backed off right away or were made to feel really unwelcome.

But they made an exception for me. Probably not because of any quality of my own, much as I'd love to think so. More a sort of honorary deal, like I got an exemption because I was dating Chance. Admission into the members' lounge was like a perk that came with the position. And they were both so much fun and so interesting, it felt like a real privilege. A lot of people don't know how funny Chance could be when he was in the right mood, but he was a riot sometimes, and Willy was always good for a laugh. And they set each other off. Sometimes one would catch the other's eye and they'd just start giggling. It was great to be part of that.

And all my girlfriends envied me. They envied me being with Chance of course, but also my being allowed to hang out with both of them. Independent of the romantic aspect. Hanging out in their dorm room, which was against the rules but I did it all the time and we never got into serious trouble for it, just chatting away or listening to music—Willy had this great collection of jazz LPs and they were on the Victrola all the time—and hanging out in the commissary or picnicking in the quad or whatever. And then, the next year, spending most of my free time in their apartment off-campus.

And this isn't a very noble reason to enjoy anyone's company, but when other people envy your being able to do it, that does add to the appeal. You know, from what I've read, it was really boring to be part of, say, Frank Sinatra's entourage, or Elvis Presley's, you just sat around waiting for the king to express a desire and then you had to hop to, but still, the fact that everybody who *wasn't* in their entourage wished they could be made it feel like you were the luckiest person on earth.

What was Chance like as a lover? You mean...not from a romantic point of view, but from the physical side? Holy cow, that's an awfully personal question. That really crosses a line. I'm certainly not going to answer it. Except I'll say this: We were young, we were ardent, and we were...beginners. Okay?

Wilson Denny

NANCY FINALLY CAME ACROSS toward the end of May, as I recall. A huge relief for all concerned. It's my understanding that the deciding factor involved *her* roommate, *Nancy's* roommate, almost as much as it involved Chance. She found out this girl—they had become good friends, not inseparable buddies like Chance and me exactly, but they were pretty close—she found out that her roommate had been having sex with her boyfriend on a regular basis since high school. It must have been eye-opening for Nancy. A shock. Her roommate, and I can't even remember the girl's name anymore, but her roommate was a straight-A student and a fine upstanding citizen and a big Eisenhower supporter and went to chapel every Sunday, so I guess finding out that such a person was also enthusiastic about fucking caused Nancy to reassess her options.

And while it no doubt was a cause for jubilation for Chance, it sure as hell made *my* life easier too. This roommate—oh wait, I remember her name all of a sudden, it was Elizabeth something. [pause] Elizabeth Copeland! God, in what part of your brain are these data stored? She lived an hour or two from campus, I mean her folks did, and she often went home for weekends. In order to have sex with her boyfriend, I think that was the main motivation, although of course her parents thought it was to visit *them*. But now, Nancy, finally realizing that sex wasn't necessarily a badge of shame, that even Republicans and Christers do the nasty, Nancy finally felt okay about it. More than okay. She became a devotee. She started sneaking Chance into her room on weekends and whenever her roommate was out—I don't know if they used the towel-on-the-doorknob trick or not—and as a result I finally could rely on being able to sleep in my own bed. Sometimes during the week they'd have an afternoon tryst in our room, but that wasn't the same kind of inconvenience. In fact, it probably improved my grades, since I used to hide out in the library to let them do their business, and once I was there, there wasn't much to do but study. So maybe I owe making the Dean's List to Nancy's newly liberated libido. And since my grades helped me get into NYU Med, I suppose you could say I owe my whole career to Nancy's decision to let go of her virginity.

Nancy Hawkins

EARLY JUNIOR YEAR, A couple of weeks before Christmas break, Chance told me he was quitting State, he was dropping out. He was just wasting his time at college, he said. His mind was made up. He was going to go to New York, maybe apply to the Actors Studio, maybe even try to find an agent. He knew what he wanted to do with his life, and he had some notion of what he needed to do to make it happen, and nothing he was doing at college was helping him get there.

He asked me to come with him. It was as close to a declaration of seriousness as he'd ever gotten, but frankly, I don't think he really meant it. I didn't think so even at the time. I was touched, kind of, but I also found it hard to take seriously. Here's how I interpreted it, what I thought he was saying: "Listen, I'm not breaking up with *you*, I'm breaking up with my life here. And to prove it, I'm asking you if you want to come with me." It was sweet in its way, considerate, he was making it clear that it wasn't a personal rejection, but of course it kind of was. I was part of the life he needed to leave behind. I'm not sure I could have put it into words back then, but on some more basic level, some non-verbal level, I understood. Whatever he was after, whatever kind of life he wanted for himself, it sure as heck didn't include me. Or it might have at first, and then wouldn't have. I knew that, knew it without having to think about it.

And frankly, I wouldn't have been tempted regardless. I didn't want to go to New York. I had no business in New York. And I wanted to finish school. I had my own life to consider. Plus, it was clear I'd just have been a drag on him if I'd gone. He was going to be hoeing a very rough road for the next couple of years; you didn't have to be sophisticated about show business to know how tough it would be. Plus, a whole new life would be opening up for him whether he was successful or not. The last thing in the world he needed was some girl from back home depending on him.

And maybe I didn't love him. Not like *love* love, anyway. We had fun together, and I cared about him, and I knew he was a pretty remarkable guy, but since I wasn't really tempted to follow him to New York, not for more than a couple of minutes anyway, I have to conclude my feelings for him didn't run all that deep.

What? You think that was mature of me? That's nice of you to say, but I don't think I was especially mature. Not at that age. I think I just knew, maybe I'd known all along, that Chance was going to be going places where I wouldn't be able, or even eager, to follow.

George Berlin

CHANCE CAME TO SEE me one afternoon. He wanted some advice. He was thinking about dropping out of school and going to New York to try his luck. What did I think? He claimed to want my opinion, but in retrospect I think his mind was made up. He knew what he was going to do. What he wanted was my blessing. Which is kind of touching, I guess. We'd become close, I was very encouraging toward him, I thought he might be a major talent. You could even say I kind of mentored him, although not in terms of acting instruction—I was in no position to do that—but just providing validation and moral support.

Anyway, I had to think fast and search my own conscience. Ordinarily, I would never tell a kid it's okay to drop out. Never had before, and this wasn't the first time I'd had one of these conversations…kids have identity crises in college, it's kind of a thing, and they feel a need to run away. Just snap the umbilicus and split. But I *believe* in college. I believe in the value of a broad education no matter what you want to do with your life. And Chance wasn't only a talented actor, he was a very bright guy. His mind was like a sponge. Plus, I think, even for actors, the more you know the better you'll be at your art. Stuff—knowledge— things that have to do with history and literature and art and even science, stuff can influence your work in ways that are indirect but profound. Hemingway used to cite as influences not only Tolstoy and Shakespeare, but also Mozart and Cezanne. It all goes into the mix. If you're receptive enough and smart enough and have the sort of integrative temperament an artist needs, it all goes into the mix.

But with Chance…well, he was so motivated, and not only about acting, but about everything. The quintessential autodidact. He didn't need us. So I shook his hand and told him I'd be very sorry to see him go and I would miss him, but I thought he was probably making the right decision.

Wilson Denny

SOPHOMORE YEAR, CHANCE AND I rented an apartment off campus on the bad side of town, and trust me, that town didn't have a good side. Our place was an incredible hovel, but we both liked the idea of having our own space and putting some distance between ourselves and the school authorities. Guys that age don't notice how lousy their living space is, but they know whether or not adults are in a position to supervise them. That was much more important to us. Also, we found a place with two bedrooms, so we didn't have to worry about hanging any damn towels on any damn doorknobs anymore.

Did we consider not being roommates that year? You mean living alone, or rooming with other guys? Well, either way…I mean I can't speak for Chance, and we obviously can't ask him now, but I know I didn't. We were pals. Like I said, there were hardly any black folk on campus, so I didn't have an obvious other place to turn. But that's neither here nor there, really. Chance and me, we were tight. Maybe even best friends. We were incredibly lucky the school assigned us to the same dorm room freshman year. I can't imagine either of us would've been happy rooming with almost any of the other guys in our class. Me for obvious reasons, and Chance because…because they were the kind of guys he went to high school with, and he didn't have any friends in high school. Or so he told me.

So I was more than a little pissed off when halfway through junior year he suddenly announced he was splitting. For one thing, it kind of left me in the lurch in terms of the apartment. I couldn't afford the rent all by myself, and we'd signed a year lease. But it wasn't only about the apartment. Chance was my best buddy at State and the sad truth is I didn't have a second-best buddy. Being black at a lily-white place like that, you were pretty isolated. People might be nice to you—I mean, it wasn't like I felt the full weight of institutional racism directed my way most days—but they didn't get especially close either. It was a nod in the hall, a quick hello, how's it goin'? Even the girls you slept with, they mostly kind of withdrew afterward. I'd reconciled myself to feeling isolated when I'd first arrived as a freshman, but then I'd been incredibly lucky in terms of Chance being my roommate, and now, over the course of a couple of years, I'd been spoiled. I didn't relish being a recluse for the next year and a half, plus probably four years of med school. And in addition, I thought Chance should probably have talked this over with me first instead of just dropping it on me. Isn't that what friends do?

Nancy Hawkins

I DON'T KNOW IF you know this, and I don't know if I should even tell you, but...see, after Chance left for New York, me and Willy, we had a little...a little thing. A little fling. And it didn't end well. For *anyone*. Willy and I barely spoke afterward, which was awkward, since we saw each other all the time. It was impossible to avoid each other at such a small school. And when Chance found out...well, he pretended it was cool, his letters said he thought it was great, that he always knew the two of us had this mutual attraction and were bound to act on it sooner or later. But the truth is, things weren't the same afterward. Between Chance and me, I mean. Fewer letters right away, and pretty soon none at all. He stopped writing. Now, that could have been for all sorts of reasons, I suppose, but given the timing, it seems clear to me it had something to do with me and Willy. So, I mean, that wasn't a good idea from a whole bunch of points of view. I mean, obviously. And looking back, I think maybe Wilson and I were both mainly trying to keep in indirect contact with Chance, that's how come it happened in the first place. And it just didn't work.

NEW YORK

Leon Shriver (actor)

CHANCE FAILED HIS AUDITION at the Actors Studio. It was a crushing experience for him. Lee told him he seemed to have some talent, but he just didn't have enough maturity or professional experience to benefit from the Studio. He didn't have *any* experience, in point of fact, although he may have lied a little on the paperwork we had to fill out before we performed. People do, all the time. But let's face it, he was a college dropout who'd done some community theater and a couple of college productions, and that's it. Now, professional experience wasn't strictly speaking a requirement at the Actors Studio, not officially, but they kind of frowned on amateurs, or people whose résumés made them look like amateurs.

On the other hand, I mean, come on. This was *Chance Hardwick*. A totally great actor. A natural. Without any training at all, he was already better than almost everyone studying at the Actors Studio. Almost anyone working on Broadway. And he gave a great audition. I know, I was there. And to some extent we were even competing with each other, so you can imagine how hard it is for me to say that.

The thing is, Lee was just...he was being Lee. Pulling rank, playing the guru, arrogating unto himself the role of ultimate judge. I think he resented the fact that...see, all of us in the room knew we'd seen something special, there was that kind of sharp, unconscious, collective expulsion and intake of breath when Chance finished his scene, the sound every actor hopes for, the one that signifies the audience has been transfixed by something onstage, they've been holding their breath without even knowing it, and they all let it out at the same time. It's a glorious validation of the whole theatrical enterprise. And it happened that afternoon when Chance auditioned, and I think it bothered Lee. He felt they should have waited for his reaction, he wanted to reassert control of the situation. Felt the need to set us straight, you know? So he rejected Chance with that patronizing rhetorical pat on the head.

And Chance never forgave him for it. I mean, in retrospect, rejections of that sort early in your career can be a funny detail in your biography. Like all those publishers who rejected *Moby Dick*. Here you had one of the best actors of his generation, if not *the* best, turned down flat by the most distinguished acting school of its time, and by its most famous instructor. But that kind of story is funny only in retrospect. When it happens to you, you don't know that within a couple of years you're going to have a huge career. When it happens, it's nothing but a devastating setback.

Lee did tell Chance he should come back in a year or so and try again. I guess he viewed that as a small concession. Chance said— although under his breath, so I may have been the only person to hear it—he said, "Sure, and they say pigs'll be flying by then."

We auditioned together, Chance and me. Each agreed to be in the other's scene. You were required to play a scene with someone else—that was the rule. No monologues permitted. The scene had to be from a contemporary play and it had to involve a change in attitude or emotion and it had to be in English. We were both waiting tables at the same Village dump in those days, and we both had high hopes of seeing our name in lights—[laughs]—and we'd become workplace pals. Casual pals, but friendly. 'Cause we were both dealing with a lot of the same shit. Sometimes we'd go out for a beer after our shift, and, you know, cry in said beer about how tough things were. So we agreed to audition together—a little mutual encouragement, because we were both apprehensive about the whole idea, aghast at our own temerity—and to help each other prepare. I'm not sure Chance even had anyone else to turn to. He was still pretty new to New York, I don't think he knew a lot of people. And as for me, I had other options, but I just trusted him. As a guy, I mean, not as an actor so much. I didn't realize how good he was yet, I'd never seen him act except when we rehearsed a bit for our auditions. I just had a good feeling about what sort of person he was.

He chose a scene from *Long Day's Journey*, I did one from *All My Sons*. We were hitting dysfunctional family life pretty hard, weren't we? [laughs] But that's what most American plays were about in those post-war years.

The irony is, I passed the audition, he didn't. But credit where credit's due, he forgave me. [laughs] All kidding aside, it's not so easy to accept another actor's success when you've struck out. Acting may not be a zero-sum game, but it is when you're actually competing for the same one part. And even when you aren't, it sure can feel like it sometimes. Because the odds are so long, you start feeling like, well, if one of you made it, then the other's chances must have shrunk.

But like I say, Chance was a good guy. A generous colleague. More generous than I would have been in those circumstances. Congratulations, you deserved it, that sort of thing. Big handshake. He was a stand-up guy when it couldn't have been easy, even if things finally did work out for him in a way anyone else would envy. As I say, no one could've been confident about *that* at the time. For all we knew, it might have been the burial ground of all his ambitions right there. And of course, considering how things ended for him, maybe what *did* happen later wasn't so enviable after all.

So Chance forgave me for my lucky break. The only person he *didn't* forgive after that deflating experience was Lee Strasberg. Where Lee was concerned, he held a grudge, a deep grudge. A few years after all this happened, and after Chance had become a star, they bumped into each other at some event here in

New York, and Lee approached Chance and introduced himself and told him how much he admired his work. He didn't have any memory of the audition. He had no idea they had a history. And Chance looked him up and down, ignored the outstretched hand, and told him to fuck off. I've never seen Lee look so shocked. Except maybe when he was acting, *playing* somebody who was shocked. I mean, he was so shocked at that moment he was too shocked even to be offended. I doubt anyone had ever told Lee Strasberg to fuck off before.

Michael Strachan (writer)

WE WERE CASTING MY first play, a little off-off-Broadway production. And Chance came in to read for one of the parts. One of the smaller parts.

I wanted to cast him. I thought he was great. But the producer and the director disagreed with me. "Too fey," they said. "He's all wrong for it." I was amazed at how obtuse they were being. I mean, it seemed so obvious to me. "Are you kidding? The kid's an amazing talent! He can be anything we want him to be." But they won the argument. I still want to kick myself for not sticking to my guns. Might have made a lot of difference. To me, not to Chance. The guy they eventually *did* cast…well, let's just say he went into another line of work soon after we closed. And we closed after about five performances.

Before we opened I contacted Chance to tell him how much I liked his reading and how sorry I was that we'd gone in a different direction. And he wrote back a while later. He was generous about the play, told me he thought it deserved a better fate. Of course, that could be interpreted as a dig for our not having hired him, but I think he meant it sincerely. And we kept in touch after that. In fact, he's the reason I ended up coming out here to California.

This was a couple of years later. He knew I'd been having a rough time in New York. He wrote to say there was work to be had in pictures and money to be made—they were always looking for good writers—and I ought to give it a shot. Seeing as I had nothing to lose, I took a chance and came out here to scout around. And never looked back.

Ellie Greenfield Lerner (girlfriend)

I SUPPOSE, LIKE THEY say in the movies, Chance and I "met cute." Still makes me giggle when I think of it. See, I used to work part-time in a little record store in the Village. Little hole-in-the-wall place. Long narrow room crammed floor to ceiling with racks of LPs. I was a student at NYU at the time, so the location was convenient, and the owner was good about being flexible when it came to my hours and everything. And it was a neat job...I'd be alone in the shop most of the shift, I could play whatever records I liked, deal with customers when they came in, do schoolwork behind the register when things were quiet.

Chance used to drop in a lot. I'd come to recognize him as a regular, even though he almost never bought anything, just flipped through the LPs. I think we were a kind of regular stop on his afternoon wanderings. He'd come in and head straight to the jazz section at the rear of the store and see if anything new had come in. Of course I noticed him right from my first day. Good-looking guy like that. I mean, gorgeous. Obviously. But really ratty. He was going through a difficult time back then, and he totally looked like a bum. Like the handsomest bum on the planet, mind you, but still, pretty disreputable. In dirty torn jeans and this filthy torn army coat with God knows what kind of stains on it. He was usually unshaven. Couple of days' growth of beard. Hair kind of tangled up. Believe me, you have to be awfully handsome to still look handsome in the shape he was in. But in a funny way, that might have added to his allure. To a girl who's nineteen years old, at any rate. He was kind of mysterious, do you see, kind of romantic, this guy who was so great-looking and obviously down-and-out at the same time. Like Arthur Rimbaud or somebody.

But other than my saying hello to him when he'd come in, we didn't speak. I mean, I'd say hello and he'd kind of mumble something back or give me a furtive nod. He didn't ignore me, but he didn't make conversation, that's for sure. Occasionally he'd come in, notice the music I was playing on the store system, and kind of wrinkle his nose. A little show of disapproval. He didn't like my taste, I guess. Which was pretty unformed at that time, admittedly. Cornball stuff. Your Hit Parade stuff. Once in a while he'd even roll his eyes. That was as close as he came to communication. It was hard to tell whether it was humorous disapproval or pure unvarnished scorn.

And then one day, I noticed in the big store mirror—there was a mirror over the entrance reflecting the entire room, I guess for just such an occasion as this—I noticed Chance, in the jazz section way in the back, slipping an LP under his coat. I've got to tell you, it was shocking. I had no idea how to deal with something like that. It had never happened before, not in my experience, and I was naïve enough to believe it never happened. But there it was, right in front of my eyes. Well, behind my head, actually, but reflected in a mirror right in front of my eyes.

So I was stumped. What was I supposed to do? The manager hadn't given me any guidance about how to handle shoplifters. It hardly seemed worthwhile to call the cops. I mean, how much did LPs cost in those days? A buck, maybe? Two? This wasn't grand theft. And I wasn't exactly in a position to overpower him physically. Chance wasn't a big guy, it's true, but I *was* a little girl. Still, I was steamed, I didn't feel like just letting this go. It was so brazen. So...

so…it struck me as almost *contemptuous*. I wasn't going to let him get away with it without at least letting him know I knew. I didn't want to seem stupid, a dupe, like he'd somehow pulled the wool over my eyes. Also, I wanted him to know that in my opinion it was a really lousy thing to do.

So as he headed toward the front entrance, sauntering out as casual and cocky as you please, even giving me a little wave, I said, "You hold it right there, mister."

He could have bolted, of course. If he *had* run for it, by the time I got out from behind the register and through the front door to chase him he could have been down the street and around a corner and been lost among the crowds in Greenwich Village. But instead he froze. "What is it?" he said. First time I'd ever heard his voice, other than those mumbled "hi's." His voice was deeper than I expected.

"I saw what you just did," I said. "I saw you take that record."

"Huh? What record?"

It's funny: For such a great actor, he wasn't much of a liar. He sounded just about as guilty as he obviously was. "Come on, bud, don't treat me like an idiot. I'm from around here, I'm not some out-of-towner sap. Now hand it over." See, the thing is, since he wasn't running away, I sort of felt like I might have the upper hand even though there was no reason for that to be the case. He still could have run, but for whatever reason, he didn't. Guilt? Inexperience? He somehow was enjoying himself? Beats me. I went on, just, you know, improvising. "It's store policy to prosecute shoplifters to the full extent of the law." I made up that store policy on the spot, incidentally. "You could be in big trouble. But if you hand the record over right now, I'm willing to let it pass."

I had no cards to play, not really, but he seemed a little cowed. He said, "Okay, okay," and pulled the record out from under his coat. He looked a little sheepish. As he handed it up to me, he said,

"It's Sonny Stitt's latest. I just had to have it. I'm a little short right now, I would have come back and paid for it eventually, honest I would have, but I couldn't wait, I had to have it right away." And then, as I took it from him, he went on, "Are you a Sonny Stitt fan?"

"I'm not really familiar with him."

"Not familiar with Sonny Stitt? You're kidding, right?"

"Is he a singer?"

Chance snorted. "No, he's not a *singer*. You must be confusing him with *Johnny Ray*." This was a dig at the kind of stuff I'd been playing in the store some of the other times he'd come in. "Sonny Stitt plays the saxophone, for your information. Alto and tenor. He isn't some crappy pop singer, he's a serious artist. A genius."

"I don't really listen to jazz much."

See what he'd done? He had somehow suckered me into a conversation, almost a normal conversation, within seconds of my having caught him stealing. I sometimes wonder if it would have worked if he hadn't been so handsome. Although he had plenty of charm to go with those looks. Those incredible eyes, that mischievous smile, that confiding manner. But if he'd been some old, dirty, toothless homeless guy who'd just boosted a record, would I have given him the time of day? Probably not, charm or no charm.

"Jazz is the great American music," Chance said. He sounded almost indignant, like, how could I not like jazz? What was the matter with me? Pretty cheeky, to sound indignant right after being caught stealing. But he almost pulled it off. "It's America's major contribution to world culture! You can't just say you don't listen to it. You *have* to listen to it. Like, if you lived in Vienna a hundred years ago, you'd have to listen to Beethoven."

"But I don't like it."

He recoiled. Humorously. You know, in an exaggerated way. And damn it, he made me laugh. "I'm just going to pretend I didn't hear that," he said. And then, more earnestly, he said, "It's because you haven't heard much of it, there simply can't be any other reason. Tell you what: I'm a little short right now, I guess you've figured that out. Being an out-of-work actor can be rough on the pocketbook. But next time I get a paycheck, let me take you to one of the clubs around here. Okay? There's a lot of great music happening in New York. You'll hear what you've been missing. It'll change your life."

So that's what I mean about "meeting cute." I busted him for shoplifting and like two minutes later he was asking me for a date.

Leon Shriver

SO I'M AT THE Actors Studio, doing scenes and improvs and digging into sense memories of family trauma and dental visits and unhooking some girl's bra strap in high school, and Chance and I are still waiting tables at that little dive in the Village, on and off—sometimes they'd can us, then they'd find they were short-handed and rehire us—and then all of a sudden he gets lucky. Well, I'm not sure he saw it exactly that way. Not in the long run. He did at first. He got a job, and no actor scoffs at a job. Chance might have bitched about it, but he could also be a very practical guy. He wasn't any prima donna, not when he couldn't afford to be. Work, work, work, that was his credo back then, even if it was crap, because no actor ever thrives by going hungry, and no casting director ever notices you when you're sitting home brooding about *not* working. Work leads to more work. And it's an opportunity to practice your instrument.

So as a matter of policy he went to almost every open casting call in town. And kept striking out. He said to me, "They're not gonna discourage me, Leon. A pretty face like mine, somebody's got to want me sooner or later. I'm gonna wear those fuckers down." So he just went out and pitched himself. Parts he was perfect for and parts where the whole thing was ridiculous. I mean, hell, he was no more modest about his talent than about his looks. He figured he could be anything a script called for, could play old men and pimply adolescents and probably one of the witches in *Macbeth* if it had come to that. He never put a limit on what he could do. So he just girded himself for battle and went out every day. And absorbed all the punishment actors are used to receiving. Like, you know how Hitchcock once said "actors are cattle?" Well, that was right on the money. It's no accident casting calls are called cattle calls in the business.

But then, one day, Chance read for a continuing role on a soap—three weeks guaranteed, with an option to renew—and even though the corridor outside the producer's office was lined with good-looking guys in their twenties sitting on the floor waiting for their turn to read, guys who to any superficial observer were indistinguishable from Chance, this time his ship came in. The kid brother of one of the principals, newly released from prison and come back to town under a cloud of suspicion. Lovable but menacing. A sweet misunderstood loner or a serial killer? To be determined. It was a part he could play in his sleep.

Ellie Greenfield Lerner

SO CHANCE DIDN'T COME into the store for a couple of weeks after I'd caught him trying to steal that LP. Could he have been embarrassed? Or maybe he was waiting for the right moment. And then one afternoon he turned up. All smiles. "Hey!" he said. "How you been?" Like we were old pals. Like he'd just come back from his junior year abroad.

I was a little wary. The guy was a proven thief, after all. "Yeah, hi," I said. "Haven't seen you in a while. How'd you like Riker's?"

Twisted smile. "Not even close, honey. But I have been kind of busy. Auditioning and things."

"You still claim you're an actor?" See, I hadn't believed him when he'd said it before. It's such an easy thing to say. Every waiter, every courier, every schmo in New York and LA says he's either an actor or a writer or both. What makes someone an out-of-work actor rather than just a schmendrick who's out of work? And as I said, he had the appearance of a street person. Usually smelled like one too. So I was a little skeptical. Although, to be fair, he had cleaned up pretty good on this particular day. He didn't look nearly so scuzzy. And he smelled like Zest soap, which was at least a small step up.

"You think I was bullshitting you?" he said. Looking kind of hurt. "Not at all. In fact, smarty pants, I just got cast in something. You can catch me on your TV machine starting next week." Big smile.

So this was a surprise. I said, "Really? You're gonna be on TV? Or is this just more bull?"

"No bull. *The Proud and the Bold*. Weekday afternoons at two thirty p.m., channel seven. My part starts next Monday."

"Well…gee. Congrats." I still wasn't sure he was telling the truth or not.

"Yeah, thanks."

"Is it a big part?"

"That's not a question you should ever ask an actor. But, yeah, it's actually a pretty big part."

"Not that there are any small parts, just small actors."

"There you go."

"Well, okay, congrats again."

"Yeah, thanks again. But listen, the truth is, I didn't come here to tell you about that. I came here today for two completely different reasons."

"I'm all ears."

"Well, one of them is, now that I'm drawing a salary and all, I want to buy that damned Sonny Stitt album. With real money. Out of my own pocket."

I couldn't help smiling when he said that. "That's fine," I said. "Go grab one. I'm sure you don't need my assistance finding it."

Which got that one-sided grin out of him again, the one that later became almost his trademark. "Okay, okay."

As he started toward the back of the store, I said, "You said there were two reasons. What's the other one?"

He turned to look back at me over his shoulder. "Oh, to invite you to come out with me tonight. Clark Terry's playing at the Vanguard. He's really good. We could get some dinner, you can finally see what you've been missing."

"Uh huh. Who's paying?"

He laughed out loud at that. "Why, me, of course. I'm a working actor, for Christ's sake."

So that's how our relationship got started. I wasn't sure I should say yes to him, but I did anyway. One of those impulse things. I liked the ping-pong rhythm of our conversation, that might actually have had more to do with it than his looks.

And PS, I *hated* the jazz. God, what a racket! *Squawk squawk squawk.* But I fell in love with Chance, so I guess you could say the evening was a wash. And of course I lied to him about hating the jazz. Didn't want to disappoint him.

Don Barlow (director)

WE CAST CHANCE FOR *The Proud and the Bold.* There was some controversy about it in the production offices. Some people thought he wasn't quite menacing enough. You know, we wanted to keep the character's true nature a mystery to the audience for a while. Hell, it was a mystery to the *writers.* [laughs] They hadn't figured out what they were going to do with him. It partly depended on how he went over with viewers. He could be the sensitive, misunderstood loner who was wrongly convicted and who ends up saving the day, or he could be a serial killer. I think the writers were inspired by *Shadow of a Doubt* or *Suspicion* or one of those. We were keeping our options open, and as a result the actor had to convey both possibilities at once. For a process actor, something like that can present serious problems. When Chance had questions about his motivation, when he asked me for guidance, as happened more than once, I had to say to him, "Beats the shit out of me."

Which made it a huge acting challenge for him. Actors, especially actors who work from the inside out, need to know what their characters are trying to achieve in every scene. That's the way they build a performance. But with Chance's character, he was trying to achieve either one or the other of two totally contradictory things, and we couldn't tell him which one was right.

It was like the poor guy'd been thrown into the middle of a pool without having been given any swimming lessons. And listen, on the one hand, some of the staff didn't want to hire him in the first place because he struck them as too sweet, and he was aware of that and had to work against that impression. And on the other hand, we'd put him in this terrible position of not knowing whether he was supposed to be sweet but confused, or sly, malevolent, and nuts. Quite a quandary.

But once the camera started to roll, any misgivings anyone had disappeared. Chance could be damned menacing, but always with that winsome, ingratiating little crooked smile. And charming in a kind of insinuating, unsettling way. It was a beautifully modulated performance, honestly. Straddling all the possibilities, giving nothing away, leaving all options open. He complained about the position we'd put him in, complained to me, complained to the producers. He wasn't a prima donna about it, he wasn't a Michael

Dorsey, but he had legitimate questions. "How can I give an honest performance if *I* don't know what my character knows?" Not many day players in a soap opera would be so concerned about artistic truth—[laughs]—but Chance was never less than conscientious about his work. And we couldn't really help him. "Just do the best you can" was the upshot of what all of us advised. He had to rely on craft. Although I think he worked out some elaborate notion of having a divided consciousness so that his character didn't know the truth either. If you look at old kinescopes—a few have survived, terrible quality—you can see it in his eyes in some of his close-ups, this anxious confusion. But I'm just guessing, really. At a certain point, he must have given up on us, because he quit talking about his process. But whatever he came up with, it worked.

And the camera simply loved him. And it wasn't just the *camera* that loved him. The fan mail started pouring in from the first day. If you want objective proof of star quality, that was it right there. One appearance on an afternoon soap and the letters started arriving by the carload. "He's innocent, he just has to be!" A lot of them said things like that. Others even proposed marriage.

And of course that meant his character *was* innocent. Because now we wanted to keep him. He was a hit. We wanted him to be a regular on the show. We offered him a contract. His agent at the time was some fly-by-night stumble bum who couldn't have negotiated his way out of a paper bag, but Chance didn't need someone to drive a hard bargain for him. We wanted him. We made a generous offer.

Leon Shriver

I MIGHT BE WRONG about this, a typical actor thinking he's the most important thing in the show no matter what the credits might say, but it always seemed to me that a big turning point for

Chance was when I got the second lead in *Medicine Man*. A real Broadway show. I'd been struggling, just like Chance, working at the Actors Studio, going on auditions, getting a few call-backs but no parts other than a couple of commercials, and then, suddenly, the tide seemed to have turned. A good role in what promised to be a successful play. Established writer, established director, a real star heading the cast.

This was around the time Chance was doing that daytime soap. And it's kind of ironic, because when he first got that part, I envied the hell out of him. But then I got my shot at Broadway. And that seemed to upend everything. For him as well as for me.

Ellie Greenfield Lerner

So IT TURNED OUT to be a heck of a time in life to start dating a guy. In *his* life, I mean. When I agreed to that first date, he was a down-and-out record thief with clothes no second-hand store would touch and who on his best day smelled like cheap soap. I definitely felt that saying yes to him was an act of mercy. And then everything changed. It was maybe on our third date. Second or third. We hadn't slept together yet, so it was early, definitely. I think we'd been to a movie—it took some doing, but I'd talked him out of taking me to another jazz club—and we were at some little joint in Little Italy, checkered table clothes, candles in Chianti bottles on the table, the whole cornball shot, it was like *Lady and the Tramp*, and we were sharing a pizza. He was still such a newbie to New York that he regarded pizza as exotic fare. [laughs] I'm not kidding! Remember, this was a long time ago, pizza hadn't entered the Middle American bloodstream yet, not the way it would in a few years' time—at that point it was almost like what sushi would be in the seventies, at least if you didn't come from some place with ethnic neighborhoods, and…

wait, where was I? I've lost the thread. Remembering this stuff, it all comes flooding back, sort of overwhelms me just thinking about it. Haven't given any of these things a moment's thought in a long, long time.

Oh yeah, thanks. Right. Okay, so we were eating this pizza—I was showing him how to fold the slice over and eat it with his hands—and he was analyzing the performances in the movie we'd just seen. And that was actually interesting, his manner could get a little pedantic sometimes, a little lecturey, but what he had to say was real sharp and insightful, and because so much of it was new to me I always learned a lot when he started explaining acting to me like that—so that was going on, and I think we were drinking wine, which was also a novelty for him; he was still mostly a beer kind of guy at that point in his life, he let me do the ordering, but drinking wine and eating pizza made him feel frightfully sophisticated. And anyway, suddenly this kid came up to us, she couldn't have been more than sixteen or so, and she asked Chance if he was Lance Foster—that was his character's name on the soap—and could she have his autograph?

That was kind of funny and kind of exciting, that first time. He still felt anonymous, I think, and as for me, even though I'd seen the soap—I made sure to check on that first Monday to see if he'd been telling the truth—but even though I knew he was an actor on TV by now, I still mostly thought of him as the bum who'd stolen a record from our store. It takes a little bit of time to make a big mental switch like that. So I wasn't intimidated or impressed by him or anything. Not yet. I didn't consider the situation special, I hadn't shifted gears in that way, he was just a guy I'd flirted with who'd asked me out under bizarre circumstances. And then this teenager asked him for his autograph and...and...well, you know. Suddenly you realize you're in a different world from the one you thought you were in.

But at the time, that night, we both laughed at how amazing it was, and Chance was sweet to the girl and signed an autograph and chatted with her a little. Introduced her to me, invited her to sit down for a minute, even offered to buy her a Coke, which she declined. She was obviously nervous and excited, and he tried to put her at her ease. It was as much a novelty for him as for her, after all.

But what neither of us realized that night, this is how innocent we both were, is that this was going to become a regular occurrence. It just seemed like a funny kind-of-charming one-off. But we were quickly disabused of that notion. Within a week or so, we couldn't go out in public very easily anymore. People would spot him, they'd make a fuss, they'd crowd him, they'd want an autograph or to talk about the show—they took the show very seriously, I have to say, and didn't seem to make much distinction between the show and real life, kept assuring him they knew he was innocent and stuff like that—and he'd be torn between his natural good manners and simple gratitude on one side, and a powerful desire to get the hell out of there on the other. And I suppose to protect *me* too, since a lot of the girls who came up to him would kind of maneuver me or even push me aside to get to him. It could get ugly real fast.

Kendell Fowler (actress)

A LOT OF PEOPLE forget—or maybe never even realized, never made the connection—that Chance Hardwick was a regular for a time on *The Proud and the Bold*. It's not something he mentioned in interviews after he became famous in Hollywood. Now, he didn't have a hugely long run with us, but he left a mark. We did the show live, it was all very on-the-fly and high-pressure, rehearse in the morning, air it in the afternoon, maybe do a rehearsal afterward for the following day if the pages were ready. So I hadn't met Chance yet when he showed up for rehearsals and make-up Monday morning. I'd read the day's sides of course, I knew the Lance Foster character was going to make his first appearance, but I had no idea who was going to play him. And the part as written… well, it could have been played by any sort of type, Lance could have been some nebbishy nothing, some hairy gnome, really any type at all, so I wasn't prepared for the Adonis who showed up on the floor that day.

I wanted to like him. We were a happy set, generally speaking, and there was a pretty good atmosphere on the show. People were friendly, and we were welcoming to newcomers and even day players. I give a lot of the credit to Don—Don Barlow— he was a nice guy himself, and in addition he believed a happy set was an efficient set, so even though he was dealing with all these temperamental types and under really enormous pressure, he kept things on a nice even keel. Even if you screwed up, forgot your lines or your blocking or whatever, he would be pleasant and encouraging after we wrapped. "It happens," he might say, or "Nobody's perfect," or whatever. "Try to do better tomorrow. Give somebody else a chance to be the fuck-up next time." Some little joke to make you feel safe. You know, doing the show live like that, it's a high-wire act. You're going to lose your balance occasionally. And keeping the atmosphere on the set light-hearted and collegial, it actually made for fewer slips. We were all less stressed, less taut, more relaxed about performing. And mutually supportive. If, say, somebody went up and we could see it was happening, we'd improvise a line that fed the actor *his* line. Stuff like that.

But you want to know about Chance. Right. Okay, so he came on that first morning, and right away there's *agita*. He wasn't nasty, I don't mean to suggest that, but he was obviously unhappy with the show and uncomfortable being on it. He was such an *actor*, you know what I mean? We had a job to do—we weren't the Moscow Art Theater, we weren't putting on *The Cherry Orchard* every afternoon—we were making a disposable artifact for housewives and old ladies. Nobody on the show thought this was high art or the pinnacle of our careers, we all aspired—or had aspired once upon a time, those of us who had already given up—to something higher. But this was a job, and a job isn't something to be sneezed at in this profession. There are lots of hungry actors out there. And the show had its purpose, not to save the world or illuminate the human condition, just to provide some diversion for people who liked that sort of thing. So we mainly needed to get on with it and not take ourselves too seriously.

But from the very first day, Hardwick was all, "Why am I doing this?" and "What's my objective?" and all those tiresome Method questions. And it was pretty obvious he heartily disliked the scripts, which didn't exactly endear him to the writers. "People don't talk like this!" he'd say. "This dialogue is awful!" He'd suggest line changes, new language…it was annoying, it wasted time, it was… it was like, for the rest of us, "Who the hell cares?" You know? Sometimes he was right, sometimes he was wrong—I'm willing to admit he probably was right more often than he was wrong—but so what? Was there a single person watching who would care, or would even notice?

Now, it's only fair to add that it wasn't all prima donna stuff. Not in that limited sense that it was always about *him*. Like once or twice he'd even say to Don, "This line of mine, this attitude, wouldn't it be better coming from Kendell? Wouldn't that be more in character?" Actually offering me a line or even a whole speech that was originally written for his character. Unheard of! It showed a certain integrity, or that might be one way of looking at it. But it also meant that the time when we could be doing something else, something useful, was spent discussing shit that honestly wasn't worth the effort. And forcing me to memorize new lines, which never came easy to me.

Don was very patient with him. Infinitely patient with his shit. Seemed to have taken a liking to him. He was willing to have these long conversations, accept suggestions, smooth things over between Chance and the writers or Chance and the other actors. But most of us got fed up with him pretty damn fast. He wasn't really making the show better, he was just making the process worse.

Robert Bluestone (actor)

YOU'VE TALKED TO KENDELL? Yeah, I thought so. [laughs] Chance really got under her skin. Drove her nuts. [laughs] Lots of muttering under her breath, lots of eye rolling between scenes. And I can't deny the guy could be a pain, especially during rehearsals. Slowed things down, argued endlessly.

And the writers hated him, hated him even worse than Kendell did. The poor writers were grinding out five scripts a week, it was a really brutal schedule, probably harder on the writers than anyone else connected with the show, and here's this young *pisher* comes along and says their work is crap. Which it often was, mind you. Not always, sometimes they'd come up with a scene that was kind of funny or kind of poignant, or a story line that had some vague resemblance to real life. But come on...five scripts a week, big dramatic buttons at the end of every half-hour, new story lines every couple weeks...of course the shows were often dumb. It wasn't the writers' fault—it was the whole enterprise.

So yeah, he could be a real pain in the ass. But on the other hand, you had to make allowances. He was very young, very green, and very, *very* serious. He wanted to do his best. He cared.

By comparison, the rest of us were just cynical old routiniers. And he wasn't mean or selfish about it, he was actually quite generous as a performer. Playing scenes with him was a pleasure, as a matter of fact. He *listened*, you know? Listened and reacted. Knew his lines, knew your lines, was totally in the moment when the camera started to roll. Met your eyes, plumbed them, revealed his own emotions. *Real* emotions, no indicating. Working with him was like playing ping pong with someone who's better than you are. It ups your game.

Which may have been what irked Kendell so much, frankly. Don't tell her I said so, but it was pretty obvious he was acting on a different level from the rest of us. It wasn't just that he cared—ridiculously, given the context, but he did care—it was that he *delivered*.

But I have a theory about him. See, if you grow up on the Upper East Side, say, or in some big city, someplace sophisticated, someplace with museums and theaters and concert halls, and let's say your parents are educated people, then high culture is just part of the air you've breathed all your life. You know it, you value it, but you also kind of take it for granted. Your interest in it doesn't have the force of a religious conversion. It just *is*. But if you come from a small town in the Midwest, if your background is pretty provincial, if you don't encounter all this stuff until you're in college, or even later maybe, then it takes on a different coloration, it plays a different role in your life, it seems magical, it becomes… it's the most important thing in the world. Central. Crucial. An organizing principle. And you consider yourself a missionary, partly because you assume most of the world is like the place you came from.

To my mind, Chance simply burned with all this new stuff he'd just discovered precisely because he'd just discovered it. He burned with it to the exclusion of all other considerations. Acting especially, acting most of all, acting and theater. But also jazz... he could go on for hours about Bird and Dizzy and all those bebop guys. He worshipped them. And painting—he'd apparently become friends with some gallery owners down in SoHo, he'd started to haunt the Met and MoMa—and all this stuff was new to him. He was consumed by it...like that Gershwin song, "How Long Has This Been Going On?" You know that song? [sings] "Now I know how Columbus felt/Discovering a new world."

It's like, you discover it all for yourself for the first time, and you start to feel like you're the first one it's ever happened to. Same thing happens the first time you fall in love, right? You may know better, but that's what it feels like. And you can't imagine not making it the most important thing in your life.

I mean...this is a crazy example, but there's a novel by a Canadian writer named Simon Gray, it's called *Simple People*. And the protagonist is this very naïve guy. And in one scene he finally, belatedly, loses his virginity. And he's over the moon about how great the experience was. And he's so enthusiastic about what's just happened, he says to the woman he's had sex with, "Why don't people do this all the time?" And she says, "They do."

I think high culture was kind of like that for Chance.

Ellie Greenfield Lerner

THE THING I'VE COME to realize about Chance is that he was basically an unhappy person. Maybe even clinically depressive. I don't mean just unhappy with me, or with that show he was on, or with New York. I think it was a permanent state for him. When I read about his death, and that was years after I'd last seen him, I thought right away it might be a suicide. He was a very troubled guy. It's part of what made him so appealing...you wanted to take care of him. You felt he needed to be cared for.

David Bayer (acquaintance)

I'D OCCASIONALLY SEE HIM at Julius's. I mean, I *think* it was him. Jeez, I always just assumed it was him, that's why I contacted you, but...I mean, it *must* have been him, the resemblance was too striking for it not to have been, although...I mean, it sure as hell looked exactly like the guy on the soap. But it's also true this guy had a mustache, and I don't know that Hardwick ever had facial hair. Although it could have been fake, that's another possibility. A little disguise. And he always came in wearing a fedora, which wasn't quite as unfashionable then as it would be now, men still wore hats, but still, you mostly didn't wear something like that indoors. So I'm thinking it probably was him, and maybe he thought he could go to gay bars incognito.

We'd nod hello, maybe say good evening. I'd say something, he'd mumble something back. That's about as far as it went. He'd come in around 11:00 p.m., midnight, have a drink or two, and leave. I never saw him leave *with* anybody. I don't think he came in to trick, just to absorb some of the atmosphere. Maybe to reassure himself that gay bars, a gay community, actually exist, demonstrate to himself he wasn't the only queer on the planet. Like maybe where he came from nobody knew about that stuff. Don't get me wrong, wherever you came from fags walked among you, but they kept their identity secret. It was a secret society.

Well, whoever he was, Hardwick or a lookalike, he kept to himself. But like I say, I'm pretty sure it was him. He'd sidle in kind of late, sit alone at the last seat at the bar, keep his head down and his hat on, sip his drink for a half-hour or so, sidle out again. His whole demeanor, his posture, his bearing, everything, said, "*Ne touchez pas.*" So of course people left him alone. You've got to respect someone's privacy, even out in public. No one asks for autographs in a gay bar.

Leon Shriver

MEDICINE MAN—MY CAN'T-MISS, SURE-TO-BE-A-HIT Broadway show—closed after six performances. Brooks Atkinson *hated* the play. I mean *really* hated it. Wrote a venomous notice. A classic of the genre. Now, as it happens, he loved *me*—gave me a positively glowing review—but also said I was the only good thing in a horrible mishmash and my performance alone wasn't enough to redeem a miserable evening.

The odd thing is, even though I was in a huge flop, I sort of had the feeling I was on my way. And Chance had a similar reaction. He took me out to dinner the night after the show closed and told me that with the review the *Times* had given me, fuck the play, I was going to be in demand. And he was right. I think he was probably jealous, but he was also being a good guy, bucking me up. And I got cast in another show within the month. And when that happened, he said to me, "See? I told you." And he also said, "You know, it's lucky for you that you're a good guy. Because otherwise I'd really hate your guts."

And I said, "You're one to talk. You're in a successful TV show, you're making real money, you don't have to worry about when you'll get your next shot, you don't have to go out for auditions all the time and pray for a call-back. You're set."

He rolled his eyes. "Have you seen the show, Leon? *Have you seen the show?*" I admitted I had. "And you think highly of it, is that what you're telling me?" Well, I had to concede I didn't regard it as possessing superlative artistic value. "So tell me: Would you be happy doing that five days a week every week, and seeing those five days a week stretch out past the horizon?"

Well, he had me there.

Eppy Bronstein (widow of agent)

MURRAY ADORED CHANCE. EVEN when he first showed up at Murray's office, when he didn't have a pot to pee in, Murray took a shine to him. This must have been real soon after he first got to New York. Another cockeyed kid from the boonies hoping to make it in show business. But Murray liked his face, liked his all-American manner. Just had a good feeling about him, you know? Thought he probably had talent. No professional credits to speak of, but Murray could tell there was something special about the boy. I remember he came home that night and said, "I think I just signed the next Montgomery Clift." I asked him what the fellow had been in, and he said, "Nothing yet. But I got an instinct."

Signing him was a real act of faith. I mean, besides that instinct, Murray had absolutely nothing to go on, no reason to take a chance on...on Chance. [laughs] But Murray was like that anyway. Even when he wasn't enthusiastic about a talent, the way he was with Chance, he still was more inclined to take somebody on than turn him down. He used to say, "This is a crazy business, it's like playing the slots, you never know what machine's going to come up cherries. Might as well spread your bets and increase your odds." Forgetting that it was also a way to increase your losses.

But aside from that, he mostly just had a special feeling for Chance. See, Murray and me, we had two daughters. Murray loved 'em to death, both of 'em equally, totally doted on 'em, but I think he always wanted a son too. And that didn't happen and I think it was an ongoing disappointment to him. So a young guy like Chance coming under Murray's wing...that meant something to him. Meant the world to him. Touched his heart, not just his wallet.

Ellie Greenfield Lerner

THE ONE THING CHANCE and I never discussed was the nature of our relationship. We probably should have—I mean, looking back, it's amazing to me we never did—but I was too shy to ask him about how he felt, and he was either too shy himself or too self-protective to volunteer anything. Maybe he was out of touch with his feelings, or maybe he just didn't feel that much. But we never used the "L word." By which I don't mean "lesbian!" [laughs] *You* know the word I mean. I was too young, too intimidated, and maybe too much in love myself to dare, and much too nervous about how he might answer to ask him anything of that nature directly.

Now, as far as I know, he wasn't seeing anyone else during the months we were together, and I definitely wasn't. I don't even know if that would have been against the rules since we never talked about the rules. But it's my impression we were both monogamous during that time. Although, now that I think of it, who knows what he was up to? If you fall in love with the silent type, you can't expect them to tell you anything. So I just kind of assumed we were going steady. I guess I assumed all sorts of things, and maybe, as the saying goes, I was just making an ass of you and me.

Maybe this was a hint, though. A straw in the wind. My parents were eager to meet him and I wanted him to get to know my folks. My mom and dad offered us a standing invitation to come to Sunday dinner in Hempstead. My father—this was typical of his humor, by the way—said, "You really should bring him around. We'll give him a taste of Jew food." But Chance never wanted to go, always made up some excuse why it wasn't feasible. He had to learn lines for the coming week, he was tired, he had an early Monday call...whatever. So we never made it up there. As far as my folks were concerned, Chance was just a rumor. My mother started watching his show every afternoon out of a sort of weird sense of maternal loyalty, but they never met him.

But on this monogamy question, the thing is, Chance and I were seeing so much of each other, I don't know how, between me and *The Proud and the Bold*, he would have had time for anything or anyone else. He had long days, and we got together most nights.

Usually at my place. I'd make him dinner or he'd bring some take-out. And a bottle of wine. He'd developed a taste for the stuff. Yeah, we usually stayed in. Going out was kind of a rarity. Partly because he was usually exhausted after a full day of rehearsing and shooting, he just wanted to kick off his shoes and relax, and also because, as I said, it was hard to go out without being mobbed by fans. Mostly older ladies. Not exclusively, but they made up the bulk of his fan base, so it wasn't exactly *threatening* to me, not in the sense that someone might steal him away—it was just an annoyance.

Don Barlow

A MONTH OR SO into his contract, Chance asked me if I thought it'd be possible for him to be in a play while doing the show. Could we find a way of accommodating that kind of schedule? I think he was going to read for a part in some Broadway production, and it was apparently one he really hungered after and he thought he had a pretty good chance of scoring. I told him it was fine with me, I'd be glad to help any way I could, but that it wasn't my decision, he'd have to talk to the producers. Not only was it finally up to them, but they had to deal with *all* the aspects of producing the show, they had more elements to juggle than I did. Technical crew, unions, craft people, craft services, everything. Putting on a thirty-minute show every day is like planning the Normandy invasion. Only riskier. [laughs]

So several things happened, and ironically, it was in this order: Chance asked Hilda and Ben, they were the ones who produced the show, he asked them if they could work around his being in a play, then he read for the part before they answered, he got a call-back but didn't get the part, and only at that point did Hilda and Ben, who didn't realize he'd been passed up, tell him no, it just wasn't possible. That even if he were the star of the show, it would be too hard to manage, and for someone who was just a supporting player...

And I think that pretty much clinched it for him. On the other hand, he probably wasn't displeased to have an excuse to walk. It was obvious he wasn't overjoyed about being on the show, was almost ashamed to be part of it. He used to refer to it as *The Loud and the Old*. And listen, I always liked the guy, he was smart and could be funny, and he obviously took his craft very seriously, and you have to respect that, but let's face it, he was also a grumbler. A troublemaker, even if his motives were pure. So when he asked his agent if it would be possible to break his contract, I don't think Hilda and Ben were inclined to resist very strongly. I'm not saying it was an unmixed blessing—he was turning into the most popular thing on the show, he was getting tons of fan mail, our ratings were up—but he wasn't the easiest guy in the world to work with. A lot of the cast were quite content to see his back.

Ellie Greenfield Lerner

PEOPLE SOMETIMES ASK ME if I'm the woman in black. You know who I'm talking about? That woman who puts flowers on his grave every year? [laughs] She's almost more famous than Chance now. But it's ridiculous. Frankly, I don't even know how anyone knows we were ever a couple. I guess it's been mentioned in a couple of biographies, but that happened way before he became well known. I was witness to the start of his fame, but it came as a surprise to me, it had nothing to do with my dating him. If anything, it just got in the way. I've never written anything about him, God knows, and this conversation right now is the first time I've ever talked about Chance to anyone other than my parents and a few close friends. I've turned down lots of requests for interviews.

I'm a private person. It isn't anyone's business. I didn't date him for reflected glory. I wasn't dating a *movie star*, for goodness sake, I was in love with a *guy*.

I guess there's just so little known about Chance's personal life. He was so…I don't want to say secretive, but just so private—and maybe he *was* secretive—but I guess any name that becomes known, any person who is on the record as having been romantically linked with Chance, that person automatically becomes a suspect. It's like when people guess who was Jack the Ripper or something, they always pick someone famous from those times because those are the only names they know. The idea that it was just some anonymous madman never seems to occur to anyone. It has to be the Crown Prince or Walter Sickert or whoever. Not that I'm famous, of course. I'm anything but. Still, after people somehow found out we'd been involved once upon a time, my name got added to the list.

But I mean, honestly, the idea that it might be me is idiotic from almost any point of view. [laughs] For one thing, I live in New York! Do they honestly think I fly across the country every year just to make such a…such a silly, *theatrical* gesture? So…*look-at-me*. In order to let the world know I'm bereaved, because if the world doesn't know it maybe I'm not so bereaved after all. Nope. Sorry. If I had to guess, I'd guess it's an actress. That's where I'd look if I really cared about finding out who it is. Maybe someone who had an affair with him or maybe just someone he worked with. Or maybe someone who had a crush on him from afar.

But that whole mystery nonsense, that whole display, it's the kind of gesture you make if you're not content to experience your emotions in private but feel you have to let the world know about them, even if you do it incognito. So no, I have a feeling it isn't just some random fan. I suppose it could be, but I think it's probably someone in show business. Not necessarily anyone we've heard of—probably not, a person like that wouldn't need the attention—but someone on the fringes. I'm amazed no one's found her out. She's been photographed often enough, even if it's from a distance. Hasn't anyone approached her or tried to talk to her?

Eppy Bronstein

CHANCE ASKED MURRAY TO try to get him out of his contract on *The Proud and the Bold*. Murray was very upset. He'd been so thrilled to get the boy that job, and it had worked out so well, turned into a regular part. Chance was a real success story, which not too many of Murray's clients were. He planned to negotiate much better terms when his contract came up for renewal. He was pretty sure his negotiating position was really strong now, he was confident he could get a lot more money for Chance. So he tried to talk him out of doing anything rash. But Chance's mind was made up, and he argued with Murray, and finally insisted. And Murray had to eat crow and go down there and get Chance out of his contract, which he just hated to do.

But what was worse…after he'd done what Chance asked, Chance fired him. Just upped and fired him. Told him he was going to look for new representation. He wasn't thrilled with how Murray had handled everything, he wanted, he said, to "go in a new direction." That just about broke Murray's heart. I don't want to over-dramatize, I'm not saying that's what killed him—I mean, he didn't die for another seven or eight years, so obviously it wasn't what killed him—but something went out of him forever after that. He seemed a little broken. Murray loved the boy and he loved being associated with him, it was as simple as that.

And he was also…I mean, Murray felt Chance was going to be big, a star, and of course Murray turned out to be right on that score. So he'd taken a gamble on the boy, it was an act of faith, the gamble was about to pay off, and suddenly Murray was out of the game. It had been hand-to-mouth for us for years, barely getting by, and this was his shot at something bigger. So losing Chance was doubly devastating to him. Financially as well as personally.

Leon Shriver

So Chance and I had dinner one night at this Chinese place he liked—it wasn't very good, to be honest, but he didn't know from good Chinese food, and he liked the fact he could eat there and nobody bothered him—and he suddenly announced he was giving up on New York. He was going to split. I was shocked. It seemed crazy. He had the show, he had a girlfriend, he'd kind of established a life for himself here. He hadn't been in the city much more than a year, but it already looked to me like a natural fit.

I tried to talk him out of it. He was a friend, for one thing, I liked hanging out with him, but also, he was so talented I figured it was only a matter of time before people started to sit up and take notice. He just needed to be patient. But his mind was made up. He said something along the lines of, "I've put myself out there, I've given it a shot, I've shown what I can do, and all I've had to show for it is this lousy soap. And the soap is becoming a trap for me. It's steady work, it's easy, the pay is good, but I could find myself doing it for years and suddenly wonder where the time has gone. It's a dead-end. I've got to save myself."

So I asked him what alternative he had, and he said he was going to give Hollywood a try.

Well, that kind of startled me. He was such a fanatic about theater, I didn't think movies would appeal to him at all. So he gave me some rigmarole about how the popularity of TV was going to force movies to become better, more serious, more grown up. That was his story, but I don't think that was really it.

I think he needed a change of scene. New York had defeated him, that's how he saw it, had knocked him down and chewed him up, and he'd had enough.

Ellie Greenfield Lerner

ONE NIGHT, AFTER WE'D had dinner—he'd cooked up some spaghetti, one of his specialties, with a tomato sauce with anchovies and capers and crushed red pepper, really delicious—he suddenly announced he was leaving. Just like that. I waited for him to ask me to go with him, but it didn't happen. This was basically good-bye. I was devastated.

He wasn't curt or dismissive about it. You could even say he was sweet. But still, it was all so abrupt. There'd been no warning at all. I cried all night, and he held me and said, you know, "There there," that sort of thing. But it didn't make any difference. He wasn't going to change his mind and he did not say our relationship was going to continue. He was packing up and splitting at the end of the month and that was that. When he left New York, he'd be leaving me as well. I was heart-broken. I mean really crushed. One of those once-in-a-lifetime heartbreaks. It took me more than a year to get over it. Maybe I've never completely gotten over it.

His first year away, he wrote me a couple of times from California. Just chatty letters, nothing personal.

I didn't answer. I didn't think those letters deserved an answer.

Dorothy Goren Mckenzie

AFTER HE LEFT NEW York, before he went on out to Hollywood, Chance came home for a spell. Not an extended spell, mind you, just a little over a week. We were a stop *en route* is all. A way station. Still, he did bother to stop, so that was something. He didn't have to.

Maybe he needed to do his laundry.

He'd been away a long time. Years. He must've felt it was only right to come by and say hi to me and to our mom and to Aunt Mary, especially seeing as how we were practically halfway between New York and California, and barely out of his way at all. There was a detour of maybe an hour or two, not much more than that. So he dropped by to say hello, give us all a hug, reacquaint himself. He didn't have anything to do with my dad, though. I mean, he *did* say hi to him, he was perfectly polite, at least at first, maybe until the last night, but it's not like he would have crossed the street to do it. No hug, that's for sure. My dad meant less than nothing to him. To be honest, I was beginning to feel the same way, and heck, the guy was my dad, he wasn't Chance's.

I'd barely seen Chance since he'd left for college. Maybe two Christmases before he dropped out, quick holiday visits, not much more than that. He didn't come home for summer vacation. Instead, he got some sort of job near where he was going to school. Waiting tables at a local restaurant, I think. So even though he was my brother, or my half-brother to be precise, he was more like a stranger than kin to me by the time he was heading out to La La Land. There'd been some letters along the way, some phone calls. He used to send me a card and some sort of present on my birthday—he always remembered it, which is kind of surprising, considering his rocky relationship with the family—but frankly, I'm not sure he would've recognized me if we'd bumped into each other on the street.

That's an exaggeration, of course. We sent pictures back and forth, and of course I sometimes watched his TV show, so I certainly knew what *he* looked like. Seeing him on TV, seeing my own brother on TV, was a real mind-blower, as you can imagine. It made my girlfriends squeal. But basically, from any realistic point of view, we were strangers to each other.

He stayed with Aunt Mary and Uncle Earl while he was here. There wasn't much room in our house. He would have had to sleep on a couch in the living room, and there was only one bathroom, so it made sense for him to stay with Mary and Earl, where he'd lived for quite a few years anyway. But also, I don't think he wanted my dad to be one of the first things he saw in the morning, before he'd even had his first coffee, and I'm positive dad felt the same way about him. So it was better all around.

Mom was thrilled to see him again. They hadn't seemed to me to be so close back before he left us—although honestly, what did I know? I was just a little girl, nothing made a lot of sense to me—but when he came for this visit, she couldn't get enough of him. She practically begged him to stay with her and Daddy. But he was firm about not doing it. I think that awoke some painful memories for her, when she'd felt caught between the two of them. She was over at her sister's all the time, though, just so she could spend more time with Chance.

We'd all been aware of that TV show, of course. It was like... like he'd been to Jupiter and back. A whole different, distant world. Where we come from, you don't know anyone on TV. Unless they've been arrested for armed robbery or manslaughter or something like that, or nowadays maybe for operating a meth lab, then you might catch a glimpse of them on the local news at five.

My dad was kind of ho-hum about it, or pretended to be. He'd just say, "Boy that's dumb!" Or, "How could anyone waste time watching those lowlifes?" You know, Mr. Refined Taste, Mr. Drama Critic. As if we were watching the show because we *admired* the characters or were *riveted* by the dramatic artistry. I'm not saying the show was especially bad, by the way—my mom kept watching after Chance left it, she'd sort of gotten hooked by then—but that obviously wasn't the reason we were watching. We were watching because Chance was on TV. Any idiot would have understood that unless they chose not to. But anyway, the point is, for Mom and Aunt Mary and me—and sometimes even Uncle Earl, although he tried not to act *too* impressed, he thought that might make him lose face, especially in front of my dad, 'cause being critical always makes you look smarter than being enthusiastic—it was just beyond anything any of us had ever imagined. Our own Chance on the TV!

So I was antsy about his visit at first. It was more like meeting a celebrity than reuniting with a member of the family. I think we all had that feeling a little bit, but probably me most of all. The last time I'd talked to him face-to-face I'd been a little girl. He'd become a stranger. A famous stranger, as we saw it.

And sure enough, his first night home was super awkward. We had a family dinner, buffet style, Mom and Aunt Mary cooked, kind of potluck, Mom brought over casserole dishes, and both of them cooked up a storm, every dish Chance had liked as a boy. Nobody knew if his tastes had changed, nobody thought to wonder about that. Mom made macaroni and cheese with ham and some weird salad with marshmallows in it, and my aunt made a pot roast and mashed potatoes and a cherry pie for dessert. This was not a dinner your cardiologist would approve of. And judging by the look on Chance's face...I mean, his eating habits clearly weren't what they'd once been. But he was a good sport, he dug in, he made all the right noises.

Everybody was there that night, and Chance seemed a little overwhelmed by the fuss, and as I said, it was all pretty tense. My dad was acting pissed off, as was his way, only more so than usual, and Uncle Earl was...I mean, he was already showing signs of the Alzheimer's, although we didn't call it that then. "A tad forgetful" is how my aunt described it, but it went way beyond forgetful. He was confused a lot of the time. And Mom was twittering around, anxious and hovering, forcing food on Chance and asking him if he was okay and if he liked his dinner and how was the macaroni and so on, and Aunt Mary was…well, in a funny way, I think she and Mom had a little competition going, a little unspoken contest about whose dishes he liked the better and which of the two of them was closer to him and who'd been the main grown-up in his life. And no one knew if we should mention his TV show or act impressed or even ask him about his life in New York. What I'm saying is, no one knew how to act around him at *all*. No one could tell if this was a…a resumption of an old relationship or a completely new thing. I just stayed quiet and let the adults make fools of themselves. I was too shy to make a fool of myself.

But after dinner, after Earl had gone up to bed and Mom and Dad had gone home, and Mary had fallen asleep in her easy chair in the living room, I stuck around—I'd driven there separately—and me and Chance cleared the table and washed the dishes. I was surprised he did that. Men didn't usually do household chores in my limited experience, but he didn't make a big deal of it, me and him just started clearing the table and taking the dishes to the kitchen, and then he put them in the sink and started washing and I started drying 'em as he handed 'em to me, drying 'em and putting 'em away. And while we were doing that, he said, "So, how are you, sis? How are things?" And he sounded like he was interested, like he cared.

And I don't know, there was something in his tone, something in the way he asked…I just started crying. It was like…see, nobody had ever asked me anything like that before. Nobody showed any interest in how I was feeling or what my life was like. We didn't ask those kinds of questions. We weren't supposed to think about those things. And I was going through some tough stuff, and the idea that this guy who was my brother but who also was on the TV and who seemed more like a stranger than a brother, the idea that this guy even thought to ask…well, I just crumbled, you know?

I was having lots of problems with my dad at that point. Maybe that's typical when you're a junior in high school, but it didn't feel like some sort of general adolescent thing. I started describing what was going on to Chance. He was surprised. He said, "But Steve adores you! When you came along, it was like his whole life changed. I was there. I saw it. Hell, I was a victim of it."

And I told him, I said, "Well, that might've been true when I was a baby or a little girl and didn't have any personality of my own. It was easy for him to adore me then. But once I started thinking for myself, he didn't like it one small bit." And then I noticed what he'd said, and I said, "Is that when you and he started fighting? When I was born? I never knew that."

Anyway, we suddenly had something to talk about, the two of us. And we talked and talked. It was just amazing. This guy I was thinking was a total stranger to me, but we were talking about people and experiences we shared, and really opening up to each other, and it was great. I felt like a huge burden was being lifted off my shoulders, just being able to say what I was feeling to someone who seemed to understand.

For the rest of his visit, we were almost inseparable. As I told you, we hadn't been close before—I mean before he'd gone off to college, we were too far apart in age and we lived in different houses and so on—but now, for the ten days or so he was with us, we saw each other pretty much every day. We went for walks, we went down to the drugstore for lunch, we caught a movie, and after the movie he started telling me about the acting in it, who was good and who was bad and why, and that was really amazing, he pointed out stuff I'd never noticed before. And we stayed up late after dinner, just gab gab gab. I finally felt like I had a brother.

Mary Bennett

HE DROVE FROM NEW YORK to Hollywood. I never could fathom making that kind of road trip, but hey, I'm kind of a stick-in-the-mud gal when it comes to going places. Back then, people made that drive pretty regular. It was the main way of getting from coast to coast, either that or by train, change in Chicago. Four or five days on the road, minimum. Most people didn't fly in those days. Air travel was still a big deal. They didn't have jets for commercial travel yet, you had to take a propeller plane. Flying seemed a little...I don't know, exotic-like. Something rich people did. A little scary too, like, if God had wanted man to fly, that sort of notion. People still thought that way. And besides, Chance was moving himself lock, stock, and barrel, he was moving his whole life from one place to another, and even though I don't believe he owned much, no furniture at all, just his clothes and some books and those jazz records of his, it was probably easier to take all of it with him than try to ship everything. Especially since he didn't even know where he was going to be staying. So ship it to *where*, you see what I mean?

But anyway, he stopped here for a little visit on that trip. A week or two. Stayed with Earl and me. Sally hoped he'd stay with her, but that really wasn't practical. Not enough room in that tiny bungalow, and Steve would probably have nixed it anyway. And besides, Chance would rather have slept in a parking lot than stayed in the same house as Steve.

It was wonderful to have him with us, even for so short a time. But it was a little peculiar, too, and it still makes me sad to think about that aspect of it. He'd been part of our household, and I thought of him as being almost like a son, which of course upset Sally no end. But I did, I adored that boy, and now he was more like a guest than a family member. What with his having gone to college and having lived in New York—which was like another country to us, might as easily have been Belgium or Saskatchewan—and then on his way to Hollywood, also like another country, and having been on a show on the TV and everything...well, we hardly knew whether he would be *our* Chance at all, or just some person who looked like him but acted completely different, somebody who looked down on us for our small town ways.

And I have to say, it *was* a bit like that. Not that he looked down on us, but it took a while to get used to having him among us again. Sally was as nervous as a kitten around him, her own son, and Steve pretended not to be impressed, which only showed how impressed he actually was, and as for me, well, I kept wanting to hug him and kiss him and kept feeling like he'd find that unwelcome. And it was hard to know what to talk about to him. Lord knows life around here is pretty dull, or we figured he'd think it was, you know, after all he'd seen and done and everywhere he'd been, so we didn't want to bore him with our own dreary lives. But it was hard to know what to ask him about his own. Every question felt like prying. Like prying or like…like we were country hicks asking about life in the big city. [laughs] Which I guess we were, but still…

And he *was* different. Not in real obvious ways, mind you. He was still quiet and polite. He never acted high-and-mighty or hoity-toity. And if anything, he was more helpful around the house. I guess living alone he'd learned about household chores. But there was something else…it's hard to describe, maybe someone smarter than me could do it…his mind always seemed to be yonder, even when he was talking right to you. I don't mean he wasn't *in* the conversation, because he was, but you got the feeling he was talking to you on automatic while his real self, his soul, was somewhere else. Or like he was worried about something, something you couldn't guess at and wouldn't understand.

I think Sally felt it more than I did. He was living in our house, he *had* to deal with Earl and me. With Sally…well, he still called her "Mom," he kissed her hello when he saw her, he took her out to dinner once or twice—without Steve, incidentally, I don't know how he managed that—I mean, how Sally explained it to Steve that made it all right, so it didn't provoke some sort of blow-up—but anyhow, when Chance was with her, there was just something missing. Some special degree of, of, of *devotion*, I guess you'd call it. We all could sense it, but I think Sally really *felt* it.

And on Sunday morning—he was here through one Sunday—when we all were getting ready to go to church—we used to all go together, Sally and Steve and Dot and Earl and me—he said he wasn't going. That was a little upsetting. When I asked him why not, he said he just didn't do that anymore. He said it real mild, not argumentative, but still...and after, there was this pause, and I wanted to ask him if he'd become like an atheist or a, a, I can't remember the word anymore, whatever you call it when someone doesn't believe in God exactly but isn't real militant about it, but anyway, I didn't have the nerve to. Maybe I was afraid of how he'd answer.

But I'll tell you this. The next week, after Chance had already gone, Dot announced she didn't want to go to church anymore either. She said she figured she was old enough to make up her own mind about things and she didn't feel like church was for her. She wasn't sure she still believed in Jesus, she said. Well, Steve wasn't having it. They went back and forth a few times, so Mary told me, and then he slapped her pretty good and forced her to go. So I don't know if Chance was to blame for all that, but I kind of think he must've been.

But on the other side, I gotta say this: Chance was wonderful with Earl. Earl was beginning to get forgetful around this time, asking the same questions over and over, telling the same stories, looking confused about this and that. And Chance was real patient with him. Lots of people weren't. Including Steve, by the way. Steve used to make fun of Earl, which was downright cruel. And it hurt Earl's feelings. He wasn't so confused that he didn't know he was confused, didn't realize something was wrong. But Chance was super-patient about it. Pretending to be interested when Earl told the same story over and over, and repeating his answers over and over when Earl kept asking him the same questions. And it's interesting, because, as I think I mentioned, Chance and Earl were never especially close. I never got the feeling Chance felt much in the way of warmth toward Earl, which was fair enough, since at best Earl was kind of lukewarm about Chance. But on this visit, Chance was, you could even call it saintly when it came to Earl.

Dorothy Goren Mckenzie

So LIKE I SAID, things were mostly okay this visit, a little uneasy maybe, we none of us were exactly sure what to expect from Chance, but things mostly went pretty smooth. And like I also said, Chance and me, we actually became close while he was around. It was the grown-ups—by which I mean my mom and dad and Uncle Earl and Aunt Mary; because of course Chance was a grown-up by then too, but he wasn't part of the grown-ups' *generation*, if that makes any sense—they were the ones who seemed queasy around him. Unsure how to act, unsure what to make of him. They were more used to dealing with him in a way that no longer made any sense, they had to figure out what way *did* make sense. But for all that, things were on a pretty even keel for most of the visit. He was nice to our mom and he restrained himself with my dad—although I could see my mom wanted more from him than she was getting, which was a little heartbreaking to watch—I'm not sure what would have satisfied her or what she expected, but whatever it was, she wasn't getting it—and he seemed appreciative of Uncle Earl and Aunt Mary, if not exactly doting. He was helpful around the house in thoughtful ways that he hadn't been before, making his bed, doing the food shopping without being asked, various household tasks, making coffee in the morning if he got up first, stuff like that. Things Uncle Earl didn't ever do. He would've dismissed that stuff as *woman's work*.

But the stuff really hit the fan on his last night in town, just when we were all breathing easier. There'd been so much apprehension before his visit, but it had seemed to go fine, and we were feeling really sad to see him go. Especially me. Well, Mom and Aunt Mary too, it looked to me like Mom was coming to terms, or at least trying to come to terms, with the way she'd sort of let her relationship with Chance slide when she first married my dad and when I was born, it was like she was discovering all this motherly feeling toward him that she'd denied or—what's the word?—*suppressed* when he was younger. And wanted to make it up to him. But still, even considering my mom and aunt, I think it may have been hardest on me. Like I said, I felt I'd finally found someone who understood me. Someone I could really talk to. I'd been having a pretty rough time in high school—not so different from what Chance had gone through, I guess, or at least that's what he told me, he said in those days he felt like someone who didn't even speak the same language as the kids he went to school with—and it had been fantastic to finally have someone who seemed to be on the same wavelength. Who understood what I was trying to say. To finally have, like I said, a real big brother, not just in name, not just as a formality, but in the way he treated me and in the way I looked up to him. But now it was his last night with us, he was all set to drive on to California the next day. His car was all packed up and gassed up, he was planning on getting an early start. So it was a bittersweet occasion.

My mom—*our* mom—insisted we have Chance's farewell supper at our place. I don't believe Aunt Mary put up much of a fight about that. Not that time. Chance had been staying with her, he'd been having most of his meals at her house, and she wasn't so mean or so competitive with her sister that she was going to begrudge her the opportunity to give Chance his last meal before he left us for Hollywood. And of course mom made something special. Not macaroni and cheese this time, she wanted it to be fancier than that. So she made this leg of lamb thing for him, a kind of complicated dish with some sort of spicy tomato sauce, I think she'd found the recipe in a magazine years before, and she recalled that when she used to make it at Easter he'd always ask for second helpings. And she wouldn't let Aunt Mary bring anything except a salad. She wanted this to be her show.

Well, my dad was in a pretty grumpy mood all day. Where Chance was concerned, Dad was often grumpy, and today, since it was totally devoted to Chance, to giving Chance a big send-off, he was especially grumpy. Complaining about how elaborate the preparations were, and how expensive the meal was, and making fun of Mom's nervousness. Not making fun *in* fun, either. *Mean* making fun. Putting her on the defensive, which of course made her even more nervous.

"I want it to be a nice evening for him, Steve," she told him. Almost pleading. "It's his last night here till goodness knows when, maybe till forever, and I want him to remember that we told him goodbye in a loving way. I want him to want to come back sometime."

Dad just grunted, but if you knew Dad well, you knew how to parse his grunts. This was an ominous grunt.

So Chance came over at about five thirty with Aunt Mary and Uncle Earl. They all came together. She brought what passed for salad in those days: Some iceberg lettuce, a sliced tomato, some sliced cucumber. A Russian dressing she made herself that was just ketchup and mayonnaise mixed together, nothing else. And Chance brought a bottle of red wine he'd bought in town. I don't remember anything specific about the wine except that it was French. The specifics wouldn't have meant anything to me, partly because I didn't know the first thing about wine and partly because I was too young to drink alcohol, my parents were really strict about that. But I'm guessing it probably wasn't the cheap stuff. I think Chance wanted to make a handsome gesture on his last night, so he might have been a little extravagant. He probably got the best bottle that was available in the town liquor store, which, you know, wouldn't have been like one of those Rothschild things, but probably wasn't swill either. Something a cut above Thunderbird or Italian Swiss Colony.

Well, bringing wine turned out to be a mistake. Or maybe it wasn't a mistake. Maybe it's wrong to believe the wine was the problem—maybe just Chance's existence was the problem. Daddy was going to find *something* to make a fuss about, and it's possible that if Chance hadn't brought wine Daddy would have picked on, I don't know, Chance's haircut, or his shoes, or his calling Aunt Mary "Mary" instead of "Aunt Mary," or pretty much anything, no matter how ridiculous. Whatever was handy. Whatever he could seize on. But what was handy that night, what first caught Daddy's attention, was the fact that Chance brought a bottle of wine.

He started in immediately. "Wine, huh?" You know, sounding suspicious, like he'd never heard of anyone drinking wine before, or maybe like it was poisoned or something. And then, "Is this what you and your fancy friends drink in New York? You all must be mighty sophisticated. Real artsy-fartsy little prancers." With his pinky in the air.

And you know, at first, Chance—and all of us—tried to pretend this was meant in fun, even though we of course knew it wasn't. Chance smiled—laughter was out of the question, but he did manage a smile at first—and answered with "Yeah" or "I guess so" or something like that. But that just got Daddy more determined. He wasn't out to be amusing, he wanted to be insulting. He didn't want things to go smooth, he wanted trouble. He wanted to provoke trouble. If Chance didn't rise to the bait then he was just going to re-double his efforts. Not let up until he got a big enough rise out of Chance to make the exercise worthwhile.

Mary Bennett

THAT LAST NIGHT, THE last night of Chance's visit, was just terrible. I try not to think about it. Thinking about it, even after all these years, still gives me the willies. Lordy. See, Steve started in, the way only Steve could, and right from the first it just put everybody on edge. And then he got worse and worse. Poor Sally suffered the most of all of us, I suppose, because she wanted so much for this dinner to be something special, to be something Chance would remember fondly. Although...you know, to be honest, now that I think about it, maybe the real victim that night was actually Dotty. She wasn't hardly out of childhood yet. She was defenseless, trapped inside that house with those people. And she couldn't even protest, she wasn't allowed a voice. She just had to watch it in silence.

Dorothy Goren Mckenzie

SO WE FINALLY SAT down to dinner. It seemed like an eternity sitting around the parlor making small talk, although it couldn't have been more than a half-hour. And of course as soon as we got to the table, Daddy announced he was drinking beer. And then he glared at my mom, kind of daring her to have any of the wine Chance brought. And as usual, she was so cowed by him, all it took was that look of his and she immediately announced she'd be drinking milk, which is what she usually drank with supper. And Uncle Earl, he was a beer kind of guy too, so without really understanding what was going on or noticing the vibrations, he signed up to be on Daddy's team. And I say Daddy's team because suddenly this was almost a political battle, you know? Like you were choosing sides. Then Aunt Mary upped and announced she wanted wine, that was how she cast her vote, but I don't even think she really did. I think she was making a statement, just like my dad was. She'd probably have preferred milk to be honest, or maybe Dr. Pepper. But she wanted Steve to know he couldn't boss *her* around, and she wanted Chance to know she had his back.

But then my mom, seeing her sister side with Chance like that, suddenly felt, I don't know, like she'd backed the wrong horse, and as I said, they'd been kind of having this unspoken contest all along, so she said, "You know, on second thought, maybe I'll try some wine. That sounds like fun." At which point my dad gave her a really dirty look and said, "You said you wanted milk and that's what you're going to have, Sally. We don't drink wine in this house." It was so ugly and brutish and childish and bullying, I didn't know where to look. But he always was able to lord it over her, so although she looked upset, almost like she was going to cry, she nodded and waved her hand at the wine bottle Chance was offering her, waved it away.

Mary Bennett

So THE WINE BUSINESS was already nasty, childish, and unpleasant, and surely gave us all the indication we needed that this was going to be a miserable night. But it turned out to be just…just a…what's that word for a drink before dinner? An *aperitif*. [laughs] I mean, I'd already seen Chance start to stiffen when Steve ordered Sally not to have any wine—that was the first time he let on in any way, even silently, that Steve was bothering him, no doubt because he hated to see his mom bullied like that, but he still kept his peace. It was borderline, mind you. I think he was biting his tongue, but he kept his peace.

But after Sally brought out the lamb and the mashed potatoes and the Brussels sprouts and we started passing 'em around, that's when Steve started in on the TV show Chance had been on. How stupid it was and how bad it was and what a load of crap it was. He actually used the word "crap," which was pretty shocking, since Steve didn't approve of cussing. He even said things like "h-e-double hockey sticks" instead of that other word. As if that somehow made him a good person!

Well, Chance just shrugged. "No one has to like it," he said. Not getting riled.

And, look, he surely knew what Steve was up to. I think he just wanted to stay as calm as possible for as long as possible, if only to make it clear who was responsible for any dust-up that might erupt. "You can like it or not," he said. "It's a free country."

"Yeah," Steve said. "Thanks for the permission. I don't like it. No one in his right mind could like it."

And Chance shrugged again.

Chance's shrugging like that was probably more obnoxious to Steve than if he'd yelled. After all, getting him mad was what Steve was all about that night. So he tried something else. "Did they fire you? Is that why you ain't on the show anymore? Couldn't cut it?"

"Nope," is all Chance said.

You have to understand that the rest of us were watching all this without a peep. And without moving a muscle. No one was eating, no one except Earl, who was chewing away without a care in the world. But no one else was stirring. We were barely breathing. It was all too nerve-wracking.

And Steve went on, "Not that it matters if you were fired or not. Doesn't signify. Those idiots in New York, those Jews and fairies, they don't have a clue what's good entertainment and what isn't." See, all of a sudden he was an expert. "They think they're so much better than us, when they're...I mean, they're just a bunch of—" and then he used some words I don't care to repeat. Not swear words, not like "crap" and "damn," but, you know, slurs about groups of people and other things you're not supposed to say out loud. No true Christian should say things like that. It's not just rude, it's unkind.

So there was this long tense wait. Dead quiet. You could hear the traffic outside coming from the major road all the way at the end of their block. People were looking down at their plates 'cause they didn't know where else to look. Nobody wanted to meet anyone else's eyes, that's for darn sure. Things had gone way beyond our being able to pretend everything was okay. The dinner was ruined.

And please understand, we may not have been too enlightened back then in our little town, things have changed a lot in the years since, a colored man even ran for president not too long ago, for the nomination I mean, that Jesse Jackson person, and I surely would never have voted for him, I didn't take to him at all and besides, I would never vote for anyone from that party of giveaways, but he ran and the world didn't crumble to pieces or anything…but the point is, even sixty years ago you didn't *have* to be too enlightened to know you just don't say some things. You could *think* them— I'm sure plenty of people did—but it was shocking to hear that kind of language at the dinner table.

And of course we all could see what Steve was up to. He had a goal, you know? He wanted to get a rise out of Chance, and he was going to keep pushing until he succeeded. The only thing I don't know to this day was whether he was mainly trying to ruin the evening for Chance or for Sally. But the truth is, it was kind of a bank shot. You hit one, you've taken out the other at the same time. I snuck a glance at my sis. She looked like she wanted to disappear. Her lower lip was trembling. She didn't have it in her to be mad, though, only to be miserable.

And then Chance said something like—and his voice was still quiet, nice and even and steady; he wasn't going to give Steve the satisfaction of getting him to shout—he said, "You know, Steve, I assume you're already aware of this, it can't come as news to you, but just to be clear, you're behaving like a tremendous asshole." Those were pretty much his exact words, a nicely composed, kind of complex sentence. Chance was always a good talker when he chose to talk at all. And what he said now made us all...I mean, we just gasped. Everybody at the table. No one ever said things like that to Steve. It was, you could almost say it was unthinkable. Until, like so many unthinkable things, until they happen, then all of a sudden they aren't unthinkable anymore. Steve himself was so startled he didn't have a ready comeback, so Chance went on, "I mean, look, I'm in town to visit my mom and my sister and my aunt and uncle. You really didn't figure in my plans at all, you were just part of the package. Not an especially appealing part either. So if you're not happy being here tonight, if you have a problem with the company, why don't you fuck off? Trust me, you won't be missed."

You'll have to pardon my French there, Mr. Frost. I'm not comfortable with that kind of language myself, it's how I was brought up, ladies didn't talk like that back then and neither did gentleman for that matter, but I'm trying to tell you what Chance said to Steve, and I believe the words he used counted in this situation. I surely haven't forgotten them. And I have to tell you, shocked as I was, offended as I maybe even was, I also...some part of me wanted to applaud. It was about time somebody talked back to Steve, put a spoke in his wheels. He was such a bully, and we were all afraid of him. It's hard to say *what* we were afraid of—he wasn't physically abusive so far as I know, and while he may have spanked Dotty if she was naughty, I don't believe he ever struck Sally or anything of that nature—but there was just something menacing about the man. So then, into that silence—and the room wasn't exactly silent, since it still seemed to be echoing with what Chance had just said, the sound waves seemed to be bouncing off the walls—Dotty laughed. That was a mistake on her part, but she most likely couldn't help herself. Partly nervousness, partly delight.

Well, she was a much easier target than Chance, of course. By now Steve obviously had come to the conclusion that Chance was no pushover, that he could give back at least as good as he got. So he wheeled around on Dorothy. "Go to your room!" he said.

"Uh uh," Chance said. "Don't pay him any mind, honey. You stay right here."

"Butt out! She's my daughter and she'll do what I say."

"Not this time. Nope."

Steve stood up. Suddenly. Violently. That was really scary. It rattled every dish on the table. And almost immediately, Chance stood up too, and they were facing off across the table. Sally had already begun to cry, and Dorothy turned pale pretty much instantly, and after a second or two she started to cry as well. Earl looked confused. He started to say something—probably to ask what was happening—but I shushed him. I said, "Not now, Earl." And he minded me, as he tended to do at that stage of his life. Meanwhile, the two fellas stared each other for what seemed like minutes, although it probably wasn't even a single minute. And finally Steve said, "Get out of my house."

"Right," Chance said. "I plan to. After I've finished my supper." And at that he sat down again and quietly started eating. And a second or two later he said, "By the way, Mom, this lamb is delicious. I'll probably want seconds."

Well, it was funny—no one laughed, mind you, we weren't in a laughing situation—but it was funny how Steve just couldn't figure out what to do next. He stood there watching Chance eat, and you could see the gears turning in his head as he tried to come up with his next move. He couldn't use force—Chance could probably take him if things actually got physical, and would likely have jumped in if he'd tried to get rough with Dotty—and more yelling and growling wasn't going to accomplish anything. So he was standing there fuming and looking ridiculous, and Chance was casually eating his lamb, and in spite of having made all those threatening noises Steve didn't have any way of coming out on top in this little battle of wills. So he finally plopped himself down in his chair again.

And then Chance rubbed it in a little. It was mischievous of him, maybe even a little spiteful, but I couldn't find it in my heart to blame him. He said, "Say, Steve, could you please pass the sauce?" It was clever...Steve could either do what Chance asked or look like a petulant child. There was no third choice. So he grunted and passed the dish with the sauce. "And the wine, while you're at it? But go ahead and pour a little for yourself first. It's good stuff. You should try it." Chance was enjoying himself, you see. He was kind of...kind of spiking the ball, you might say. "And Mom, you really should have a sip. You'll thank me. Right, Mary?"

And now I had the guts to say, "Absolutely. It's scrumptious." Chance was so merry about standing up to Steve, it was contagious.

Dorothy Goren Mckenzie

So right after that awful dinner, one of the worst meals of my life let me say, when Chance was about to leave with Mary and Earl, after giving our mom a hug and a kiss, and waving good-bye to my dad with a big grin, saying "Thanks for dinner, Steve, it was swell," he got to me. He was going to give me a little pat and a kiss on the cheek, but I couldn't stand to see him go. I really couldn't stand it. He'd be gone in the morning, I knew that, and I'd really fallen in love with him this visit. He'd become, he'd almost become a mainstay in my life. Yeah, that fast. He was the first person I ever felt I could talk to and be *understood*. So I threw my arms around him and I held him tight. I was crying again. I'd cried earlier a little, when he and Daddy were going at it, but now I was really sobbing, getting his shirt all wet and everything, and I said, "Please, Chance, take me with you. Please. Let me come with you. I won't be any trouble."

He was startled. So was everybody else in the room, needless to say. There was a moment when no one knew what to say. And then he stepped back and looked me in the eye and he said, "Come out to the porch." So the two of us went outside—it was a lovely warm night—leaving everybody to wonder what was happening, and he shut the door behind us and he said, "Look, honey, you know I can't do that. I wish I could, but I just can't. It isn't practical, and it probably isn't legal. And what would I do with you?"

"But I could even be helpful," I said. I was kind of pleading. Willing to say anything. "I can clean house for you and maybe even cook while you're out trying to be an actor, going to try-outs and things. Are they called try-outs?"

"They're called auditions." He was smiling, but then he frowned and said, "I'm sorry, baby, but it's just not going to happen. It can't. Mom would never forgive either of us, that's one thing, and I can't be responsible for you that way. I've got my own struggles to get through. And like I said, it's also probably against the law."

"But I hate it here!"

"I know. I know you do. I did too. So here's what you need to do. Stick it out and finish high school. Work hard, get good grades. It might seem like graduation is a long way off, but then all of a sudden, before you know it, you'll be marching down the aisle to Elgar." I didn't interrupt him to ask what that was. He said, "And then go away to college. Pick one as far away as possible. College'll change everything. It did for me."

"But you quit."

"I had a good reason to. You won't. And besides, I got a lot from it while I was there. So go to college and never look back. Okay? You'll be done with this town and these people for good. You'll be free. And able to decide for yourself what you want next."

And that was it. He left for LA early the next morning. Really early. Aunt Mary told me he was already gone by the time she got downstairs. But he'd brewed a pot of coffee for her before he left.

HOLLYWOOD

Gil Fraser (roommate)

I'D PUT ADS UP on various bulletin boards around town. "Actor seeks roommate for two-bedroom apt. in West Hollywood. Split rent, food, utilities. Easygoing a requirement." The fellow who'd been sharing the place with me had finally given up and gone back to...to wherever. Kansas or Iowa or Sweden or wherever he was from. He came out to Hollywood, like all of us, to make it in the business, but he got discouraged fast. I don't think he was hungry enough to put in the time or put up with the rejection. Good-looking guy, I'm sure his friends must have told him he looked like a movie star, so he figured, what the hell, what have I got to lose, nothing much else going on in my life, I'll give it a shot. And then it didn't happen right away and he got discouraged. But the truth is, coming out here to be a star is a mug's game. Every guy and gal who makes the move is probably better looking than you, even if you're the best-looking person ever to come out of wherever you come from. Which isn't true of me, by the way. As no doubt goes without saying. I never hoped I'd be a star, I just wanted to *act*. No glamour boy aspirations.

But anyhow, the thing is, if you're smart, you come out here for the experience and 'cause you care about the work itself. If you can make a successful career, great, but if not, you're part of this world, you've got friends who care about the same stuff you do, you take classes, you do small theater productions, you audition for commercials, you eat all sorts of shit, but you keep going for it. This dude, my ex-roommate, I don't think he cared much for acting as such. He was a good guy and a hassle-free roommate, we got along fine, but he didn't have the...what's the cliché? The fire in his belly. It was just a single throw of the dice for him. *Snake eyes!*

I was living in this pretty nice two-bedroom in West Hollywood at the time. Much nicer than my situation warranted. I was barely scraping along. West Hollywood wasn't incorporated yet, of course—it was just a neighborhood. And not even a happening neighborhood. Middle-class, a little staid. Lots of single-family houses, many more houses than apartments at that time. The gays were maybe just starting to move in, it didn't have that vibe yet. Couple of bric-a-brac shops along Santa Monica around San Vicente had already opened, but that was just the thin edge of the wedge. The wedge itself was still a few years away. My building was on Holloway, a couple blocks west of La Cienega. Near the Strip, but you weren't too conscious of the Strip unless you walked up there. It was pretty quiet on Holloway. Stretches of it hadn't even been developed yet. There were still some big empty lots. It wasn't far from where Sal Mineo was murdered, but that was a long way in the future.

The rent was reasonable. They probably could have charged twice as much and gotten away with it, but luckily for me they didn't seem to know that. Still, I couldn't afford the place all by myself. And I didn't need two bedrooms anyhow. But I didn't want to move—apartment hunting and moving are such a miserable business—and I liked the apartment, and the location was super convenient. Near the canyons, near Hollywood. Every studio a short drive away, short by LA standards. So I advertised for a roommate. Always a risk, but when you're young, you're willing to take risks. A number of people answered the ads. But there were two things about Chance that made me decide on him. One is that he was an actor too, and a struggling one. He told me he'd been in a soap in New York for a few months, but, you know, that didn't cut a lot of ice in this town. He'd be starting cold for all practical purposes. So we'd have that in common, could talk about what we were going through, run lines with each other before an audition, consult about approaches to parts, that sort of thing. And the other—[laughs]—this doesn't speak well for me, maybe, but the thing is…see, he was so fucking handsome, I immediately thought, my very first thought, was, hell, if we go out for a beer or something, the girls will swarm around him like flies, and if I'm in the vicinity, maybe I'll be able to choose among the rejects. [laughs] Pretty piggish, I know, but hell, this was the fifties. *Everyone* was piggish in the fifties. And not just guys. Women too. Piggish wasn't even a category. And you know, we were young then, we were horny, we were hungry, we were pretty much slaves to all sorts of unruly appetites. And this was LA, there was all this pussy around. It was like a candy store. We wanted some of that candy. And when I say "we" I mean me, of course. And like I say, it's not like I'm proud of this, I'm just telling you how it was.

Chance liked the apartment, and we came to terms right away. None of this "let me think about it" bullshit. I helped him move his stuff in. He didn't have a car back then—he'd driven out to California in some flivver he'd bought for the purpose, but it had apparently died soon after he got here—so I went over to the fleabag near Skid Row where he'd been staying and drove him and his stuff back to the apartment. We managed it in one go. He didn't have a lot to his name back then.

I told him right away he'd need a car in LA. Can't really manage without one. He said he was aware of that. He had a little money saved from the show he'd been on, enough to keep his head above water for a few months and definitely enough to buy a used car to replace the heap he'd driven out in. It was the first item on his to-do list after finding a place to live.

That first night, I told him dinner was on me. A sort of welcome-aboard gesture. We walked down to Barney's Beanery, a few blocks down the hill from the apartment. The walk back up was a lot tougher than the walk down, I can tell you that, especially with a few drinks in us. Anyway, once we got there, it was the usual scene, noisy, bikers and musicians and tourists and Hollywood fringe types all thrown together, guys playing pool, the jukebox blaring, people jabbering. Chance took a look around and said to me, "Good choice, Gil." Big grin on his face. He was thrilled to be there, entranced by the atmosphere. It was like, "Hey, I'm really in Hollywood!" Or maybe, "Hey, I'm sure as fuck not in Kansas anymore!" Or maybe even, "Sure glad not to be in New York!" I don't think he'd lived there for very long, maybe a year, but he seemed happy to be gone. Because, you know, that's how the world divides: people who love New York—I guess that's the hip position—and people who can't stand it, at least over the long haul. Chance was in the second camp. He was hip enough not to worry about being hip.

So we're in Barney's, and he's all smiles. I pointed out the "Fagots – stay out!" sign over the bar and told him not to worry about it, they mostly kept it there for its historical quaintness and its notorious misspelling. The policy, if you could call it a policy, wasn't enforced or anything. It's not that I suspected he was gay, by the way, I wasn't warning him from that point of view, I just didn't want him to think I'd taken him to some hotbed of homophobic bigotry. That wasn't an impression I wanted to give him on his first night as a roommate. You're in the arts, you can't afford to indulge that kind of prejudice. Or any other, really. Tolerance for all sorts of people comes with the territory, is my philosophy. We're a fucking Benneton ad is what we are.

As to whether Chance *was* gay...I know there's been all sorts of speculation about that question, both when he was alive and since. There always *is* in this town, isn't there? Plus there's that awful memoir that slimeball hustler wrote, which frankly I think is a bunch of crap. But all I'll say about that whole business—and I'm someone who had a ringside view of his life for a couple of years, remember—what I can tell you for a fact is that he definitely liked to screw women. Whether he also liked men…I never saw any evidence of it, but that obviously doesn't prove anything. You can't prove a negative.

But, for example, I've heard people say that that woman in black—you know the one I mean? The one who puts flowers on his grave? You do?—okay, well I've heard people say she must have just been a fan or someone with an unrequited crush, no way she could have been a lover, because he played for the other team. Well, that's horseshit. I have no clue who she is or what she meant to Chance or Chance to her, but anyone who says *that* doesn't know what the fuck they're talking about. Women loved the guy, and trust me, he loved them right back. Even before he was a star, when he was just an unknown schmuck like the rest of us, he had…well, he had those good looks, of course, but let's face it: good looks aren't so rare in this town. They're the coin of the realm. Pretty people come here in droves. But he had something else too, some sort of special appeal. Something winsome and sweet and maybe even a little needy, something that seemed to cry out for mothering. And some mysterious quality, something withheld and murky and dark. He was just catnip to the ladies. Like they were moths and he was a flame. A dark flame. A smoldering flame. And trust me, he took advantage, he thoroughly enjoyed himself. Whatever else he may have been, and that's anybody's guess, he was not a guy who *only* liked guys.

And anyway, who really gives a shit? Like Lenny Bruce said, a guy will fuck *mud* if he's horny enough.

But that's another thing about Chance, and I'm sure you've been hearing this a lot from the other people you've talked to. He just wasn't an easy cat to know. I was probably as close to him as anyone, at least in those days—hell, we shared an apartment for a couple of years and we were good friends all along—but even

I can't say I knew him real well. He had...I don't want to call them secrets, because that sounds like he was *keeping* secrets, and I don't think that was the case. But you just knew there was a lot more to the guy than you could see. He was like an iceberg. The part you could make out was the small tip with the main part submerged. He was...I don't think *slippery* is the word. There was nothing dishonest about him. But he was almost impossible to figure out. You could never be totally sure what he was thinking or feeling. All he showed you was a smooth surface.

Like, just for instance, there was this huge overgrown vacant lot near our apartment, around where Westmount runs into Holloway. Really huge. I mean acres, literally. It was like a jungle in there, trees, weeds, huge brambly bushes, hills, big declivities in the ground, gullies. When you were in it, you had no sense there was a city around you, you could have been in the Amazon basin or something. This was back before developers got their hands on it, obviously. I think it's a parking lot now. Such a shame. LA is like that Joni Mitchell song. Anyway, there were times when Chance would cross the street and head into that place and just disappear for an hour or more. And if I asked him what he'd been up to, he'd say, "Oh, nothing. Just thinking." See what I mean? Who goes into a vacant lot to think?

So okay, where was I? Oh yeah, Barney's.

We got a booth, had a couple of shots and then some chili and a couple of beers. And we hit it off right away. Scoped out the women, made coarse comments the way young men do, shared a few war stories. I could see right away it was going to be a good arrangement. He may have been a little reserved—although I mostly became aware of that side of him later—but he was friendly, he was funny, he was *present*. You know what I mean by present? I mean when he talked to you, he was totally *there*, in the moment, listening and reacting, paying full attention. Just the way he was when he did a scene. It's part of what made him such a good actor. And we had a lot to talk about, a lot in common. Chance was a little shy at first, but a genuinely nice guy. He was a good friend if you gave him a little room and a little time. And had something to offer.

And he was very levelheaded. He knew pretty faces like his are a dime a dozen in this business. LA attracts good-looking people the way shit attracts flies. It's full of beautiful gentiles and smart Jews, they come here in droves, and then they intermarry and have ugly stupid kids. [laughs] Just kidding. Anyway, Chance knew his face might open a few doors here, but it wouldn't be his fortune. He had a good sense of what it could do for him and what it couldn't. And he was shrewd enough to realize that while a featured spot on a New York-based soap was an okay item on his CV, it gave him some legitimacy, it wasn't anything more than that. At first, when he mentioned it, I thought he might be bragging about it, might think it was a big deal, but no, he had it in perspective. It was just an incidental detail. He knew he was starting an uphill climb. He didn't expect to soar.

And I'll say this for him too: He didn't forget his friends. After he made it big, I mean. We didn't see a lot of each other once he became a star, but I always knew he was there for me if I needed him.

Dorothy Goren Mckenzie

A COUPLE OF WEEKS after he left, I got a postcard from Chance. A picture of the Hollywood sign. The note on the other side said, "The air here is brown, but otherwise it's paradise. Beautiful weather. Beaches and mountains. Got a place, got a car, got a roommate, now I'm looking for a job." God, it sounded so exciting, so...so totally different from where I was. I was glad to get it, but it made me positively ache with longing. Longing for Chance himself, and for another kind of life.

Irma Gold (agent)

CHANCE CAME TO ME looking for representation. As I recall, I'd been recommended to him by Gil Fraser, another client of mine. I had a pretty good roster. No huge stars but a fair number of working actors and actresses. I kept them busy, they paid my rent.

When he showed up at my office, he looked pretty bedraggled. Like someone who might ask you for spare change down on Selma. Jeans and a torn T-shirt—at first I thought it might be some sort of Brando affectation, but the truth is he might not have had anything better—and his hair was a mess and obviously hadn't been cut in months, and he looked like he hadn't been sleeping much. But still, signing him was a no-brainer. Even in that bedraggled state there was no mistaking he was a beautiful boy, and he'd been in a soap so I knew he wasn't a complete wannabe, he'd had some experience in front of a camera, and then he read for me—this was before actors had demo reels, there was no such thing then, it was all very hands-on and low-tech. So he did some Chekhov thing if I'm remembering correctly—from *The Seagull*, maybe?— and it was obvious he could act. At least adequately…I won't claim I recognized how amazing he was at that first meeting. I won't pretend to have realized he was a genius, but I definitely could see he had skills, he wasn't just another handsome lox. This town is full of 'em, and sad to say they sometimes manage to have careers. It isn't only tits and ass that can get a person work. Biceps and pecs and a strong chin can go a long way too.

Two words: Lex Barker.

I try not to represent people like that, though. I'm not a purist and I'm not a saint and I know this is a business and movies aren't the Sistine Chapel or anything, but still, when I pitch a client to a casting director, it's my reputation on the line just as much as the client's, and my business depends on my reputation. It would be a bad thing if casting directors start regarding me as a bullshitter. If I call and say, for example, "This or that person would be perfect for your project," he or she better at least be plausible for their project or they'll stop taking my calls, or they'll take my calls and shine me on but never hire anybody I send to them. So I try to be, within practical limits, I try to be selective. I have to believe in my clients. If I don't believe in them, I can't fight for them.

Not that it's a science. We make mistakes, we trust our gut and our gut might steer us wrong. Sometimes someone will come in and I'll hesitate, I'll say I have to think about it. At that point it isn't much more than a coin toss. And sometimes someone will come in and I can immediately see there's nothing there and I'll say no right off the bat. It's heartbreaking, but this is a tough town and it's a tough business. "Sorry," I'll say, "but I don't think I can help you. Maybe you'll have better luck with someone else. I wish you the best." Usually I never hear about that person again, but once or twice the person has gone on to have a pretty decent career. I called heads and it came up tails. That happens. And I'm happy for them. Truly. I freely admit I'm not infallible. There's no such thing in this business. As William Goldman says, "nobody knows anything."

But I had no hesitation with Chance. I won't say I knew he was going to become a *screen idol*, but I had no doubt I'd find him plenty of work right away, and had a notion that there might even be star potential there. But like I said, I'm no purist. The first thing I got him was second lead in this awful space opera thing. Total crap. Even by its own nonexistent standards. But hell, it was a job. I wasn't too high and mighty to send him in to read for it, and he wasn't too high and mighty to take the part when it was offered.

Or even those TV commercials I got him. He played a college student with a splitting headache in one—that was for aspirin, of course. He did another for dog food. A few others I can't even remember anymore. And I scored him a couple of smaller roles in TV plays, which were a thing in those days. Nothing memorable...I mean, some really good writers used to get involved in those: Rod Serling, David Shaw, Reginald Rose, Paddy Chayefsky. But there were some mediocrities too, mediocre writers and mediocre plays, and I'm afraid those were the ones Chance got cast in. One *Playhouse 90*, a couple of *Studio Ones*. Forgettable plays, but the important thing is, his work got noticed. He was really good in them, and he was developing a small reputation in the business.

But we were just getting our feet wet with those early credits. I knew I'd invested in a property that was going to appreciate. It didn't feel like a coin toss this time. I was just glad he knew Gil and that Gil was already one of my clients. Chance would never have come to me otherwise. Life is like that. Everything that happens, good and bad, happens by accident. Don't let anyone tell you different.

Matthew Devon (actor)

HARDWICK WAS A PUNK, all right? A total fucking punk. We're not supposed to speak ill of the dead, is that what they say? Well, piss on that. You came to me for the truth, right? Well, that's the truth. I hated the little prick.

No, we were never buddies. Hardly. We were in a film together, that's all. A cheapo horror thing. Trust me, you wouldn't have seen it, probably can't even find it on IMDb—but hey, it was work, right? A gig is a gig. And the producers were signatories to the MBA, and that was a big deal. The SAG health plan wasn't anything to be sneezed at, not even in those days. You needed credits to stay covered. The director was some blacklisted guy working under a fake name. I think he might have been hot shit once, I'm not sure about that, but now he was reduced to cheapo crap and grateful for the gig. The producers were willing to turn a blind eye if the guy was minimally competent and willing to work for scale.

I don't think Hardwick had been out here very long, but I'd been kicking around LA for over ten years. Waiting for my big break, like everybody else. Scrounging, mostly. It was tough. A few B-pictures, one or two small speaking roles in a couple of bigger productions. I had a walk-on in a Duke Wayne Western once. Walked on, muttered a few threatening words, got dragged out. To Boot Hill. The Duke upped and shot me. 'Course, I had it coming. I was a no-good varmint. But anyhow, the point I'm making is, gigs were few and far between. I waited tables occasionally, did a little beefcake modeling—fruitcake modeling, I used to call it—anything to pay the rent.

So one day my agent landed me this starring part—a *starring part!*—in *Martians from Venus* or whatever the son of a bitch was called. Some stupid thing. Outer space, rubber suits on the monsters, threats to destroy the earth. The usual crap. But still, I was gonna be the star. That meant something. Looks good on the bio, right? And it gives you bragging rights when you're trying to score with some chick in a bar. "Oh yeah, I had a starring role in a picture." They look at you with new eyes. You're not obligated to give them the title. In my case, I could honestly claim I didn't remember it.

But that starring business was in my contract. The credits had to read, "Starring Matt Devon as..." as whoever. Flash Montague, Butch Bladeworthy...I can't remember my character's name either. The money was short, natch, not much above scale, but hey, you never know what might lead to bigger things. You want to be *seen*, that's the thing we all tell ourselves. Never say no to a job. If you think something's beneath you, you're not an actor, you're a hobbyist.

So this newbie was hired to be my spaceship copilot or vice admiral or whatever it was. Chance Hardwick. The juvenile role. To appeal to teenage girls, I guess. The heartthrob. Dickie Jones to my Jock Mahoney. Edd Byrnes to my Efrem Zimbalist. And listen, I was fine with that. The part was in the script, and it didn't step on my toes. He was there to grab a different demographic. Fine. I got the moms, he got the ones who were still waiting for their first period. Fair exchange. No prob.

Or so I thought.

After the first day of shooting—a location shoot up in the Santa Monica Mountains; the place was supposed to be Mars or Venus or Pluto or the moon or some foreign body that wasn't a clearing just off Mulholland Drive—I suggested to Chance we go grab a beer. Just being collegial, you know. And he stared at me for a few seconds and then he said, "Why?" Which was already kind of...I mean, I was a little taken aback. And then, before I could come up with a reason, he said, "Nah." No excuse or explanation or anything. Not "Thanks, but I've got a date," or "I'm really beat," or "I have to work on tomorrow's lines." Just "Nah." I mean, what an asshole, right? Who does that?

But that wasn't such a big deal. I could see he wasn't exactly the warmest, most sociable guy I'd ever worked with, but you don't have to be best buds. I prefer to put things on a friendly footing, it makes for a happier set, it helps resolve problems more easily if they happen to occur, but hell, it isn't required. The real problem was... see, I don't know, maybe he was blowing the director or something, but somehow his part kept getting bigger and mine kept getting smaller. They kept giving him my lines, they even started giving him my heroics. This skinny little pipsqueak is suddenly grappling with space monsters in hand-to-claw fighting. I mean, I used to go to the gym daily, I was pumped, I'd been a fucking male model, I was much more believable as a scourge of extraterrestrials. But no, they wanted him to do it. In other words, to make a long story short, he was stealing the picture from me, right out from under me, in broad daylight, and with the connivance of the hack director we were working with. A schmuck who made Ed Wood look like Orson Welles.

I finally spoke up. This was maybe the second week of shooting. Or rather, I didn't actually speak up, because I don't like to make those sorts of complaint public, it makes you look like a prima donna, and besides, it adds to the tension, and there was already plenty enough of that, so I pulled the director—whose name I've also thankfully forgotten—I pulled him aside, we went into his trailer, and I said, "Look, what the hell is going on here? Why are you building up this kid? Those lines make a lot more sense coming from my character. And I'm obviously built more convincingly for the physical stuff." I think I even made a joke and said, "Besides, I've been fighting Martians all my life." Something like that. Just to leaven the mood a little, 'cause directors don't like to have their authority challenged. Especially the insecure ones. And this one was plenty insecure. With good reason.

He just gave me gobbledygook back. "We think it works better this way," he said. I wondered who this "we" included. The producer? Maybe, although I never saw the producer on set. Or was it Hardwick himself? Did he have something going with the director, like I kind of hinted before? I don't know the answer. And then he said, "Don't worry, though, we've got some additional stuff for you later, you'll see. The script needed a little restructuring is all." Needless to say, that part never happened. In the finished picture, the kid probably ended up with more lines than I did. Conniving little bastard.

Fortunately, nobody saw it. Even for a crummy drive-in date flick it was a piece of shit.

Gerhard Fuchs (musician)

I met Chance Hardwick at a party at, let me see, I think it was the Prices'. Vincent and Mary's. Yes, definitely at the Prices'. Vincent, you see, was one of those rare Hollywood people who didn't restrict their society to other show business people. This was very refreshing to me and Frieda. And unusual in this town. There were always plenty of movie stars present, too, of course, many in the way of show business royalty, they were willing to rub shoulders with us commoners if it was under the Price aegis, but it was at least possible at those parties to talk about things other than grosses and studio deals and who had been cast in what. Vincent enjoyed a mix of people—he had, I think, a life subdivided into many distinct compartments, if you catch my gist—and his interest in culture was genuine and serious. Mary's also. So one found painters, of course—Vincent was an art historian with basically a professional level of expertise, as you probably know—and writers, by which I mean novelists and playwrights and even poets from time to time, not merely screenwriters, although in those days Hollywood screenwriters were a far more erudite group than you'd find today. And musicians like myself, and professors from UCLA, and so forth. Those were lively—you say frolicsome?—they were frolicsome parties.

Lots of Europeans in those days too. We were everywhere during the war years, and remained a presence in the decade after. Many people don't realize that Los Angeles was something of a mecca for refugees who were fleeing Hitler or the Bolsheviks. They think of it as LaLa Land, but that is a very incomplete picture of the city, at least during that particular period. I arrived in '38, in the nick of time as you might say. And for a while...well, as a cultural capital, it could give Paris or London serious competition. Rachmaninoff lived in Beverly Hills—died there too, in point of fact—and Stravinsky's house was just off the Sunset Strip on Wetherly Drive, and Schoenberg, whom I'd known rather well in Vienna, was in Pacific Palisades. Rubinstein was here, Heifetz, Piatigorsky, Thomas Mann, Brecht, the Werfels, Wilder, Garbo, not to mention almost every extra and bit player in *Casablanca*. [laughs] Even Eisenstein was here early on, a bit before my time unfortunately. I believe I would have enjoyed speaking with him. And he should have stayed, of course. Those who went back to the Soviet Union, from wherever they'd emigrated to, often ended up regretting the decision. Those who went back to Germany too, at least to the DDR. I never learned how Brecht felt about his repatriation, but of course he was escaping McCarthyism by then, he was fleeing *from* rather than returning *to*.

Plus there were all the Brits. Aldous Huxley, Christopher Isherwood, James Mason. If foreigners constituted a Hollywood colony, the Brits, typically, were a colony within that colony. Englishmen simply adored it here. Couldn't get enough of the sun and the flesh. Everything they couldn't find at home. Available apparently without guilt or shame. A miracle! [laughs] Not to mention the additional, traditional colonial advantage of feeling superior to the natives. [laughs]

But I was telling you about meeting Chance Hardwick. Frieda and I were at this party at the Prices', as I said, and as usual I felt a little...I felt like I didn't exactly belong. Like a fish out of water, is that the idiom? Yes? It's a lovely expression. It conveys exactly how I used to feel. My English wasn't so good in those days, and that was one reason for my discomfort. It's got much better since, I believe. I've been here so long now, you know? Practice, practice. Like playing scales, so it becomes automatic. By now I've lived in

California so much longer than I ever lived in Austria, much, much longer, so even though those early years are usually decisive, I now, for example, think in English most of the time. Although I sometimes *dream* in German, which is itself interesting, is it not so?

Now, I don't say my English was not already serviceable from the start, I'd studied English in school, a difficult and demanding school, one of the best in Vienna—they taught British English at the *gymnasium*, they took their cue about correct pronunciation and usage from the BBC, and sometimes even today people ask me if I'm English, can you believe it?—but what I mean is, although I could function here in practical ways from the arrival, I could go shopping for groceries and consult a doctor and fill my petrol tank and help Frieda deal with the authorities when it was necessary, but in that setting, at the Prices' I mean, with that erudite company, I was hesitant about attempting to express myself. These were some of Europe's great minds, and there were some rather intelligent Americans there as well, and they were often discussing politics and philosophy and science and so forth, and for that a high school vocabulary did not seem altogether adequate.

Also, we were struggling a little financially, Frieda and I, money was short—I'd lost my job in the Warner Brothers studio orchestra a couple of years before, quite unfairly let me say, I've always suspected anti-German sentiment played a role which in my case was ridiculous, after all, Frieda is Jewish, it's the reason we had to emigrate. But I am not, and therefore was perhaps a little suspect. But there was nothing to be done about that, and so I was giving lessons and we were trying to cope that way—and as a result we were always the poorest guests at these fancy social occasions, and while that doubtless bothered Frieda more than me, it bothered both of us. We felt like poor relatives receiving charity sometimes. Not that the Prices ever made us feel that way…it was all our own distress, not anyone else's fault. Some people could be snooty about that sort of thing, no question, but the Prices were always welcoming.

So…Frieda was off talking to some of the wives, or at least standing with some of the wives while *they* talked—Frieda could be very shy under the best of circumstances, and especially around important people, maybe that was a carry-over from having been a second-class citizen in Austria during her formative years, you learn to accept such a judgment of yourself even when you know in your mind it's wrong—and besides, she was even more self-conscious about her difficulties with English than I—so she was in another room, and I was in the living room taking a canapé from a passing waiter and wondering to whom to talk or whether we should just leave, and suddenly this extremely good-looking young man approached me. He was dressed very casually, no jacket, no tie, which you might think was typical for Hollywood, but it wasn't, not in those days and not at this kind of gathering, and I right away assumed he must be the one person at the party who might be more destitute than I. Which—[laughs]—immediately endeared him to me, of course.

He introduced himself. The name Chance Hardwick meant nothing to me. It meant nothing to *anybody* at that point in his career, I don't believe. I'm not sure how he managed to get himself to the party. He was even less known than I at the time, and I was a complete nonentity. Perhaps he'd encountered Vincent somewhere random and Vincent had taken a shine to him and impulsively invited him.

I told him my name, we shook hands, and then he said, "Someone told me you're a musician."

"That I am."

"And that you were trained in Vienna."

"Vienna and Brussels, yes. At the Conservatory, and privately with a gentleman named Eugène Ysaye."

"The way you say it…am I right in thinking he must be famous?"

That was rather astute of him, I must admit. My studies with Ysaye were a point of pride for me, I cannot deny it, and my tone must have conveyed that pride even while I endeavored to sound matter-of-fact. And as a result, I immediately began to regard Mr. Hardwick, whose self-presentation was so unprepossessing, I began to regard him a little differently, with a measure of respect for the chap's intuition. For what is now rather pretentiously dubbed "emotional intelligence." I answered, "Well, yes, Ysaye had a…a certain reputation. He was, in point of fact, a great man."

"I'm really glad to meet you," Hardwick said. "See, when I heard you were a musician, I wanted to ask you something. I'm just beginning to listen to classical music, and I'm getting very interested in it. I'm starting to realize what I've been missing all these years by not knowing about it. And I wonder if you could tell me something—anything, really—about…uh…is the name Barcock? A composer. Very modern. I've just discovered him. His music seems terribly exciting."

"Do you mean Bela Bartok?"

"Yes, that's the one!"

So I had to laugh. Barcock! [laughs] But he was very eager to hear what I could tell him. Bartok was still considered quite avant-garde at that time. By now he's just part of the canon and that's all there is to it, but then he was regarded as…as…thorny? Is that the right word? Difficult, anyway. A little…rebarbative? [laughs] You mean to say you don't know that word? My English vocabulary is superior to yours! [laughs] And you're a *university professor*! Well, you've certainly made my day, Professor Frost.

[laughs for several seconds]

So Hardwick asked about Bartok—or Barcock [laughs]—and I was surprised that this young man might be interested in someone so forbidding, and I must say I was in general very impressed with his seriousness. You don't expect that kind of seriousness in one so young. Let alone in a handsome young Hollywood actor. We talked for over an hour. At one point, Frieda came to me from the next room and made one of those "I'm ready to leave now" gestures that husbands and wives learn to make to one another, and I had to shake my head to indicate I wasn't ready. I was enjoying myself, and thoroughly enjoying Mr. Hardwick's company. As he seemed to be enjoying mine. We talked about the music he should listen to if he wanted to know more, and he asked me many questions about my training and my experiences and my life in LA. His curiosity about practically everything seemed voracious.

And meanwhile, Frieda kept going out and coming back in, looking increasingly desperate. I suppose I should have been a better husband, more attentive to her whims. But it was so rare for me to have a conversation like that in those days, it was very hard to tear myself away. When we finally did leave…well, Frieda wouldn't talk to me for the entire drive home. I was…you say *in the doghouse?* I was very much in the doghouse.

Gil Fraser

WAIT, YOU'RE SAYING SOMEONE told you Chance was interested in classical music? [laughs] Nah. [laughs] Ridiculous. Must have been a classical musician, right? Yeah, I thought so. See, Chance had this way…he had this way of talking to people. A sort of…trick, I guess, although he'd never have called it a trick himself. Pretending to be interested in what people did. Asking a lot of questions. I don't mean pretending to be interested in *them* so much, that would have been too obvious for Chance, but pretending to have been interested for a long time in what they did. It was a way of getting them to talk. And no, he wasn't being sociable. For Chance, it was *research*. People who knew things he didn't know, or acted in ways he hadn't seen before, he always felt he could pick up something from them that might come in handy later. He wasn't especially interested in the information *per se*, in what they actually said—I mean, sometimes it was interesting, sometimes it bored him to tears—he was interested in watching how they acted and sounded while they were saying it. So he could use that specific emotion and behavior when something along the same lines arose in a script.

Pretending to be interested was a sort of confidence game. He did it all the time, and people were always taken in. Because you want to believe people are interested in what you have to say, right? I saw him do it scads of times. I'm sure there are still people out there who think he was passionately interested in astrophysics or Polish history or agricultural economics. He became what he thought you wanted him to be. And he could be totally convincing. He'd pick up on what you were telling him and give it back to you in different words as if he'd been thinking about it forever. He was a chameleon, see? And he'd be studying you closely the whole time in order to be an even *better* chameleon next time.

You'd be hard-pressed to say who or what the real Chance Hardwick was. For a few years back there, I probably knew the cat better than anyone, and even I can't claim I really knew him. We were good friends, but down deep he was always a mystery to me. He was...I think I'd say...jeez, not deceptive. Maybe just *baffling*.

Maybe Briel Charpentier knew him better than me. It's possible. She's the only one besides me who you might reasonably say got close to him. Have you talked to her? She's around somewhere. And I'm sure *her* Chance Hardwick was completely different from mine. You ought to give her a call. You have? Well, that's good. She can probably tell you things I can't. I mean, heck, she can even describe his dick.

But as to your question, the simple truth is, in the entire time we roomed together, I never once saw Chance listening to any classical music. That was just completely not his thing. We shared an apartment for over a year—I know what I'm talking about. It was mostly jazz, he listened to plenty of jazz, and he knew a lot about it. I think he'd picked up the bug in New York. We'd go to clubs occasionally, him and me. Shelly's Mann Hole, the Lincoln Theater, a couple of others in town. Including places where we were the only white guys in the joint. Didn't faze Chance, and nobody ever made us feel unwelcome.

There were great players around in those days. The whole West Coast jazz scene was cooking. But going to a club...it was always his idea...you know, "Hey, Gil, so-and-so"—a name I didn't necessarily even know, but Chance obviously thought was hot shit—"so-and-so is playing in the Valley tonight, let's make ourselves presentable and head out there." Doing something like that would never have occurred to me, it wasn't the way I usually chose to spend my time, but if Chance suggested it I'd usually say yes. He was fun to be out on the town with, for one thing, plus I trusted his taste. I can't honestly say he made a convert out of me, but I dug the atmosphere. I dug being in the club, checking out the women, getting half-potted, shooting the shit, listening to the music. I enjoyed the music okay, not the bebop stuff so much, but some of the more melodic players, some of the quieter tunes. But the thing is, if any music was *his* passion, that was definitely it. At home, he'd often have a record on while going about his business. Always jazz, never classical.

Or if he was with a date in the living room—I'd give him space under those circumstances, go out somewhere or retire to my room, and he'd always do the same for me; it was an unwritten rule between us, it's the way roommates stay on good terms—if he was with a girl in the living room, he might put some Sinatra or Nat Cole on the record player. Something to put her in the mood. He had nothing against those guys, but for him they were mostly a means to an end.

I wouldn't say Chance and I ever became *friends* exactly, but we always got on well. Still, other than the occasional lunch to talk business, or a round of drinks to celebrate a good bit of casting, or one of the big holiday parties Marty and I used to give, we rarely socialized. Different generations, different worlds. Mutual respect—and over time I came to feel more than respect for Chance, it became something closer to awe—but outside of business, we weren't in each other's lives in any significant way.

But with one exception, we never had a cross word between us or anything like that. He trusted me, he knew we were allies, and he seemed to appreciate what I was able to do for him. And I believe he respected me as a person as well as an agent. So our relations were always amicable and cordial and even warm. Except for this one time, and it still pains me to recall it. It was the only time we lost our tempers with one another.

This was early on. I'd already gotten him some smaller parts, he was working a little. Including one Western…I got him an audition without even being sure he knew how to ride a horse. Usually I was more careful than that! Fortunately, it turned out he was actually a really good rider. He'd loved horses since he was a boy. But anyway, he was working some, small roles in this and that, some commercials, like I said, some TV, a couple of pictures. He was starting to make a living, but we were still waiting for the big breakthrough.

And then a well-known director—I probably shouldn't tell you his name—saw him in something, recognized his potential, and asked me to arrange a meeting. This was great news. It seemed like it might be the break we'd been waiting for. The fellow was a veteran, you could even say an old-timer, hell, he'd gotten his start in the silents, but he was still super-respected and still active, still A-list. So when he suggested Chance come to his house and they could discuss possible projects over a drink, Chance was excited. *I* was excited. The man was a force in the industry. He got movies made.

I told Chance that before he went he should shower and shave and dress respectably and comb his hair and so on. Show some respect. He still needed that kind of guidance. I don't know whether it was rebelliousness or plain old slovenliness, but he didn't always put his best foot forward. Sometimes it didn't matter, but there were times it could matter quite a lot. And this time, because so much might be riding on the meeting, and because the fellow he was meeting with was kind of old school, I insisted Chance come to my office for inspection before he drove over to Beverly Hills. This director had a reputation for exquisite taste, both in his work and in his person. He was famous for having a certain casual elegance, good dresser, suave manners, beautiful house, fine art collection, and I didn't want him to be offended by Chance before they'd even had a chance to talk. See, I knew Chance was bound to make a good impression once they started discussing movies and acting. I just wanted to make sure things got to that point.

When he showed up, he looked okay. I mean, honestly, he was so handsome he could get away with stuff like a couple days' growth of beard or faded jeans and a torn T-shirt and still be totally gorgeous, but that wouldn't do this time, and he'd followed my advice and taken care of some personal grooming. He still looked informal—khaki pants, a striped sport shirt, no tie—but the gestalt was respectable. Almost collegiate. What would later be called preppy. Not, in any event, *zhlumpy*. So I gave him my stamp of approval and sent him on his way.

And it may have been an hour or so later when I got a call. On my home phone. I'd already gone home. It was Chance, and he was speaking so quietly he was almost whispering. I'm guessing he'd asked to use the fellow's phone and gone to another room so he could talk to me without being heard. But even though his voice was very low, he sounded panicky, with that quavery quality. The director was moving on him, he said. He said the guy had sat very close to him on the sofa, had looked deeply into his eye, had put his hand on Chance's knee and told him if he wanted to succeed in the business he needed to be flexible. Chance knew what he was being told, of course. He might have been fairly new to Hollywood, but he wasn't a babe in the woods. When you look like Chance, you get hit on a lot, you learn to recognize the signs early in life. The guy told Chance he could make him a big star, said he'd helped a number of young actors in his time. He mentioned a few names. They weren't obvious ones by any means. Some macho types, some legendary ladies' men. Of course, the fellow might have been lying about some of them. No way for us to check, is there?

Now, Chance didn't come right out and ask me for advice, but that was pretty clearly why he'd called. So when he finally stopped babbling—he'd been talking a mile a minute—I said, "Listen, Chance. Listen, hon. He's a powerful man in this town. He isn't talking through his hat. He's in a position to do us a world of good."

And Chance sort of grunted and then he hung up without saying goodbye.

Now I should tell you right here and now that I had—and continue to have—no idea about Chance's sexual tastes. That certainly wasn't anything we ever discussed. If it had emerged he was queer I wouldn't have been shocked, but I can't say I necessarily thought it was the case either. I had no opinion on the matter. And to be honest, I didn't think it was relevant in this particular situation. People do all sorts of things that wouldn't be their first choice if there are compelling reasons for it.

But anyway, he hung up on me. And about a half-hour later, my doorbell rang. That was a shock. I didn't expect any visitors,

I was already in a housecoat and mules, my husband and I were preparing dinner in the kitchen. So I answered the door, and it was Chance, looking furious. Steam coming out of his ears, virtually. It was obvious this wasn't the right time to suggest we wait and talk in the morning, so I led him into the little room at the back of the house Marty and I used as a study.

"How could you put me in that position?" he said. Almost shouted. He was in a rage. No hello or anything.

So I told him I didn't know that that was the position he'd be in when I set up the meeting. So then he said, "But when I phoned you just now, you told me to go through with it."

I defended myself by denying I'd told him that. I'd just explained the situation because he needed to understand what might be at stake.

Which didn't placate him. "I thought you were an ethical person," he said. "I can't believe this."

Well, that stung. "It's not like I *like* it," I said. "But I *am* in the business, and this is how the business sometimes works. It's been this way from the beginning. It's nasty, but it's the world we're in."

"It's not the world *I'm* in," he said. "I'm an actor, not a whore. I sleep with people I want to sleep with. I don't have sex hoping for a payoff." And then he said, "And I thought you were my agent, Irma, I didn't think you were my pimp. I'm honestly surprised at you."

Well, he was right, of course. I'd been looking out for his career, maybe, but I hadn't been looking out for *him*. You get so inured to that kind of bullshit that you stop noticing how ugly it is, how dehumanizing and degrading. Treating artists like...like *meat*. I felt deeply mortified. So I steeled myself and apologized to him. Abjectly. And I was sincere, I honestly felt terrible, and I think he could see I was sincere. I didn't know how this would turn out or how he'd react, in fact I initially thought he'd probably fire me—

which I probably deserved, at least from one point of view—but he didn't. We got past it.

At the time, standing in the study with him, I felt a little desperate, so right then and there I suggested—almost begged him—to sit down for dinner with Marty and me, we had enough food, and Chance surprised me by accepting, and…well, we actually had a pretty pleasant meal, all things considered, and soon, after a few glasses of wine, we were even laughing about the whole incident. Chance started acting out the scene, and, you know, he was brilliant at that sort of stuff, he played both parts, the director and himself, to perfection, oily and sweaty and insinuating as the would-be seducer, timid and shy and virginal as himself, and he had Marty and me in stitches—and by the time he left he realized he had a great story to dine out on as long as he disguised the identity of the director.

James Sterling (acting teacher)

GIL FRASIER BROUGHT CHANCE to my class the first time. It was the one in the evening…I was teaching several a day. After I was blacklisted I couldn't work in pictures, so I had to really scramble to make a living. Ran myself ragged for a while, three or sometimes even four classes a day. Usually one in the morning, one in the afternoon, one after dinner. It was grueling work. When you teach something as intimate as acting, you have to make a huge emotional commitment to each student. You can't just sit back and watch, you have to engage. It's very personal, very active. When a class ended, I'd often find myself drenched in sweat. I'd have to take a nap before the next class started. And we started eating our dinners at a ridiculously early hour so that I wouldn't have to expend all that emotional energy on a full stomach, and to give me time to get back to the little theater I was renting in Hollywood.

My wife wasn't thrilled about that, but she understood. My kids kind of liked it...they were always hungry anyway, so from their point of view, the earlier we ate the better.

Gil had been studying with me for more than a year. A good student, an enthusiastic participant in class, and a fine solid actor. The kind of guy—he might not give you brilliance, there might not be any blazing moment of insight or illuminating display of emotion, but you could rely on him to give an honest, intelligent performance. He had a pretty good career over the years, and still works now and then—I see him occasionally in a TV drama or an indie film—but I'd say he deserved to be better known. One of those character guys who are indispensable to a good production even if you don't pay much attention to them.

He and Chance were friends.

They were roommates? I didn't know that.

Anyway, he brought Chance along one night. Chance was curious, I guess, and I'm sure Gil told him good things about the class. He came in that first time just to observe. I had a policy in those days, people could sit in for a couple of classes for free before deciding whether they wanted to attend as a student. Many did. They liked what they saw. After watching for a while, there was this itch to participate, to be part of the action. What we were doing in those classes was exciting, it was hard to just sit on the sidelines and watch other people throw themselves into it.

So Chance came a couple of times, and then he signed up. I think for both him and Gil the expense wasn't negligible. Neither of them was working much at the time. I didn't charge a hell of a lot, but even that small amount was a large amount if you weren't earning anything.

Students sometimes brought monologues or scenes in to class and we'd work on those, but my basic teaching technique was to work with improvisation. Not free-form, not just get up there and start winging it. That would be too unstructured to be useful. I wanted to teach *focus* and *concentration* along with the free exercise of imagination. So instead, I'd give them written-out scripts, only with some of the lines of dialogue missing. And they'd have to improvise those missing lines, fill in the blanks as it were. And my rule was, their improvised lines couldn't directly address the overt substance of the scene. They had to talk about something else, something apparently unrelated that might reveal subtext, might show us what the characters were thinking and feeling. It's a lot harder than it sounds, believe me. Some quite good actors weren't good at it at all, some were mind-blowingly great. But even the ones who weren't good at it…their acting definitely benefited from the exercise anyway. Because it didn't just teach them how to improvise. It helped teach them to *act*.

The first time Chance performed in class, it was a monologue, not an improv. Something from *The Tempest*. And it was very good. We worked with it line by line, the whole class pitching in and asking about why he'd made this choice or that, commenting on possible alternatives. He had trouble answering—he worked intuitively, his process wasn't intellectual—but he wasn't especially defensive about the suggestions. And everybody agreed it was an excellent piece of work. We had some questions, we had some criticisms, but there was no doubting the fellow had a lot of talent.

But the next time he got up, it was to do one of the improv scenes. The set-up was a blind date, a first date between a guy and a gal that had been arranged by some mutual friends. And the written dialogue was pretty realistic, the way people would behave on a first date when they don't know each other at all and feel a little exposed about needing to be set up with each other. Awkward, but putting their best foot forward. Expressing curiosity about one another even if they weren't especially interested. We'd done that scene in class lots of times.

So after the first few written exchanges, the boy's script has a blank...an indication he should improvise. And Chance said, "What's that weird smell?"

Well, that was startling. Nobody had ever gone quite *that* far afield with an improvised line. And then he edged away from her in this very gingerly way, as if...you see, the way I interpreted it, his character didn't want to be rude, didn't want the girl to feel insulted, it was a subtle, almost invisible sidling away, but it was as if the smell was so unpleasant he needed to get some distance from her. And the girl—I don't recall which one it was, and that should give you some idea of what made that particular class memorable— the girl just stared at him. Because she was supposed to improvise something back, but his line flummoxed her completely. She moved a little closer to him—I don't even think she was aware she was doing it—and he sidled away again, and because she hadn't come up with a line, he went on, "Oh, that's right, Chuck told me you just had an operation."

So at that point the whole class laughed. No doubt because it was so unexpected as well as so socially unacceptable, they assumed Chance must have intended it comically. But his affect was totally earnest, puzzled and troubled if anything. And the girl recovered enough to say—see, in improv you're never supposed to contradict anything any other actor has said, you have to accept it and build on it—she said, "Yeah, they released me from the hospital last night."

Not exactly a brilliant comeback, it didn't take us anywhere new, but at least she said *something*. And Chance said, "They did? Usually when someone smells like that they keep them overnight for observation."

And at that point they were back into the written script. And it went on like that, with Chance, whenever it was his turn to improvise, throwing out the most bizarre, out-of-left-field lines.

The poor girl couldn't keep up, that I do remember, and also looked offended at some of Chance's choices, as if he was insulting her personally, as if he was putting her down, not acting a character.

When they were done I did what I always did, which is throw the class open to discussion, ask the students for reactions. And the initial response was pretty hostile. Some people said he'd been mean, some accused him of not taking the class seriously. Others wondered if he'd had any idea what he was doing or was just desperately free-associating. Finally his pal Gil spoke up, not offering an opinion, but saying, "Tell us what *you* think, Jim. What were your feelings about it?" Maybe he asked just because the mood was turning ugly, and he wanted to take some of the pressure off his buddy.

So people seemed shocked when I said, "I thought it was dazzling." I even heard a few gasps. I think they expected me to be much rougher on him, partly because they had no idea of what he'd been aiming for and figured I didn't either, and also because I was capable of being pretty harsh when I felt students weren't working at their peak. And also, to be honest, I was ordinarily pretty chary with praise. People shouldn't come to class expecting to be complimented, they should come hoping to learn. But I thought this was an astonishing performance, especially considering it was Chance's very first time up, and it deserved to be recognized as such.

I went on to talk about how people feel on first dates, how self-conscious they are about themselves, their appearance and their behavior, how unnatural and ill-at-ease they are, and underneath, perhaps even unbeknownst to themselves, how judgmental they are about the other person, wondering if the date is worth the anxiety they're putting themselves through, whether it's worth the effort and maybe even worth the expense. Plus how they feel, especially if things don't seem to be going too well, how they feel a little angry, and maybe the anger's directed at themselves but often at the other person too, and they might suppress it, but it's still there. "I think Chance was totally in touch with all those emotions, the self-consciousness and the self-loathing and the hostility and the anxiety, and was externalizing them, turning them into a theatrical reality." Then I turned to him, up on the stage, and asked, "Is that what you were thinking?"

And he gave me that famous lopsided smile and said, "Maybe something along those lines. Insofar as I was thinking."

So right from the start I knew he was special. And he kept coming to my classes, even after he'd become a star. And in interviews, he was always very generous about what he learned in my class.

Sir Trevor Bliss (director)

I FELL INTO FILMMAKING more or less by hazard. I daresay that's how it often worked in my generation. No one thought of filmmaking as a profession in those days, you see. Back then, no child in Britain—I imagine no child anywhere—dreamt of becoming a cinema director when he grew up. We didn't even realize there *was* such a thing.

But after my stint in the RAF—I'd had a pretty good war as such things go, a bit of excitement, only a few brushes with serious danger—which isn't to say I wasn't scared to death every waking moment, but the fear was rarely justified by the facts on the ground, or, to be more precise, in the air—certainly I was relatively safe compared to the chaps who faced genuine life-threatening jeopardy on a daily basis—but in any case, after the war, and after a couple of years at Swansea University, which I left without taking a degree, I found myself...well, first, I should say that while serving I'd been assigned to do aerial photography and reconnaissance over Germany, often as a follow-up to bombing missions, in order to survey and assess the effectiveness of each raid, so I definitely knew my way around cameras and things. I'd continued with photography at Swansea. And so after I'd left Wales and returned to London, after a few weeks there penniless and utterly confused about what to do with my life, I found my way, through some friends I'd made in the service, to the Documentary Division of the BBC, where I learned the ins and outs of motion picture camera work. I stayed for a bit, and then landed a position at Pinewood Studios, first as a cameraman, and then, having earned a measure of trust, I was allowed to try my hand at directing a few things.

And because they were rather well-received, more work followed, and then Hollywood expressed an interest, and that seemed like quite an attractive proposition after the privations of the war years and post-war rationing and so on, so I popped over to California for a rather long period. I never took American citizenship, although [laughs] I did take an American wife, and soon had two American children as well. Legally speaking they're both nationalities, they carry both American and British passports, but no one who meets them would mistake them for English. My parents, when they finally met their grandkids on a visit we made one Christmas, were loath to acknowledge my paternity.

[laughs]

And I also acquired an American partner. After I'd made a couple of films as a hired gun, so to say, I decided I'd really prefer more creative control over the work I was doing, and teamed up with a bloke named Saul Lindauer, and we formed a production company. Saul was more on the producing end, I was responsible for the directing side of things. But to be fair to Saul, we both played a creative role at the development stage of any given project. He had sound story sense and made exceedingly valuable contributions in our initial discussions with the writers. So I don't mean to suggest he was simply the finance fellow. But once filming got underway, he generally stayed away from the set.

We had a project in development at United Artists, a good one, we entertained high hopes for it, we'd optioned a quite distinguished war novel—there were so many good ones, weren't there?—the Second World War, whatever else it was, turned out to be a boon to American literature, so many of those returning GIs had been through hell and had gripping tales to tell. We were too late with Mailer and Jones and Shaw, or in one case were simply outbid, but we managed to option Chuck Leveret's *Plains and Hills* before anyone else could get their hands on it. It was a good novel, rather Hemingway-esque, but if you're going to be–*esque* that's not a bad–*esque* to be, particularly if you're writing about combat.

Saul managed to round up the financing without too much difficulty—it was what Hollywood calls "a prestige property"—and we began casting it, and we were going to go with Orson Bean for the younger brother, he was just beginning to make a reputation in New York, mostly in comedy, but he was a good, versatile actor, and we were going to bring him out. But then he got named in front of HUAC, and that was that. It was a terrible period, those blacklist days. Many careers and reputations were utterly destroyed. Orson wasn't destroyed, thankfully, he managed to bounce back in theater, where the blacklist didn't have the same degree of sway, and he ended up doing fine for himself. But casting him in a movie at the time was out of the question. And from what I understand— not that it should matter—he wasn't even a Communist at all. But once you say something like that, as people often do these days, you're almost conceding the government's right to examine people's conscience, you're simply criticizing them for doing sloppy work, and that isn't a position I'm comfortable taking. The entire operation was corrupt from its inception. That's why I never took American citizenship, and why I ultimately returned to Britain, although admittedly my divorce had something to do with that latter decision as well. But I'd been considering naturalization for a time, it had seemed like a sensible step, and now it no longer seemed like anything I'd want to do. Britain never had anything resembling a McCarthyite episode, you see, and that was enough for me to keep my nationality and my passport.

But as I was saying, we were forced to give up on Bean, we had to find a replacement. And since this was the younger brother of the protagonist, we were willing to cast an unknown…indeed, it almost *had* to be an unknown. Returning veterans who were already established actors would likely be too old to be convincing in the part. So the word went out, and Irma Gold sent us Chance Hardwick to read for it. Along with another of her clients as I recall, although I can't for the life of me remember his name. But she sent along the two of them. Hedging her bets, you might say. [laughs] This was for the role of Chip, troubled younger brother of the lead, who at that point we thought was going to be Alan Ladd, although Ladd eventually dropped out. We replaced him with Jeff Harte. A compromise choice, although Jeff turned out to be marvelous in the role. Quite the best performance of his career, I daresay.

But Chip was a great part, and that may in fact have been the reason Ladd bailed on us. Meatiest role in the script, in my opinion. Not a lot of lines, but a number of bang-up scenes, and at key plot points. We looked at a good many young actors, some of whom became quite successful soon after. Russ Tamblyn came in, Nick Adams, Steve McQueen, Roddy McDowall, Dean Stockwell. Many actors who were to make their name in the near future, as things turned out. Well, I suppose Roddy already had a name, as did Dean—he'd been in *The Boy with Green Hair*, hadn't he?—but some of the others, their success was a few years off. But my point is, the way things unfolded in Hollywood in those days, the rumor mill was always churning, people somehow knew things before they were meant to know them. It remains a mystery how rumors spread in that odd town, but the word was apparently out that this was potentially a career-making role. So agents were sending us their best. In retrospect, just considering the quality of the people we turned down, I guess you'd have to say it was a damned stellar cattle call.

And we finally went with Hardwick. He had a quality. *I* saw it right away. Saul was somewhat hesitant at first, he felt the boy might be a little too soft, he said—[laughs]—"Only a fucking limey would think this candy-ass has the balls for Chip." [laughs] That was Saul for you. Not the most delicate of sensibilities. In point of fact, he could be a total twat sometimes, with all the subtlety of a two-ton lorry. He did come 'round eventually, of course. Admitted he'd been blind. By the time we wrapped, it was impossible to deny. But I on the other hand saw Hardwick's appeal immediately. Maybe because I'm a fucking limey. [laughs] It was hard to define, the nature of that appeal, although many, of course, have tried in the years since his death. Whole books have been written on the subject, haven't they? Scholarly monographs. You've probably written one yourself. Forgive me for not knowing of it. Books on cinema don't really engage me. That's often true of practitioners and theorists, don't you find? They inhabit separate realms.

The thing of it is, Hardwick had a way of giving you the feeling he was suffering from a pain so deep—so intense, so mysterious and personal—that your heart couldn't help but go out to him. Everyone wanted to mother him, even men. Even heterosexual men. And women found him enormously sexy while men didn't find him especially threatening. He wasn't a macho bruiser and yet, *pace* that twat Saul, he didn't seem like a pantywaist either. D'you know what I mean? His vulnerability didn't have the…pardon me for being so frank, but the rather sniveling quality you found in an actor like Sal Mineo. A very good actor, please don't misunderstand me, but

I think he was destined *always* to be the second lead. His kind of vulnerability was very real, and reasonably touching, but it wasn't the sort that translates into the leading man species of stardom.

During the shoot, Hardwick wasn't a huge presence on the set. He was quiet. Shy, perhaps. Sitting back, watching. Perfectly pleasant to the crew. Agreeable, accommodating, not hiding out in his trailer, but rarely initiating any interactions. He may have still been a little awed by what was happening to him, of course. This would be a huge leap forward in his career, and he must have been aware of the fact. He may not have been entirely ready for it, emotionally speaking. Indeed, considering the way his life ended, he may never have learned how to deal with it. [sighs] Such a tragedy.

During the first week or so of shooting, I had no complaints about his work, he was very professional and definitely delivering all we expected of him, but it was only when I looked at the rushes on the evening of the day we'd shot his first really big scene, a scene where he confesses to his brother what he's done, that it suddenly struck me he might in fact be extraordinary. It was in his eyes, you see. The most complex emotions, all there, transparent, residing behind his eyes. Not so visible from the director's chair, but the camera found them. He *let* the camera find them.

The next day, I sought him out. And this is possibly the thing I recall about him most vividly from that whole shoot. I had him summoned to my trailer. I offered him a cup of coffee and I told him to take a seat. He looked very uneasy, but he plopped himself down on one of the easy chairs. And I told him that, as usual, Saul and I had screened the previous day's dailies in the evening after everyone had left for the day. And he grimaced—you know the look, no doubt; it became something Chance Hardwick was known for—and he said, "Am I gonna be replaced? Is that it? Am I doing it wrong?"

[laughs]

Isn't that sweet? He thought I had called him in to fire him! He was being very stoic about it, very brave, very stiff upper lip. Maybe in deference to my national origins. [laughs] I must admit, I was charmed. "No, no," I hastened to tell him. "Not a bit of it, silly boy. Quite the opposite. You're giving me great stuff! Wonderful stuff! I invited you in to praise you." So at that his whole posture slumped. It's interesting to watch a great actor when he isn't acting, don't you find? He's *still* acting. Can't help himself, can he? I went on, "I just wanted to tell you, whatever it is you're doing, do please keep doing it. It's working a treat. You *own* this character. By the time we wrap, you may own this *film*."

And of course I was right on both counts.

Irma Gold

ALMOST EVERYBODY IN THIS town hated the blacklist. Even most conservative Republicans. Not John Wayne, not Ward Bond, not— [feigns vomiting]—Hedda Hopper. Those bastards were happy as pigs in shit. Ruining people's lives, and being able to do it while patting themselves on the back for their patriotism...it was like they'd died and gone to heaven. A place they'll never actually see, by the way. Not after the way they behaved. But anyway, most of the people in this business, regardless of how they voted, they still believed in the First Amendment. Artists tend to be like that...they have a vested interest in free speech and free thought, don't they? Hell, you take a guy like Gary Cooper. Coop was as conservative as they come, but his father had been a justice on the Montana Supreme Court—were you aware of that?—and he detested the blacklist. He didn't like witch-hunts. You didn't have to be a lefty to hate the blacklist.

And besides, just from a practical point of view, that kind of outside interference, it made it harder to get the work done. The blacklist made it impossible to hire some of the people you wanted to hire. A talent like Dalton Trumbo or Waldo Salt—no matter what your politics were, you didn't care about theirs if you could get them to write a screenplay for you. They always delivered. But now you couldn't. If you did, you might be blacklisted yourself. Hedda Hopper or Mike Connelly would write a column about you, say you were giving aid and comfort to the Reds, and your career would be in tatters.

Of course, that whole horrible period also represented an opportunity for some people. The rats, of course. They suddenly had more work. They could almost write their own ticket, taking the jobs their former comrades might otherwise have gotten. Most of 'em never paid a price for their treachery either. Lee J. Cobb, Elia Kazan, Sterling Hayden, Lloyd Bridges, Abe Burrows, Burl fucking Ives...I mean, the list is long. Their careers prospered, they never looked back, no regrets, not unless their conscience ever bothered them, not unless they woke up in the middle of the night in a cold guilty sweat, like Kazan confessed happened to him once, or like Lee Cobb and Sterling Hayden used to whine about all the time. But those *mamzers* mostly did all right for themselves. You don't always get justice in this life. There are murderers who die in their sleep.

But my point is, some of the youngsters, the up-and-comers, the new faces...nobody would have thought to subpoena them, you know? They weren't well known, for one thing, so there was no good publicity in it for the Committee, and besides, they were mostly new in town. Now, as far as Chance Hardwick is concerned, he and I had never discussed politics—for all I know, he didn't have any at that time, he might have been one of those guys who couldn't have cared less—but in any case, whatever he'd been up to before he got to town, it wasn't on anyone's radar, and there was no way he was going to be named or subpoenaed.

And *Plains and Hills* was a perfect example of the kind of thing that was happening in those days. If Orson Bean hadn't been smeared by some self-dealing prick or other, he'd have played Chip in that movie and his life would've been very different, and as a result Chance's life might've been very different too. Just another example of the way forces outside your control end up determining your fate.

Gil Fraser

CHANCE AND I WERE both up for the same part. Chip in *Plains and Hills*. It was bound to happen eventually, I suppose. We were about the same age, the same approximate type. Maybe I was more rugged, he was more sensitive, but if we'd been a Venn Diagram, there would have been a lot of overlap.

We'd talked about the possibility before that. I mean, I'd been in town a lot longer than Chance, I'd been in that situation. You and a friend, or a number of friends, are competing for the same role. It can get intense. It can get *tense*. True, you might all lose out, but on the other hand, one of you might win, which means the rest of you are going to lose. That can feel really shitty. So one night fairly early on, over a couple of beers, I warned him that something like that could easily arise. And that if it did, we had to be colleagues, we had to be friends, we couldn't let ourselves become rivals. Or, I mean, of course we'd be rivals, we're competing for a job for Christ's sake, but we couldn't let that become a problem, we couldn't let it become so destructive that it screwed up our friendship. And I told him that it was particularly important with roommates, because if things get nasty between you and your roommate and things get said that you regret, there's no chance to go off and lick your wounds in private and settle yourself down and come back with everything resolved in your mind. You're like cellmates. Or ferocious animals in a single cage.

And I'll never forget this…I was lecturing Chance about all this, carrying on at great length, you know, preachy, big brotherly, and he finally interrupted me, he said, "Listen, Gil, relax, I've already been there." So I looked at him sort of quizzically, and he went on, "Back in New York, a friend of mine and I both tried out for the Actors Studio, okay? And he made it, I didn't. He got three ones, I got two ones and a two, the two was from Lee himself, which meant come back sometime and try again, and that was that. It was a totally shitty experience, I felt horrible, but we handled it. We stayed close friends, all right? I didn't begrudge him. If you get a part we're both up for, I'll be disappointed but I'll still be happy it was you rather than some random jerk. Trust me, it's gonna be fine either way."

And then, when *Plains and Hills* came along, it was obviously gonna be such a prestige picture, and just looking at the sides when they sent them over you could tell Chip was a fabulous part, almost an actor-proof part. It was obvious to me that anyone who got cast in that role was probably gonna be a star. You'd have to be unbelievably awful to fuck it up. It almost played itself, a pre-punched ticket to the next level. No, not just the next level, a quantum leap up a whole shitload of levels. A rocket to the fucking moon.

And the irony—if you want to call it irony—is that when they signed Chance, I was a real shithead about it. I'd given him my big lecture, but I guess when I did it I assumed I was at the head of the queue and he was the one who would have to be a good sport. And here it was, a few months later, and the ball was unexpectedly in my court. And I fumbled it big time. I groused and complained and questioned his skills and in general behaved like an asshole. Said he got the job only because of his pretty face. Talked about my training versus his lack of training. Just was impossible in every conceivable way. And to his credit, Chance didn't gloat or anything like that, didn't seem to take great umbrage, didn't even defend himself. He was a perfect gentleman. He told me he thought I'd have been great in the role but he just happened to win the coin toss and that that sometimes happened. And he said he couldn't be sorry about how it had turned out, but that if it hadn't been him, he would have been thrilled if it was me. And then he gave me a lot of space to get over it. He was a model of good sportsmanship and collegiality, and I was…I was a fucking John McEnroe.

But only for a while. Let me say that in my own defense. I needed a day or two to get past it and pull myself together. Then I gave him the biggest apology I was capable of, downright *abject*, which God knows was appropriate, and I bought us a bottle of expensive champagne to celebrate his having got the part, and I took him out to Scandia for a celebratory dinner, and of course we fought over the check. He said, "Hey, I'm finally making real money here, let me get this," and I said, "No, ain't gonna happen, there'll be other dinners and you'll be buying those, you can be sure of that, but tonight's on me." And I'd really like to believe that made everything okay again. He acted like it did. But then again, he was a great actor, wasn't he?

Mike Shore (stand-in)

MY BEST BUDDY WAS Jeff Harte, who you've surely heard of. Kids today might be only vaguely familiar with the name, but you're a film guy, you must know his work. Me and Jeff were friends going back to the old neighborhood when we were kids, and we stayed best friends right up till the day he died. He was a pretty big star back in the day. Among other great pictures, he was the star of *Plains and Hills*, the movie you're asking me about. And he was a good guy. Success didn't go to his head, he stayed a good guy the whole time, just a regular guy who looked after his pals—there were a group of us who hung out together.

People sometimes referred to us as his entourage, but it wasn't really like that. Not really. We weren't like a bunch of hangers-on. I guess he *was* kind of at the center of things, being a big star and all, and, you know, if there was money to be spent it was probably going to be his, he was a generous guy that way. But he never made us feel like he was the king and we were his court. It was more free-wheeling and democratic than that. I mean, yeah, we mostly did what he wanted, I guess 'cause he was footing the bill, so if he said, "Hey, let's all go to Vegas for the weekend," no one was going to say, "Nah, take us to Rosarita Beach instead." That would've been bad form. No one ever thought of doing anything like that. But he didn't make it feel you were being bossed around or anything. And anyone could make a suggestion, you know, and sometimes, if he liked it, he'd take you up on it.

And like I say, he looked after his friends. So, for example, he'd get me the gig as his stand-in whenever he was making a picture. It wasn't a big leap or anything; we were pretty close to the same height and the same build, so for blocking and lighting and so on I was at least as good in the job as the next guy. I could stand still with the best of 'em. It was boring work, undemanding work, but it was a paycheck, and he liked having me around, you know? It was a way of taking care of me and at the same time seeing to it that we could hang out together and shoot the shit between takes. Play a little gin rummy, tell jokes, flirt with the gals on the set, reminisce about the old days.

And *Plains and Hills* was an interesting shoot, I'll tell you that. Jeff was recently back from the army—a couple of years ago, might be—he'd made a couple of pictures since getting discharged, but for all those guys who became stars before the war, they were a little nervous about where they stood now, now that years had gone by and the world had changed. Would audiences still want to see them? Would that weird chemistry that made them stars still be working? Was a new generation taking over? So this picture was damned important to him. The two pictures he'd made before this one weren't stinkers, but they weren't big hits either. Things were becoming a little iffy. I think he even took a pay cut for *Plains and Hills*. Me and Jeff didn't talk about money much, except for the times he might ask me if I could use a little help, but he kind of hinted to me that that that was the case. I guess he figured a prestige picture, if it did good, it could put him back on top. Might be worth giving up some up-front money for that. And he might collect the difference on the back-end. Which he did. Big time.

And like I suggested, there were all these new actors who'd come up in the past few years. And they were a whole new breed. A lot of 'em had trained, for one thing. Studied acting. Like it was an academic subject or a musical instrument or something. Jeff's generation, they just got up in front to the camera and did it, learned their lines, noted their marks, did the job. But these new guys, they'd been to...to...I don't know, conservatories or something. Most of 'em were from New York, I think, studied The Method or whatever. Had a whole complicated process, made a big deal about preparing themselves, they had to go through all sorts of rigmarole. The idea of just getting up there and giving a performance...it's like they sneered at that.

Well, you can imagine how Jeff felt about those people. Hated 'em. Resented 'em. Thought they made acting into something it wasn't, were all airy-fairy about it. Wasted everybody's time on the set. Put everybody through a bunch of shit so they could, what did they call it, get into the truth of the scene or the character or something. Jeff thought they were really just playing with their dicks while everybody had to stand around and watch them do it. That was his attitude.

Just between us, and I probably shouldn't say this, but frankly, I think he was probably a little scared of 'em too. Maybe I'm just talking through my hat here, and I would never have said anything like this to Jeff himself, he would've clocked me for sure, but I sometimes got the impression he was...he was afraid they might be *right*, you know? That they might know something about acting he didn't. Or worse, that he might not know *a damn thing* about acting. To be blunt, he was afraid that they might be much better than him, they might show him up.

Even before all this, even before the war, after we'd had a few drinks, he'd sometimes admit to me he didn't really know what he was doing when he was acting, he'd just fallen into it by chance—he got spotted by a talent scout when he was working as a day laborer on a construction site, height of the Depression, he'd felt lucky to have *that* gig, this movie thing was just totally random—and then it worked out for him but he had no idea why. So he might've felt he'd been getting away with faking it all those years. I'd tell him, no, no, you're really good, it comes so natural to you you don't *need* to know what you're doing, all you have to do is do it, but when he was soused he'd get pretty low and it was impossible to jolly him out of it. Compliments even made him angry. He mostly just wanted me to sit there and listen to him whine, I guess. A life-sized dummy or a cardboard cutout of me would've worked just as well.

And I also think he was sure those new boys and girls, that new breed of actors, considered him a hack and a dinosaur, which both made him mad and shook his confidence even more. Both at the same time. And believe me, it's tough for a tough guy to feel that way. A tough guy isn't supposed to worry about shit like that. A tough guy doesn't get his confidence shook.

And it could get ugly. On the shoot before *Plains and Hills*, a Western called, let's see, it was called *The Maverick*—not to be confused with the TV show that came along a few years later—there was this New York actor, I don't even remember his name anymore, and...Jeff used to call him "Mumbles." He did it enough so the guy finally got defensive and said, "Look, Jeff, this is natural speech, we're just two guys talking in a saloon, right? I don't have to elocute, it'd sound phony. If we keep things at a conversational level the mic'll pick it up." Well, he didn't say it snotty, I'll give him that, he said it kind of matter-of-fact, actor to actor, but even so, that sure as fuck was the wrong approach to take with Jeff, like you're *schooling* him somehow. And he didn't react well, that I can promise you. If you knew him, if you were a friend of his, you could see it. He kept a poker face, which was Jeff's way, you might even say it was his acting technique—[laughs]—but if you knew him well enough and knew what to look for, you could see that vein in his neck start to throb. And from that moment on, it was just close-in combat. In the middle of pretty much every scene they were shooting, every *take* of every scene, while the camera was rolling and everything, Jeff would turn to the director and say, "Would you tell Mumbles to speak up, Jack? I can't hear a fucking word he's saying."

And besides that stuff, the guy went through all this Method crap *before* each take. He had this lengthy, tortured process, and it drove Jeff bat-shit crazy. And he finally had had enough and he got the guy fired. Just couldn't stand it anymore. Couldn't stand *him* anymore. For a few days he just grumbled, grumbled so you could hear it though, then he took to complaining out loud, telling the guy to shit or get off the pot, and finally he went around the director's back, went straight to the producers, and said, Listen, life's too short for this bullshit, it's him or me. Jeff might not've been as big in '49 as he was in '39 or '40, but he was still a pretty major star, and if he wanted someone gone they'd be gone. And the next day, that's how fast it happened, the guy was gone and this other actor had taken over. Wrong sort of type, much too old for the part, too old and, frankly, too fat, but Jeff was comfortable with him—they'd done a few pictures together before the war—and that's all that mattered at that point. They had to reshoot a bunch of scenes, they lost a week or two, and I can't imagine the suits were happy about that, but Jeff got his way.

So anyway, because of that, and other things too, we were all a little nervous about this Hardwick guy they'd hired to play Jeff's kid brother. No one knew much about him, but we knew he'd been in New York until pretty recently, and that wasn't exactly a recommendation in Jeff's eyes. And we heard he'd been studying with James Sterling, and Sterling was a big Method guy, so that definitely put us on edge. It could be *The Maverick* all over again, except without horses. Jeff liked horses.

Before the shoot began, I could see Jeff was uneasy about it. Kind of antsy, and that wasn't like him at all. But *The Maverick* had been a real bad experience for him, and even though he had this tough guy reputation and could be a mean son of a bitch sometimes, he wasn't crazy about conflict, not unless he knew from the start he had the upper hand. He liked making pictures, you see, making pictures was mostly fun for him, he sometimes said he couldn't believe they paid him to do it. But *The Maverick* hadn't been fun at all, mostly because of that actor he finally got fired—that left a stench even after the guy was gone—but also because he was beginning to...to...Listen, you know the story about how someone asks a centipede how it knows how to walk, and the centipede thinks about it and then, after thinking about it, is unable to ever walk again? I think Jeff was feeling a little like that. These young actors, they were so full of craft and technical know-how and Method gobbledygook, and just by noticing them and watching them go through their process Jeff was beginning to think about those questions himself for the first time, and after thinking about them, maybe thinking about them a little too much, he wasn't sure he'd be able to act anymore.

So he was nervous. But for the first few days things went okay. Hardwick was around, he stuck around even when he didn't have a call that day, but he didn't have that much to do. A line here and there, or sitting quietly in a scene reacting to what the other people were doing, or, if he wasn't in the scene at all, just perched off the side watching. He seemed pleasant enough between takes. Polite. Quiet. Jeff was pretty rude to him to be honest, but mostly by ignoring him, not out-and-out insulting him. He'd occasionally grunt if Hardwick said something, and the grunt was meant to come across as bored or unimpressed or something like that. Like he couldn't be bothered to say anything in words, nothing Hardwick said was worth the effort.

One night during that first week or so of shooting, I was over Jeff's house, we were having a couple of drinks, and he suddenly ups and says, "So what do you think of the pretty boy?"

I say, "You mean the actor? On this picture? Hardwick?"

And he says, "Yeah, him. What do you think?"

So, to be honest, I didn't think much of anything, he hadn't really *done* anything yet. Either on camera or off. He showed up on time, knew his blocking, if he had a line—which had rarely been the case so far—he delivered it. But I knew what Jeff wanted to hear, so I said, "He hasn't shown me anything. Not sure he has anything to show."

And Jeff grunted. Same deal as when he grunted with Hardwick, I guess. He wanted more from me than that. Something meaner. But honestly, to have said much more would have been ridiculous, and would have gotten Jeff just as mad 'cause he'da known I was only trying to make him happy. It was one of those can't-win situations with Jeff. They happened from time to time. Jeff could be a peppery son of a bitch.

But then, late in the second week of shooting, they had one of their big scenes. A confrontation scene, a sort of…I mean the kid brother confesses to Jeff's character that he's killed this gal. One of the two or three most emotional moments in the whole picture. And they did it a buncha times, different camera set-ups and so on, and then each did it in close-up a few times, camera over the other guy's shoulder, and I gotta say, each time it seemed like a different scene. Hardwick did it real different each time, totally different emotional color, different line-readings, and Jeff had to change his performance a little in each take to match what the kid was giving him. Then, after a few hours of that, the director yelled "Cut!" and says, "Okay, I think that's enough for the day. Let's all go home early for a change."

So I was driving Jeff home, up Laurel Canyon and across Mulholland. And he was real quiet the whole time. Looking out the window, not saying a word. I knew better than to say anything. When Jeff was brooding like that, the best thing you could do was stay quiet and if possible be invisible. And then we reached his house, I drove up Jeff's driveway and into his garage. And he opened the passenger side door but he didn't get out right away. He just sat there for a few seconds. And then he said, real quiet, almost a whisper, "Did you see what was happening back there?"

And I didn't know how to respond. I didn't know where Jeff was coming from, and I was afraid of saying the wrong thing. So I said, "Interesting day, huh?" You know, non-committal. I was afraid if I said the wrong thing, whatever he was feeling, he'd take it out on me.

And Jeff said, still real quiet, like he was talking to himself, "It was fucking amazing." And then he said, "It was like...it was like we were playing tennis, almost. Like two seasoned pros playing tennis. And he was forcing me to cover the whole fucking court. Making me scramble." And then, after being quiet for a few more seconds, he suddenly blew out some air, you know that kind of cross between an exhale and a sigh? And he said, "I tell you,

Mike, that pretty boy's the best goddamned actor I've ever seen."
He shook his head, then he finally turned around to look at me.
"What he was doing...it was on a whole different level. It's like
he's in a whole different business than me. It felt like I was riding a
goddamn bucking bronco. All I could do was hang on real tight and
try not to get thrown."

He was nice to Hardwick after that. It was like Robin Hood and
Little John after their fight on the river. I don't mean they become
best buddies or anything, but they were on good terms for the rest
of the shoot. Jeff would occasionally clap the kid on the back after
a scene, give him a compliment, sometimes even ask him what
he thought about this approach or that. And you want to know
the most interesting thing? Jeff got great reviews for that picture.
Critics said he was really acting for the first time in his career.

Gil Fraser

AFTER *PLAINS AND HILLS* came out, it was pretty clear Chance was
going to be a star. He got these amazing reviews—and of course
later in the year he got that Oscar nomination—and he should have
won, too. He was robbed. That's what the industry is like: Veterans
who have put in the hours usually get the nod. A sentimental thing.
A reward for a career, not a single performance. But even still, he
suddenly was getting a lot of press. The movie magazines started
doing articles about him. "Hollywood's Newest Heart-Throb,"
that kind of shit. He started getting recognized when he went out.
People asking for autographs, wanting to shake his hand. I was kind
of floored by it, but he was amazingly off-hand. "I used to get this
in New York," he said. "'Cause of that soap I was on. Local fame,
you know? The trick, if you don't want to be mobbed, you just
have to be careful not to look anybody in the eye. And whatever
you do, keep walking."

After things had been building like that for a while, I said to him one morning, "I guess you're going to be moving out soon, huh? Get a place of your own?"

And he sort of grimaced and said, "Nah, not yet, Gil. I plan to stick around for a while if you can stand my company. This whole thing could be a flash in the pan. If it doesn't go away after I do another picture, then yeah, I'll probably get myself a house. I'll be sorry to leave, but it'll be time."

So that was kind of typical, that caution. He didn't trust his luck. And of course, in hindsight, maybe he wasn't so sure he really wanted the success that was coming his way. He might even have been dreading it.

Kathy Brennan (first president, Chance Hardwick Fan Club)

So WHEN WE SAW *Plains and Hills*, me and my girlfriends, we all developed this huge crush on Chance Hardwick. He was *so* cute. He was also a great actor, I realize that now of course, but back then, that aspect of things would have gone right over my head. I was just a teenage girl falling in love with a shadow on the screen. Old story, right? "Dear Mr. Gable." And I wasn't alone—all my friends felt the same way. It was mass hysteria, almost. We cut out photographs of him from movie magazines and put them on our bedroom walls, we talked and giggled about him, we read what little there was to read about him—mostly lies, of course, that's Hollywood publicity for you—and we went back and saw the movie about ten times till we had it memorized. Squealing whenever he appeared onscreen.

But I was an enterprising young lady in those days, more so than my friends, so I did a little research. I phoned the Screen Actors Guild, I found out who represented him, and I wrote him a fan letter care of his agent, and also inquired whether he had a fan club. I got back an autographed picture, which was a prized possession for several years, and also—in a separate note from his agent, not from him—an inquiry whether I would like to start a Chance Hardwick fan club since none existed at the time. I was over the moon! Of course I said yes.

So that's how I became the president of the Chance Hardwick Fan Club. There was no election or anything. It was mine by default. At first the club was just a pretty dinky operation: me, my friends, a few other girls we knew. He wasn't that well known yet. But word kept spreading, and its membership kept growing pretty steadily. It kind of built over the summer months after *Plains and Hills* came out and a whole lot of girls discovered they weren't alone in having this crush on him. Which made me feel proud, as if I had been the one who discovered him. You know, first girl on the moon sort of thing.

And then, after *Lightning Bolt* was released, MGM kind of moved in and took over the club. He was a big star all of a sudden, and the fan club was now part of their marketing campaign, so it wasn't just a kid's enthusiasm anymore, it was big business. They let me stay on as president, but I really didn't have that much to do with running it after that, I was largely president just for publicity purposes. The MGM PR department really ran things from then on, I was just the teenage figurehead. To make it seem authentic. Newsletters and announcements of special events and merchandise and things like that went out over my signature, but I didn't write them. My name was on the membership cards you got when you joined. "Kathy Brennan, President," with a reproduction of my signature. That was cool. I felt famous. I started getting fan mail myself! Seriously!

And to be honest, having operations taken off my hands wasn't a bad arrangement at all as far as I was concerned. More a relief. I could never have managed to run a real, big, professional fan club, and wouldn't have been interested in trying. I mean, gosh, at our peak we had tens of thousands of members. Way beyond anything I would have been capable of handling. I just had a girlish crush on an actor and took it an extra step, you know?

But I did get to meet him a number of times at various publicity events, and even got to attend a couple of premieres—and I have to say, he was always very sweet to me, funny and personal. He didn't make me feel like a jerk for having a childish crush, and he flirted just enough to make me feel attractive and appreciated without ever doing anything even slightly threatening. I came close to fainting the first couple of times I met him, and that isn't an exaggeration— it was almost too much for me to handle—and when he kissed me on the cheek for a publicity photo I didn't wash my face for about a week afterward, no kidding. I got Christmas cards from him too, and cards on my birthday for several years. Altogether, I'd say it was a great experience for a girl who felt self-conscious and was a little overweight and wasn't one of the cool kids at school. It gave me an identity and a sense of myself and I firmly believe it's stood me in good stead for much of my adult life.

My folks thought my obsession with him was unhealthy and didn't approve at all, but looking back, I'd say it was perfectly fine. I feel privileged to have been able to meet him, and to almost regard him as a friend. Not a friend-friend, of course. I mean, it's not like I had his phone number or anything like that, we just met when the MGM people arranged it. But over time we were sort of personally friendly, if you see what I mean. Just a little beyond what the situation dictated. He'd greet me by name at events, always had a nice smile when he saw me. It was a thrill to have him call me "Kathy" and to feel comfortable addressing him as "Chance" instead of Mr. Hardwick. He told me to. I wouldn't have done that without being told. He was just super-nice in every way.

By the time I went off to college I gave up the club. And really, gave up Chance. I mean, that fan club and everything related to it had been an adolescent activity both in the literal sense that I *was* an adolescent when I was involved, but also in an emotional sense. The emotions were adolescent emotions. I went to college and moved on to caring about other things. But still, when I heard about his drowning, it hit me really hard. All the feelings I'd thought I'd outgrown…they came rushing back. I cried and cried. I guess I still haven't gotten over it. Those early loves, the real ones and the silly ones…they stay imprinted, don't they?

Irma Gold

AFTER *PLAINS AND HILLS*, there was a lot of heat on Chance. Even before the Oscar nomination, it was obvious this was a break-out performance in a big prestige picture. The reviews were incredible, and he was getting a lot of personal attention. I told him he was ready to star, he'd gone past the up-and-comer stage with one picture. And we were already starting to field offers. And you may find this hard to believe, but that dumb little *shvantz* was crazy enough to ask me if we could wait a little, he said he was feeling kind of drained from the shoot and the publicity and everything that went with it, he'd like a few months to decompress before he took another plunge. So I could see it was time for me to give him his Hollywood 101 course. I had to get tough with him. Tough love. Read him the riot act, as a matter of fact. I told him absolutely not, he must be out of his mind even to consider it, the iron was white-hot right now and it sure as shit wasn't guaranteed to stay that way. It was time to strike, not *go* on strike. Jesus.

So the good news is, there was a bidding war. We ended up with a contract at MGM. Classiest studio and also the best terms. Win win win. He should have been thrilled, although he didn't seem thrilled. He was appreciative, don't get me wrong—he told me what a great job I'd done, he could never thank me enough, etc., etc. But he just didn't seem all that happy.

Briel Charpentier (girlfriend)

I HAD BEEN IN the United States for about five years, I think. People used to make fun of me. They thought it was ridiculous to travel from Paris to Los Angeles to study art, you know. Like you come from Newcastle and go somewhere else in search of coal. These were mostly people in California, by the way, not French people. French people were not so contemptuous of California as California people were. But it was silly. For one, UCLA's art department had a good reputation. Even in France, you know. But in fact—this was more important to me than how good was UCLA—I wanted to get out of the country. The war had not ended so long before. Paris was uncomfortable to me for many different reasons, obvious reasons and personal reasons also. And since I had studied English in school, and had done especially well in English on my *bac*, it was clear to me I should go either to London or America, where I could cope with the language. And to me, America meant either California or New York, you know, and California had much more appeal to me than New York. And London didn't much appeal at all...it too was still recovering from the war, with rationing and fog and what I imagined to be a prevailing grayness. But California seemed like a dream. For the weather, of course, the sun and the beaches and so on, but also the...the *elan* I assumed I would find there. The *joie de vivre*. The *hedonism*, to be frank. And yes, perhaps the glamour also.

So I was in Los Angeles, you know, studying at UCLA during the day and working at night in a little gallery on La Cienega. A funny little gallery...much of the art was ...not folk art, but...

how do you describe it? *Outsider art*, that's what they call it now. Like amateur art, but perhaps somewhat more accomplished than that. By people who didn't study art at a school or an academy. Didn't study at all. But who painted, so to say, rather in the style of that old woman everyone seemed to like back then. The one with the snow and the tiny people. Maybe you could say it was primitive. Unsophisticated, certainly. Some of it was rather charming, though. I began to like it, the more I saw. The innocence of it was very sweet. Not that I would want any of it on my walls.

And one night Chance marched into the gallery. Wearing sunglasses, which rather caught my attention. Who wears sunglasses at night, except perhaps drug addicts? And who wears sunglasses in an art gallery? I found out later—soon later—that he was afraid of being recognized. *I* wouldn't have recognized him, I had no idea who he was, although that would certainly have been different a year later, after *Lightning Bolt* came out. After that, *everybody* knew who he was. But the night he came into the shop, one of his movies *had* already come out even though I didn't know it, and so he later told me he was already often molested on the street. Maybe molested isn't the right word. *Hassled*. People crowding around him, you know, asking questions, wanting autographs, desiring to take pictures with him. He disliked all of that, as I was to learn. It made him unquiet.

But he came in that night and began to look at the pictures. "Just browsing," he said to me right away, as soon as he was through the door. To inform me I should not try to persuade him to buy anything. Many people used to say that when they first came in. To stop me from pressurizing.

And I—I was a snippy girl in those days, you understand—I said to him, "Perhaps you will enjoy the paintings more if you remove your sunglasses."

He smiled, that lovely, bewitching smile. He had the most beautiful smile. "You think so, do you?" A rather teasing tone in his voice.

"Yes," I said, "in fact the colors might give you more pleasure if you can see them. It's at least possible."

He took the glasses off, and he suddenly looked even more beautiful. Those deep, deep blue eyes. "I want you to know I'm only doing what you suggest because you're foreign," he said. "Like all Americans, I believe people from Europe are smarter than we are."

I think by now he was flirting with me. And by now I was delighted to be flirted with, and very happy to flirt back. He was so lovely. I was already enchanted, even though he had not yet done anything especially enchanting. "That is because we are," I said to him. "Ever so much smarter."

"You're French, aren't you?"

"*Oui.*"

"All right, smarty pants. In that case, how about you explain to me why these paintings are any good."

"'Smarty pants?' But it isn't my pants that are smart, they are just...pants." I had never heard that expression before, you know. And it sounded funny to me.

"Well, let me explain, then. 'Smarty pants' is what Americans call someone who's got a lot of sass. And you are *very* sassy. Do you know what 'sassy' means?"

"Certainly not."

"That's probably just as well." He looked around the gallery for a few seconds—it didn't require more than a few seconds, in truth—and then he said, "See, I was thinking about maybe buying one of these pictures to impress you, but the problem is, I hate them."

So that made me laugh. "You hate *all* of them?"

"I'm afraid so. They're awful." And then a terrible thought seemed to occur to him. You could see it happening behind those huge blue eyes. He said, "Unless...you didn't...you didn't *paint* them, did you? Because if you did...well, let's say I suddenly think they're marvelous."

Since we were flirting, I did not choose to defend the paintings. There were more urgent things to respond to. "No, I promise I did not paint them. I *am* an artist, but my work is nothing like this."

"I'm relieved to hear it. What *is* your work like?"

"It's...oh, never mind that. Tell me why you'd want to impress me. We don't know each other."

"Well, partly because you're French—that's rather intimidating all by itself. But mostly because you're awfully cute. *Très mignonne.*" Then he said, "See, I took French in high school, I can say all sorts of things in your language. I can tell you, for example, where to find my aunt's pencil. It's on the table, if you're curious."

"You are evidently a man of the world."

"Less so than my aunt. She has many pencils, and they're all on the table." Then he said, "In fact, I'm a man who's become interested in art recently." And then he started asking me about artists who were fashionable at the time. Did I like Mark Rothko? Jackson Pollack? Willem de Kooning? Were they for real or were they frauds? It was only later that I discovered he knew nothing about any of them other than their names. You see, he had a knack for meeting people on their own territory in order to study how they talked and acted when they were excited or enthusiastic. He could become anything. There was no single Chance Hardwick—we all met a different one. But at the time I was impressed by what seemed to be his...his...his *erudition.* Most people who came into the gallery were very ignorant. So I said again he struck me as a man of the world. Even more so than his aunt with her pencils.

And he said, "Would you be interested in having dinner with a man of the world some night?"

"But of course I would." I didn't even hesitate. I had no idea who he was, but I liked him very much already. He had a very sympathetic air. And he was *so* good-looking. "How can a girl refuse a man of the world?"

And that is how it started. We had dinner several nights later at Lawry's, which was also on La Cienega, you know, not far from the gallery, and then one thing, as one says, led to the next.

Gil Fraser

IT'S HARD TO SAY whether it was his multi-picture deal with the studio or meeting Briel that made him decide to get his own place. I mean, it could have been either. Or both. They happened at about the same time.

Suddenly he had money, and suddenly he had a girlfriend, or at least a sorta girlfriend. Not just a one- or two-night stand, anyway, unlike what had happened so many times before, more times than you could count. But now there was someone he was seeing steadily. Most nights. And even though they didn't move in together, it was clear to him—and to me—they were going to be spending lots of time in each other's company. And that my being around constantly wouldn't fit in with that arrangement at all. Three's a crowd, as the saying goes. Except at very good parties. [laughs]

No, no, don't get me wrong, I wasn't resentful at all. I thought it was the right decision, even though I was sad to see him go. Probably overdue. And I liked Briel. It was impossible not to, she had that gamine quality, almost waif-like, but *knowing* at the same time, the way French girls can be, a completely irresistible combination. Really cute-*looking* too, although not actually my type. Which is probably a good thing: Not that there would ever have been a chance of hanky-panky—friends don't hit on friends' girlfriends, that's an iron-clad part of the code—but sometimes tensions can arise even if you don't want them to. Something can sort of hover in the air, and even though you try to ignore it, over time it can turn toxic. But nothing like that was gonna happen in this case. Briel, as I say, was totes adorable, but she had that slim, almost boyish type of body, and that's a type which, while I can appreciate it, just doesn't hit me on an animal level the way *zaftig* bodies do. Even the way she did her hair, that close-cropped look that was very fashionable back then, it just wasn't...I mean, I always preferred a rich silken mane. So it was easy for me to treat Briel like a pal, like Chance's girl and my pal. And as far as I know, I wasn't her type either. I think she went for the smoother, less hard-edged type, like Chance. They made a really gorgeous couple, gorgeous and intriguing looking. You know, with both having a kind of neutral aura. They say "androgynous" nowadays, don't they? Her a little boyish, him...not feminine or effeminate or effete or anything like that, just kind of...neutral.

The three of us got along just fine. And she was a really good match for him, serious about her work, not overly impressed by Hollywood glitz, and smart-mouthed. He loved that about her, the fact she wouldn't take shit off anybody, that she was funny about it but down deep really tough. And he liked that she wasn't part of the show-biz scene. It was a relief to him, keeping that side of things separate. You hang out in this town, a lot of the people you meet are either in the business or wannabes, or even worse, hangers-on and groupies desperate for reflected glory. But Briel was none of that. In fact, when they started going out, I don't think she even knew who he was. His fame, which was just beginning back then, meant nothing to her. She liked *him*, liked him as a person, which is what you hope for when someone more or less famous gets involved with someone who isn't. People's motives in that situation are always a little dubious, fairly or not, but hers were above suspicion.

And by the way, I'm not saying it was a grand love affair or one for the ages—I know some books have portrayed it that way—but they were fond of each other, and they had a very good time together.

In addition, maybe to his surprise and definitely to mine, she turned out to be a terrific artist too. I don't think I realized till much later how good she was, but I could see right away she had talent, she wasn't just a...a hobbyist or something. And now—well, her work goes for six figures nowadays, 'nuff said? Of course, her connection to Chance doesn't exactly hurt her asking price, it adds a bit of swank, but that ain't the whole story. She's really good.

And hey, this just occurred to me, but maybe she's that old lady who visits his memorial, the one people always wonder about. Maybe that's her. Do you think? She'd be about the right age, wouldn't she? The main reason to doubt it is that she'd have no reason to be so secretive. Everyone knows about their relationship now. Not at the beginning so much, the studio wanted to preserve the idea that any girl in the country might have a shot with him. They assumed his fan base would be girls who wanted to fantasize about being with him and they were afraid that if it was known he had a steady girlfriend it might hurt his box office, so they kept Briel quiet, set him up on dates with other women, shit like that. I'm not suggesting they wouldn't let him appear in public with Briel, but they didn't want it to seem like he was out of circulation. I'm not sure he necessarily *was* completely out of circulation in any case—I don't know the details of their arrangement, I never asked, and he never volunteered—but regardless, the studio didn't want to give the public that impression.

My point, though, is that since his death there have been so many books about him, biographies and film studies, some of them trashy, some of them serious—including yours, yours was one of the serious ones, I don't want to leave the impression I don't have a lot of respect for it, hell, I wouldn't be doing this interview otherwise, I read it with interest and thought you got most things right—but by now Briel has received the attention she deserves as an important figure in his life. And she was. She was. His most important romantic attachment, at least as far as I'm aware. But since she's celebrated in her own right, the relationship has acquired this…this romantic aura. This *prestige*. It may be accorded more reverence than it deserves. As if it was, I don't know, Baudelaire and Rimbaud, Sartre and Beauvoir, Nabokov and Vera, Marilyn and Joltin' Joe. Where the legend becomes more important than the reality, where it's regarded as one of the twentieth century's great love affairs. Two celebrities from totally different worlds finding each other and coming together in a communion of mutual admiration, that sort of malarkey. Having witnessed it at first hand, I can assure you it wasn't like that.

I don't know how Briel feels about that stuff these days, it's possible she's come to believe the hype—she benefits, after all, it helped make her famous, it's certainly helped make her rich—but I'm pretty sure it would have driven Chance nuts. Would have made him laugh his head off and gotten him pissed, both at the same time. They were just two frisky kids having a great time together. Nothing fancier or more elevated than that.

Dorothy Goren Mckenzie

CHANCE AND I HAD been corresponding on and off after he went to Hollywood. His letters were mostly chatty and kind of short. He told me about that science fiction movie he was in. He was funny about that, he said it was, and I quote, "the worst piece of shit ever devised by the mind of man." I never got to see it, unfortunately. It never reached us. We only had one movie theater in town, and it wasn't a drive-in. Our theater mainly showed major studio productions. No horror flicks, no foreign films. People like Ingmar Bergman and Federico Fellini were completely unknown to us. The idea that movies could be an art form...no one had ever even considered the possibility.

We did get to see *Plains and Hills*, though. That was a year or two later, and it was super-exciting. Everybody in town went to see it. And everybody suddenly claimed to be Chance's friend. People who had treated him like dirt when he was in high school, they all claimed they'd been great buddies. Girls who laughed at him behind his back claimed they'd gone steady with him. Nothing like this had ever happened here before. We'd produced our very first celebrity!

But anyway, his letters to me were these sort of Hollywood snapshots. Not very personal, not very detailed about the specifics of his life there, but colorful. He was a good writer—I don't know if you know that about him—but he was a very good writer, and his descriptions of his life in tinsel town were vivid and fun. Very exciting for someone like me, who thought Hollywood was like Oz. Magical and distant and...and unattainable.

So his letters were short and breezy. My letters, on the other hand, were mostly full of *angst* and complaints. It wasn't fair to burden him like that, I guess, but I had no one else to talk to about what I was feeling, and after his stop-over those years before, I felt he was a soulmate, a sympathetic ear, he'd understand and maybe have helpful advice.

And then one day in my senior year in high school he wrote and asked me if I'd like to spend a couple of weeks with him over summer vacation. I guess my whining must finally have gotten to him. Holy cow, that was an exciting day. I could hardly believe it. When I told my mom and dad...well, you probably know enough about them already to guess that my mom was pleased and excited for me, and maybe a little jealous, and my dad just said nope, no way. He said he wouldn't pay for me to travel all the way to

California, that it was an extravagance no teenage girl deserved, and besides, Hollywood was full of phonies and…and other people he didn't much cotton to, let's put it that way. That's not how *he* put it, but it's how I'm gonna put it.

So I wrote to Chance telling him that my dad refused to buy a plane ticket so I couldn't go, but I really appreciated the offer, it was almost enough all by itself. And within a few days I got a letter from Chance urging me to come anyway, and inside the envelope along with the letter was a round-trip plane ticket. So Dad could grumble all he liked, and that man sure did love to grumble, but after that he didn't really have any grounds for not letting me go. He wasn't gracious about it, but after he and Mom argued in the kitchen, argued loudly, he gave in.

It was a momentous, eventful visit. The first thing that happened, after Chance picked me up at the airport and we drove to his apartment and we walked through the door, there, standing right there waiting to say hello, was…I mean, you could have knocked me over with a feather, I recognized Gil immediately! Chance had been writing about his roommate Gil, relating funny incidents about him—he sounded like quite a character—but I wasn't sophisticated enough to look at credits when I went to movies or watched TV, so although I knew the names of big movie stars, that was about it. Feature players and character actors were outside my range. But the thing is, I had seen Gil in a couple of TV shows—I think a *Perry Mason* and maybe a *Science Fiction Theater*—and in one detective movie where he played one of the bad guys. Not the main bad guy, but one of his henchmen. He usually was cast as a bad guy, which is funny, because in real life he was such a nice guy. But this was almost unbelievable to me…Chance's roommate was an actor I'd seen on the screen! I mean, what an introduction to Los Angeles! I was going to be staying in the same apartment as a real actor!

And of course Chance had been in *Plains and Hills*, so he wasn't just my brother anymore—he was almost a star. Sometimes we'd go out and someone would come up and ask him for an autograph or tell him how great he was. It made him uncomfortable, but I thought it was great. And a couple of times, women would come up and hand him a slip of paper. I'm talking about really beautiful women, women who must have been actresses or models. And I'm guessing the pieces of paper had their phone numbers on them. I have no idea if he ever called any of them, but it certainly was eye opening to see that happen. My own brother! Wow, right?

Chance and Gil were wonderful hosts. I guess I expected that would be true of Chance. He was my brother, for one thing, and he had invited me, so I didn't think he'd just abandon me once I arrived. But the surprise was Gil. He had this tough-guy exterior, and he seemed like a guy who didn't have a lot of patience for anyone else's bull, but he joined us in almost everything we did. And they were both super-patient about doing dumb tourist things that couldn't have been too interesting for them. They took me to Grauman's Chinese Theater and the Egyptian Theater, and to that Rexall on La Cienega that at the time was supposed to be the world's biggest drugstore, and up to the Griffith Park Observatory, and we had a picnic in Ferndell. We went to the Brown Derby for dinner one night and walked down to Barney's Beanery another night, we had chili at Chasen's and burgers at the Hamlet. There weren't as many tourist attractions in LA then as there are now, but they found ways to make every day an adventure. The La Brea Tar Pits, the Southwest Museum. Disneyland had recently opened, and they said it would be too crowded to be any fun, so we skipped that. But I was almost eighteen years old, so missing out on Disneyland was only a mild disappointment.

And the thing is...God, I've hardly ever mentioned this to anyone else, not even my husband—who I guess will find out about it when he reads your book, assuming he ever reads your book—but the thing is, a kind of...there was this...I mean, Gil and me, we started developing this...*thing*. An attraction. He was sort of the opposite of Chance as a type, even though they were about the same age and both babes. Where Chance was slight and light-complexioned and had a shy, almost recessive kind of personality, Gil was swarthy and muscular and macho, and he had this swagger about him, and he always seemed to have a couple of days' growth of beard on his face and his voice was real deep. He was kind of a walking, talking representation of a certain way of being a guy. The Marlboro Man way, I guess you could call it. Chance was the kind of man women wanted to mother—he brought out that caring, nurturing impulse—but I can't imagine anyone wanting to mother Gil. They'd want to be protected by him, or even, I don't know, *mastered* by him. And I found him just amazingly hot, although that isn't the word we would have used back then. We'd say...we'd probably just say sexy. He *oozed* manliness. It was almost like he used testosterone as cologne, you could smell it on him. And consider...the only males I'd been exposed to so far as possible romantic partners were the boys in my high school, with their gawkiness and their acne and their voices breaking and cracking. Gil was...it was night and day.

And maybe it's just that I was young and ripe and reasonably cute and...and *around*, you know? Constantly present in the apartment all week. It's not like I was some sort of *va-va-voom* girl. But for whatever reason, something was developing between Gil and me, and we all knew it. Me and him, we were always laughing together and whispering together, and in just a couple of days we'd already developed little private jokes, and...and, you know, we were acting the way people act when they're hot for each other. And he was attentive, more than simple good manners required. Chance may even have felt a little excluded, although he was always part of the party when we went anywhere. But still, something was going on and he wasn't in on it. I don't know if it bothered him, and I don't know whether the two guys ever talked about what was happening, or whether Gil asked Chance for permission, or whether it was just assumed that everything was okay or on the contrary it was assumed this was forbidden territory, but anyway...

It was a two-bedroom apartment, so I slept on a sofa in the living room. It was perfectly comfortable. They gave me sheets and a blanket—I didn't really need the blanket, it was hot in LA in the summer, plus there was a heat wave that year so it was even hotter than normal—and I slept on that sofa and I never had any complaints. But then one night, my last night in LA, in the middle of the night, Gil tiptoed in. I was semi-sleeping, but I heard him creeping in. And immediately my heart started racing. And then he knelt beside the sofa and began kissing me. I guess the thought of me lying on the sofa just a few feet away must have been keeping him awake, maybe for all I know it kept him awake every night I was there, and it finally, with me scheduled to leave the next morning, it finally must've become too powerful to resist. So like I say, he started kissing me, and I could feel the rough stubble on his cheeks, and I don't know if this makes any sense or not, but that part was incredibly erotic all by itself. Everything about him was bristly, hard, hairy. Incredibly exciting. Of course I kissed back. I'd been fantasizing about something like this happening for most of the time I'd been there, so it wasn't like a shock or anything. I'm not saying I expected it—I didn't—but I wasn't shocked and I sure as heck wasn't upset.

I was still a virgin. I'd messed around a little, engaged in what we quaintly used to call "heavy petting," but I'd never...well, we used to say "gone all the way." I'd never come close to going all the way. And when he realized I hadn't, he asked if he should stop, which was considerate. I think at that stage of things a lot of men wouldn't have bothered to ask. Wouldn't have listened even if the girl tried to call a halt. But he did ask if he should stop, and I said no, I wanted it to happen, I was ready. And I have to say, he was very gentle. Surprisingly gentle, I'd say, given the way he presented himself as gruff and tough. He did take control, which as a matter of fact I appreciated, seeing as how I was a total novice, but he didn't do it in a selfish or bullying way. It was clear he was behind the wheel, but it was also clear he knew how to drive, if you see what I mean. *Really* knew. It was years before I found somebody else who understood my body the way he did.

Afterward, sitting side-by-side on the couch, snuggling—it was too narrow for us to lie down on next to each other—he obviously started having second thoughts. Or at least started to feel a little anxious, started to feel that what-have-I-done feeling. Because he whispered, "Now listen, you have to understand, you live so far away, and I'm really too old for you, and—" As if I might think we were going steady or I might expect him to marry me or something. So I told him to stop worrying, I didn't expect anything more from him, it was a great way to lose my virginity, as perfect a way as I could ever have imagined, he'd been wonderful, it was everything I'd hoped it would be, and finally getting around to having sex was way overdue for me, I'd been thinking about doing it for a long time, and even though I'd developed a little crush on him over the past few days I wasn't so naïve as to think it meant anything. Quite a mouthful, but I got it all out in a rush. I didn't want him to start regretting what had happened. And I mostly meant it.

He was obviously relieved to hear all that, although at the same time he was also enough of a gentleman to pretend his feelings were hurt. "You mean you were only after me for one thing?" he said.

"Yep," I said, "that's pretty much how it was." Which at least got a chuckle out of him.

Then he told me he thought it was probably a good idea for him to go back to his own room. "For appearances," he said.

I said, "So this is supposed to be a secret? Even from my brother?"

And he said, "I think that might be best."

I don't know for certain whether Chance ever figured out what had happened. The drive to the airport the next morning was peculiar, to say the least. We tried to act normal and probably didn't exactly manage it. But comings and goings, hellos and goodbyes, are always awkward, so Chance might have just put it down to that.

For the next two or three weeks, I was afraid I might have gotten pregnant. I mean, no planning was involved, so we didn't take any precautions or anything. That worried me for a little while, although I didn't mention it to Gil. No reason to alarm him. And of course I wasn't.

A shrink—the only other person I ever admitted this episode to—suggested the experience really represented my displaced incestuous feelings for Chance. And listen, I've learned enough in my life not to deny anything a shrink says whether you believe it or not, because they'll only take denial as confirmation. I can't deny I adored Chance, so maybe that feeling had an erotic component, who can say? All *I* can say is, it sure didn't feel like that. It felt very specifically about Gil.

And either way, it was a great visit. Beyond my wildest expectations. From start to finish, but *especially* the finish. Which had the added benefit of proving all of my father's misgivings were absolutely justified. My only regret was that I didn't have the guts to tell him what had happened.

Hector Mennen (acquaintance)

YEAH, I GOT A lot of flak for my book. A *lot*. Some people called me a liar. In fact, a *lot* of people called me a liar. Not much I could do about that. I could have sued, but…well, I didn't, for all sorts of reasons. One lawyer told me it would be a waste of time and money. Besides, let them call me a liar. I've been called worse. And other people did that whole *tsk-tsk* thing, how it might be true but you shouldn't kiss and tell. *How rude!* But hell, the guy was dead, I thought people would want to know the truth. Just setting the record straight, not trying to create a scandal.

And anyhow, Chance was just one chapter. I'm not sure why that's the one that got all the attention. I outed a number of Hollywood guys. Chance might have been the *most* famous, but some of the others were pretty well-known too. But I only outed dead ones. 'Course, the law says you can't libel the dead, but that wasn't my reason. Truth is, I was being discreet. I don't know why I don't get more credit for that. I didn't want to hurt anybody or destroy anybody's career.

What? Oh yeah, right, that's true, those two were still alive when the book was published, you're right. But they were already out. Someone *else* had already outed them, a couple of tactless bastards who didn't care about what damage they were doing, so I wasn't betraying any secrets; I was just telling what it was like to be with those guys. My book was a memoir, not an exposé.

Sure I needed money at the time. I'm not going to pretend they didn't pay me for the book or that I wasn't glad to get paid. But I didn't have any reason to lie.

I met Chance at the House of Ivy, that bar on Cahuenga. It doesn't exist anymore, but it was one of the go-to places back in the day. Chance used to show up there from time to time. Always hesitated at the entrance, looked around, made sure nobody was going to react to him or do some kind of big double take. But people were cool at the House of Ivy, there was a kind of unwritten law: you mind your own business and respect everyone's privacy. People who went to the Ivy understood about staying on the down-low, especially where well-known people were concerned. And management policed people's behavior—if you didn't mind your manners, you might be asked to leave. That might be one of the reasons Chance went there instead of some of the more flamboyant gay bars in town. It was pretty low-key. You could relax. No one gawked or asked for autographs or any of that shit. And the cops mostly stayed away, and that was a pretty big deal, since the LAPD could be real bastards in those days. They liked to catch a big fish every once in a while. For the publicity. And to flex their muscle. Were they being paid off? Wouldn't surprise me. The department was pretty dirty at the time. Everybody knew it.

I was there lots of nights, looking to hook up. I was young and crazy back then, always out for a good time, maybe make a little bread. One night Chance came in, and after a few minutes I could tell he was checking me out, 'cause he was a celebrity and so I was sort of keeping track of him out of the corner of my eye while pretending not to. And then, after a while, he came over and offered to buy me a drink, and one thing led to another. The way it does. And soon we were…well, I wouldn't exactly say we were going together, he had his regular life and I wasn't part of it, but we spent a lot of time in each other's company.

Chance was majorly discreet and insisted I be discreet too. We rarely went anywhere in public, except occasionally to grab some lunch at Dolores's or Tiny Naylor's, some drive-in where we'd stay in the car and wouldn't be too visible. He had a convertible in those days, but he kept the top up, at least he kept the top up when we were in the car together. He wasn't as big a star as he was about to become, not at the time we started seeing each other, but he already was enough of a public face that he wanted to be careful.

And by the way—you might find this interesting—he was pretty inexperienced when we first got together. I don't think I was necessarily his first, but probably *one* of his firsts. He came from some small town in the Midwest, didn't really know the scene at all. So I was his guide, if you like. His Sherpa. Showed him around, introduced him around. I think he valued that. I write about all this in my book. Like the time I got him to try reefer for the first time. That was way before the hippies. Pot wasn't part of the culture yet. It was like a big secret. So I had to talk him into it. He was scared the first time. And pot was the least of it. Bunch of other stuff too. He was usually scared the first time he tried *anything*. But he was usually game after a little prodding.

The thing is, we were pretty close for a while there. I'd even say intimate. We talked about our lives and about our hopes and dreams. It wasn't just some greasy little hook-up. It was a real relationship. Maybe I even fell in love a little bit. I wish I could say the same for him, but it probably isn't true. Oh, he liked me well enough, and I don't deny he helped me out on a regular basis, a little bit here or there, but I'm not sure he was someone even capable of love. Too driven, too ambitious. He cared about acting and his career a lot more than he cared about people.

He ended things very abruptly. No warning, no nothing. One morning he just said, "Hector, this isn't working for me anymore. It's over." No explanation. No regrets. No warmth, even. I tried to have a conversation with him, maybe to try to talk him out of it or maybe just to understand what had happened. He wouldn't engage. He was done with me.

Did he—?

Yeah, he gave me some money. Yeah. He wrote me a check. A pretty sizable one, actually. To keep me quiet? Oh, I don't know...I don't think that was it. I wasn't threatening him or anything. I'm not a blackmailer. I don't think he was afraid of me talking. He probably just felt some sort of obligation. And listen, the money was welcome. I was always kind of skint in those days—

any help was appreciated. But frankly, I would have been happier with a hug.

Dennis O'Neill (detective, LAPD Vice Squad, Retired)

WE HAD A LIST. We maintained a list, constantly updated, of all the fairies in Hollywood. And by Hollywood I don't mean the district as such, I mean the industry, the people whose names you might know. It was partly for their protection, although that frankly wasn't a big part, and partly because the studios were eager to keep tabs on the people working for them and stay apprised of potential problems, and we always had good relationships with the studios— they did favors for us and we did favors for them in return; favors that included keeping them informed, giving them a heads-up if something was brewing—and partly just because it was useful to know what was going on in our beat. But also…well, I don't want to get into details, but the Department was a complicated place in those days, and not everything we did was 100 percent kosher, okay?

Anyway, you're asking about Chance Hardwick, and as far as I know he was never on any list. Now if you ask me does that prove he wasn't a fairy, I can't be that definite. It's proving a negative. The fact he wasn't on the list doesn't mean he wasn't a fairy, all it means is that none of our sources ever suggested he was. But we had good sources and our list was mighty thorough, so if I had to guess, I'd say no.

Yeah, I heard about the book by that Mennen character. I honestly don't know what to tell you about that. Mennen was on our list for sure. He was notorious. Every bartender in every pansy bar in town knew him. We brought him in for solicitation a number of times, although I think he always managed to plead out, pay a fine, and go on his merry way. But Hardwick wasn't even on our radar screen, so that's pretty much the extent of what I can offer about *him*.

The funny thing is, back then it would have been a career ender. Now nobody would give a shit. Times change.

Gil Fraser

HAVE YOU TALKED TO...WHAT does he call himself? Hector Mennen? His real name is Menendez. I'm guessing he changed it when he was trying to break into pictures himself, thought it would help him. As if the problem was his name. [laughs] That probably lasted about a day and a half. He must've thought presenting himself as Anglo would make him more acceptable on a marquee. Tell that to Cesar Romero. Hell, he could've re-christened himself Marmaduke Marmelstein and it wouldn't have done him any good.

Pictures were never going to work out for him, but it wasn't long before he discovered his true calling.

Frankly, nothing would have made him acceptable, not on a marquee, not any other respectable profession. A disgusting little hustler. A maggot feeding on the flesh of corpses. And a total bullshit artist, of course. Goes without saying, doesn't it? I don't know if he ever even met Chance. I'm reasonably positive there was never anything between them like he describes in that nasty little book of his. Like I said, I don't know for sure about whether Chance was a switcher—I suppose it's possible, if only as a kind of break in his routine or whatever—but he would never have wasted his time with a creep like Mennen. Chance had class. And he liked class in others. Especially in his romantic partners. The women he went out with...I mean, even aside from Briel, who occupied a kind of unique place in his life. But the thing is, if you're famous in this town and just want to get laid, there's no dearth of bimbos available to you. All you have to do is snap your fingers and a bevy of hot-looking tarts will come running. But that wasn't Chance's scene. I don't know if he was 100 percent faithful to Briel, maybe not, he had too many opportunities to mess around, and he was—I mean, at that age, when you're young and vital, it's hard to resist golden opportunities every time they arise even if you think you ought to. So I wouldn't discount the possibility he was out tomcatting from time to time. But Briel was the *kind* of person he was interested in. I'm not talking about gender now, I'm talking about quality. Briel was a quality person, a talented artist, a smart and accomplished woman. Whereas Mennen was the male equivalent of a hot-looking tart—only worse. It was always a commercial transaction with that guy. He didn't even have the dignity of an honest groupie. He wasn't interested in bragging rights or a notch on his gun. It was always about the angle.

But I do wonder if they ever even met. I mean, at all. That kind of nags at me. See, the thing about Chance...he played his cards close to his vest, like I said. You can call it private or secretive or what do they say these days...*compartmentalized?* I mean, there are all sorts of way of characterizing it, but the bottom line is, he was a pretty elusive cat. A shape-shifter. I'm not sure anyone really knew him. We just knew the aspects of him he felt okay about revealing.

Irma Gold

METRO HAD THIS NOTION that they were going to reintroduce Chance to the public. They knew he'd made a pretty big name for himself with *Plains and Hills*, including that Oscar nomination, so it wasn't a case of, you know, "And introducing Chance Hardwick." On the contrary, I was able to negotiate that they'd put his name above the title from the get-go, treating him like a known quantity. They didn't put up much of a fight over that one, might even have intended it all along. But still, now that he was under a Metro contract, they wanted to introduce him as a *star* for the first time. And they wanted to find the right vehicle to achieve that.

I think their sense was that it would be smart to use the "dream boat" side of his appeal for that first picture. After that was accomplished, they could proceed with all sorts of other projects, use his acting chops, but first, they wanted to establish him as a romantic leading man. A heart throb. They sent him—which means they sent *me*—tons of scripts. I acted as his filter. Read them and only passed along the ones I thought were worth considering. Most didn't come close. We went through several uncomfortable months saying no to everything they messengered over. I think they were getting a little sick of his pickiness, but between Chance and me, we weren't impressed with their choices and we didn't think it made sense to compromise on this first picture with them. A lot could hinge on how that one went, and if the picture bombed, you knew they wouldn't accept any responsibility. They'd say, "Aw, too bad, the kid just doesn't have it." You know the old Hollywood saying, "You're only as big as your last picture?" Well, in this case, since his *last* picture was going to be his *first*, his first as a star, we were determined it not be a lemon.

But when the script for *Lightning Bolt* arrived, well, that was a different ballgame. It was respectable at least, pretty well written, and with a terrific part for Chance. It played to his forehand, the sensitive, brooding aspect of his personality, but with a lot of gradations and nuances. He'd turned down other things, even the ones I thought were okay and sent along to him—"This is crap" was a typical comment—but he thought *Lightning Bolt* was okay. Good tension in the A story, nice love interest in the B. Plenty for him to work with. So that was it. He said yes and *Lightning Bolt* was greenlit immediately. Everyone breathed a sigh of relief.

Briel Charpentier

HE ASKED ME TO come with him when he looked for a house to rent. He said he trusted my eye, you know. At first I thought he might be asking for my advice because he intended to ask me to move in with him. That seemed to be a reasonable thing to think, as if he were planning a romantic surprise. And I confess I was a little apprehensive. I even considered refusing to go look with him, just to avoid having to face such a thing. But he was insistent. Which only made me worry more—why did he care so much?—but he was always very hard to refuse. And then it turned out that that wasn't it at all. He wasn't proposing we share the house, he really just wanted my advice. I was concerned about the other thing that whole day, waiting for…you say the shoe to fall? But it never did. And I can't tell you even today what I would have said. It would be nice to say I would have jumped at the possibility, although also a bit humiliating since it didn't come about, but in truth I would have been very hesitant. I did not know if we were ready as a couple for that. I did not know if we would *ever* be ready.

Why? For a great number of reasons. For one, it was clear by then he was likely to become a big movie star very soon. They were going to start making *Lightning Bolt*, which was the movie that made him so famous, and I think everybody knew that it would do so. This was exciting, but I was unsure it was wise to be so tied to someone whose life was going to change in such a fashion. And also…I loved being with Chance, but I honestly didn't know if it was a love affair that would last forever, you know. And *shacking up*, as Americans used to call it…at least back then, back in the 1950s, shacking up was understood to be a brief stop *en route* to getting married. I wasn't prepared for that. I eventually discovered I would never be prepared for that. With anybody, I mean, not just with Chance. And I do not think Chance was aware at all of how different his life was about to become. He may have known as an idea, but he had not prepared himself for the reality. The man who proposed to me—I mean, who would have proposed to me if he *had* proposed to me—would be a different man very soon. Leaving the old Chance behind. He would have no choice in the matter.

Do I have any regrets? Well, what would be the point? He never asked me, so how can I regret an answer I never had occasion to give? But no, I'm so glad to have known him, and I suppose I probably think about him every day, and I surely miss him every day, but I do not regret not living with him or marrying him. I am not sure I would remember him so fondly if we had lived together. He was not the easiest man to be with. There were so many Chances, and you never knew who was the one underneath all the others. Or whether there was such a creature at all.

We did find a very pretty house for him, though. On Woodrow Wilson Drive. A small house, almost a cottage, but neat and attractive, and very quiet. Hidden away. Small front yard with a nice birch tree, small back yard. The Hollywood Freeway—it was still new then—was just down the hill, but you had no sense of that. The sound didn't penetrate, you know.

Even though I never moved into that house, I did spent a lot of time there. And—the way these things work—he let me have a house key, and I kept a toothbrush in the bathroom.

James Sterling

A WEEK OR TWO before they started production on *Lightning Bolt*, Chance asked me if I could give him a private coaching session. This struck me as very uncharacteristic. I wouldn't ever dream of calling him cocky—he had a certain native humility about him, as a matter of fact—but he'd always seemed, from the very first class he ever took with me, confident in his abilities and sure of his instinct for finding an actor's true north. But of course I was happy to make myself available to him.

It was his first starring role, so it was a pretty big deal. But when he came to me that afternoon, he was in despair. He said, "I just don't have a handle on this guy." I'd read the script—it was supposed to be embargoed but he snuck me a copy a few days before so we could work together—and I have to say, I couldn't see the problem. It was a good script, a well-written script, and his part seemed clear. A complex character to be sure, but believable, convincing, and no more complex than plenty of others, including some he'd worked on in class. So we talked it through for an hour or two, talked about a variety of possible objectives and motivations in a number of scenes, and frankly, he seemed entirely on top of it to me. I told him I thought he was fine, and he shook his head and said "I'm completely at sea here, Jim."

Which is when it hit me. It wasn't an acting problem at all. He was just in a complete panic about his situation. About becoming a star. Or screwing up and failing to become a star when the opportunity was presented to him on a platter. He was in a full existential crisis. So when I realized that, I said, "Don't you want it?"

And he said, "Of course I want it."

"I don't just mean the part. I mean all of it."

I'd never seen him so vulnerable. I'd seen him *act* vulnerable, and do it so impeccably that you believed for the duration of the scene that he was really feeling it. But I'd never seen him actually *be* vulnerable. Which is to say, here was a guy with a personality so protean he could embody virtually any emotion you could name, but who rarely manifested any at all when he wasn't acting. He was a cool fellow whose essence seemed forever beyond your reach. But on this day, and only on this day, I saw, or thought I saw, a little kid who was experiencing sheer terror. *Real* terror, not acted terror.

So what do you do in a situation like that? I'd been through enough analysis myself, years of it, so I basically tried to be his therapist for an hour or two. Much of my teaching method was based on psychoanalysis anyway, and it seemed obvious to me that in Chance's case father issues were at the heart of many of his hang-ups. He never knew his real father growing up, never had a strong male figure. So I felt I'd almost become a surrogate father for him in recent months, and I felt maybe what he needed right now much more than coaching was some paternal guidance.

So I got him to talk about ambition in the abstract, and about his attitude toward his own ambition, asked him about how he felt about fame, about whether acting was a place for him to hide as much as a place to perform. Personal questions intended to get him to confront his fear and his confusion. And he wrestled with all those questions and earnestly tried to answer. He trusted me, and he took it seriously. And he said, when things were finally winding down—we were at it for close to four hours, if memory serves—that he felt a little better. And I said to him, "You're going to be fine, you know. You're ready for this."

And he shook his head and said, "I'm not. I'm really not. I don't know if anyone ever is, but I know I'm not."

"Listen, kiddo, you're a great actor." I don't believe I've ever told another student anything like that. My philosophy is, they don't come for praise, they come to learn. But it just slipped out of me.

And he said, "Yeah, maybe so, but that's just a small piece of the puzzle."

Briel Charpentier

ABOUT A WEEK AFTER they started shooting *Lightning Bolt*, there was one night when Chance was so nervous, he was like a Mexican jumping bean. Charged up, you know. I never saw him like that before. He couldn't sit still. Jumping up, sitting down, going over there, coming over here. Putting a record on the gramophone and then lifting the needle after about ten seconds. It was making *me* jumpy too, as how could it not? It was like being in a cage with an agitated animal.

It was concerning. He seemed so miserable. I tried to get him to relax. I gave him some wine, I asked him to talk about what was worrying him. I am not very much like a mother in the ordinary course of things, being sweet and nurturing does not come so naturally to me, but Chance was in such obvious distress I tried to be supportive and caring. As with most women, I suppose, he brought out the mother in me.

Now, he was not, from what I had seen, a person in the habit of worrying about his acting. But this was evidently different, you know. He said he had a terribly difficult scene the next day. A difficult *acting* scene that involved emotional changes he didn't know how to navigate honestly, is how he put it. He was almost in tears as he said this. He said he'd been faking it for the entire previous week's work, he didn't have a handle on the character at all, he was sure everybody could tell. And the next day there was this crucial scene and he knew it would be a disaster. He said, "I just can't find the way in." I think he meant into the head of the character he was playing. He said, "This part is beyond me. I've been relying on technique so far, and maybe that's enough to fool some people, but it won't be enough tomorrow. Technique only gets you so far. I just don't have a handle on this. At *all*."

He had already done some very demanding physical scenes. He told me they had shot some of the more challenging exteriors the first week, and he really didn't even have to tell me that, because...you see, some of them...well, the insurance company insisted they use a stunt double for the most risky things, but there were others where they'd permitted him to do them himself, he said he preferred to do his own stunts when it was possible—it seemed more honest to him, you know—and he had taken a few bad falls and…I could see his bruises, and they were pretty bad. It had been painful for him. But he was far more concerned about the scene the next morning than about any of the physical risks he had taken.

So trying to be of help, I asked him to describe his character, to say why he was having trouble. But he just shook his head. "I can't explain my process," he said. "It doesn't happen on a verbal level. Even in Jim Sterling's classes, I was pretty much helpless when we had to talk about stuff."

And I said—maybe I should not have, maybe this was not my place to say—but I said, "Is it possible this is not about the character, but about your life? Are you worried about what's happening to you?" I had a better sense of that than he did. Or a better *conscious* sense. I was aware what was about to befall him. It was already affecting my thoughts about *us*, the fact that everything was going to change. He probably knew it as well, but did not like to admit it to himself. He preferred to shut it out of his mind. So it might have been affecting him like…you know how sometimes people feel a physical pain when they are really dealing with emotional pain? Psychosomatic pain? So I thought this might be like that. Anxiety about one thing turning into anxiety about something else, something related.

He didn't say no when I suggested it. He just shrugged. My saying it out loud didn't help. He was still very agitated.

Later, I tried to make love to him, I thought that might get him to relax, or help him sleep, or take his mind off his troubles. But… oh, you understand what I'm telling you, he wasn't able to. You understand? This sometimes happened, and it happened that night. His mind was elsewhere, wasn't it?

David Osborne (director)

WE'D SCHEDULED THE BIG climactic second-act curtain scene—the most crucial scene in the picture in many ways, the linchpin—for the second week. Working out of sequence like that can be hard for some actors, especially actors whose main experience is on the stage—they have to have the intervening scenes laid out in their head before they can perform them, sometimes weeks or even months before—but I'd never seen anyone so rattled as Chance Hardwick. Things had been going fine up to then, he was doing great work, but he came to my trailer to talk to me early in the morning when that scene was scheduled, came to me right out of make-up, and he was a total wreck.

"Listen, Dave," he said. "Is it too late to replace me? I haven't had a chance to talk to Irma about this, but I just think I'm screwing up your picture. I don't have a clue what I'm doing. It might be best if I withdraw."

So for a second I just stared at him. Was he nuts? Replace the star one week into principal photography? Holy Christ. And look, I've worked with plenty of stars in my time, I understand something about temperament, I understand they're putting it all out there and they feel exposed and vulnerable and inadequate. Anyone who deals with performers knows how brutal on the psyche the work can be, what a toll it can take. You can die a thousand deaths. But this was insanity of the highest order. So I tried not to act too alarmed, which only would have made the situation worse, and I said to him, "Please, Chance, relax. Everything's going fine."

He shook his head, almost like a child refusing to eat his spinach or something. Stubborn. He said, "It's nice of you to say that, Dave, but I'm perfectly aware I've been awful so far, and today...I'm just lost. I don't know how to play the scene. I don't have a grasp on this character at all."

And I said to him, "But you've been fantastic so far." He just stared at me, wide-eyed. So I went on, "Is there anything about the scene you want to talk about? I mean, it doesn't seem to me you need any guidance, you appear to have a handle on it, but if you have any questions…"

He shook his head. "It's too late for anything like that. I'm drowning, and it's too late for anyone to throw me a life preserver. Assuming there even is such a thing."

I was just totally bewildered by this. I said, "But you've been doing first-rate work. Oscar-caliber, I'd go so far as to say. And I'm not just talking through my hat. I've been watching the dailies every evening. You haven't. They're dynamite. You're phenomenal."

And he gave me a look I'll never forget. It seemed to combine pity and scorn. Maybe even contempt. I think he lost all respect for me in that moment and I never got it back. He said, "Fine. Okay. Thanks. See you on the set." And with that he sighed rather loudly—it was a sigh intended to convey a message—and he got up and left the trailer.

So there was all this tension down on the floor while setting up and so on. I don't know if the technicians were aware of it, but they probably were. They know more about what's happening on a set than they'd ever let on. The other actors did for sure. They could sense something was amiss, if only because Chance was standing apart from everybody else, his back to cast and crew, pretty obviously…well, I was going to say "sulking," but that might not be fair. He may just have been struggling.

Anyway, it was a long scene, very emotional, with many changes for Chance's character to go through, and I could understand why he would find it challenging even under the best of circumstances. He had to start out affable, go to shock, then to rage, then deep hurt, then determination. Huge transformations separately, and a huge arc altogether, plus not a lot of space to effectuate it all. It was all there on the page—the script was very good—but really tough for an actor to make convincing. Constructing the latticework that could sustain those changes in such a short amount of time and in a believable way posed a serious stumbling block for any actor. With all his panic, Chance was definitely overreacting, but he was overreacting to a genuine difficulty.

They did one quick rehearsal, for lighting and blocking, and Chance didn't even bother to act during that, just mumbled his lines in a rote fashion, no inflection, and moved where he needed to. It threw the other actors off a little, but they were game and went through the rehearsal without a murmur. Clearly worried, since he was behaving so strangely, but professional. And then, after the usual delays with the camera and sound and so on, my AD signaled everything was ready and said the camera was rolling and I called "Action!"

And what followed was perhaps the most extraordinary acting it's ever been my privilege to witness. The scene played for almost five minutes, which is an eternity in film, and we could have shot it in pieces, of course, but we needed a master, and it was working so incredibly I sure as hell wasn't going to yell "Cut." And the camera kept rolling and they kept going. And Chance took us all on a roller-coaster ride. He was in tears about half-way through the scene; I thought the tears should be the big finish, but his instinct was better—of course it was better, the kid was a genius—and he somehow figured or intuited or just somehow *knew*, that fighting to control the tears, pulling himself together and regaining a measure of calm for the climax, was actually more honest, and ultimately more moving, than some over-the-top histrionic crescendo.

The scene ended. I called "Cut!" And there were a few seconds of dead silence, and then the entire set suddenly erupted in applause. Technicians, production staff, the three other actors in the scene. And me. I'd never seen anything like that happen before. And the applause just went on and on. Chance looked stunned. He sort of fell back into a chair—it was a kitchen set, so there were chairs around—and put his head in his hands. I went up to him, put a hand on his shoulder, and said, "See?" I thought he'd be grateful, but instead he looked up at me and the little fucker just shrugged.

Well, we did some inserts afterward, of course, some OTS's and close-ups. We were on that set until we broke for lunch, but the first take is the one we basically used. It was perfect. Chance never gave me the satisfaction of admitting things were going well—he apparently never forgave me for refusing to validate his sense of inadequacy—but we didn't have any further crises from him after that, so I suppose that represented a sort of tacit concession.

Buddy Moore (actor)

My part in Lightning Bolt wasn't huge, but it was considered a featured role because I had a couple of important scenes with Chance. Just him and me. I played his best friend. I wasn't much more than a narrative convenience, to be honest...his character confides in me, I'm the guy he turns to, and as a result the audience knows what he's thinking and what happened in the backstory. Sort of like the chorus in a Greek tragedy, only with less attitude to work with. [laughs] My part as written was probably the least interesting, the most by-the-numbers thing in the script. But I tried to give it a little oomph anyway. If you can do that with a part that's mostly just serviceable, you've really added some value as an actor. So that was a challenge, and frankly, it turned out to be a pretty interesting one as well as a tough one. A test of one's chops. So this wasn't just a job for me. Not, by the way, that any journeyman actor would sneer at "just a job." There's no such thing. "Just a job" is the entire world to an actor trying to make his way.

Besides, I was thrilled to be working with Chance. He was only a year or two older than me, but I thought of him as a senior colleague. And one I pretty much idolized. I'd seen him in *Hills and Plains*, of course, and that performance knocked me out. It seemed to define acting for a guy my age. For our entire generation. And here he was, the star of this picture, and I had these two two-handers with him, and it was like a dream come true.

But...well, I don't know. The scenes played well, I think it's fair to say. A couple of reviewers even went out of their way to mention them. But Chance...it's still painful for me to recall this. He just wasn't very nice to me. My first day on the picture, between takes, or maybe when they were setting up, I can't remember exactly, but he was sitting in the canvas chair with his name on it, sitting off to the side, alone, studying his script. He seemed absorbed, as he often did on that picture. He wasn't real sociable during the entire shoot. But anyway, I saw him there and I gathered up my courage—you probably can understand how doing something like this isn't always the easiest thing in the world, but I figured, if not now, when?—and approached him and asked if I could talk to him for a couple of minutes. He shrugged. It wasn't too welcoming, but I took it as a yes, so I grabbed a canvas chair that didn't have anybody's name on it and pulled it over and sat down next to him. And I let him know how much I admired him, and he just nodded. No thank you or anything. And I started asking him about how to approach the scene we were about to shoot—and honestly, I had a good handle on it already, I was just curious to hear his thoughts and thought it was a question that might engage him—and I said, "See, I used to think I was a pretty good actor, but you're miles better than me, so I was wondering how you see this scene."

And he just stared at me—almost glared at me, really—and finally said, "Listen, Buddy, I'm not gonna be your acting coach." At least he remembered my name. Unless he was using "buddy" the way you might say "pal" or "mac." Anyhow, he said, "If you need help with your acting, take a class. I've got my own work to do." Unbelievably unfriendly. Not the way colleagues should treat each other. Especially when they're about to play a scene together.

The only thing I can say in mitigation, and I'm not really sure it mitigates anything, is that he was pretty shitty to everybody during the shoot. Other actors, crew, director, even the craft services people. So at least I didn't have to take it personally. Although you can't help taking something like that personally. When you approach someone and they snub you, it feels like a personal rejection.

And look, maybe he was going through an especially stressful time. But it's also possible he was a full-time dick. I gather other people in other situations had much nicer experiences with him than I did, so it's possible he was just going through a bad patch while we were filming that picture. But I was in such awe of his talent—and still am of course, maybe even more so nowadays—that it felt like a slap in the face. And I really, really wish I had something better to say about him than this.

Briel Charpentier

HE WAS NOT FUN to be around when he was filming *Lightning Bolt*. He was...his mood was always dark. I don't know what that was about. It was a good movie. He was wonderful in it. Whatever was bothering him, it had to be internal. The work he was doing does not explain it.

The night after that scene I told you about, the one that worried him so much, I made dinner for him. I made something he could have almost right away when he returned home. A nice chicken ragout, which was a favorite of his, and which I cooked in advance. All I had to do was heat it up and prepare some noodles and we were ready to sit down. And he was barely speaking. He washed up and sat down and poured us both a glass of wine. All wordlessly. And he was so tense, so closed off, I was a bit scared to say anything.

But after a while, the silence was too hard to tolerate, and waiting for him to say something wasn't doing the job. So I finally asked him how the day had gone, and he said, "Fine." And that was it. Not another word, you know. And his tone was so...curt? His tone was so curt I didn't ask him anything else. We ate dinner silently. Then I cleared the table and went back to my own apartment. I don't recall his even thanking me for dinner. I definitely did not feel welcome in his house that night.

No, we weren't breaking up. I wasn't leaving for good, I just was escaping an uncomfortable situation. We saw each other a couple of nights later, and continued to see each other for...well, with a few breaks of varying length, for the rest of his life. It was just...I do not know what was happening with him at that time, but he was always in a very bad mood. For the months they were making *Lightning Bolt,* I frequently kept my distance.

David Osborne

DORE SCHARY LOVED THE picture, but some of the other execs weren't so sure. It was a tough time for studios, they were terrified about television, they thought we might be living through a period marking the end of movies altogether. The general consensus was that message pictures and dramas might be a bad bet, big musicals were what they did best at MGM, serious drama might in the future be consigned to *Playhouse 90* and *Studio One* and those shows. There was plenty of serious drama on television in those days, and lots of good writers working in the medium. But Schary thought there was still room for serious pictures, and he was an in-house champion of *Lightning Bolt* throughout the project. I'll always appreciate his support.

We had one of those test screenings in Glendale, that was the first. They're presented to the audience as an opportunity, they can view a new movie for free before anyone else has had a chance to see it, and then they fill out cards about their reactions afterward. Very tense occasions. I always hated those things; I think most of us in the creative community did. They could be very misleading and they mostly existed to give the suits back-up for the prejudices they'd started with. And sometimes we'd be forced to re-cut the picture or even shoot new scenes based on audience reaction, and that was infuriating. You live with a project for over a year, you think about it and ponder it and refine your ideas, you work with writers and actors, you shoot it in various ways and spend weeks in the cutting room getting it as close to the way you want it as possible, and then some bozos off the street with popcorn on their breath see it for the first time after having already watched some other picture and they give you their two cents' worth and the studio execs all panic and take their reactions as being meaningful in some way. I mean, fuck them. But what could we do? That's how the business operated.

So we entered this Glendale theater after the lights were already down—theater management had reserved the back two rows for our contingent—and filed in quietly. No popcorn for us! It was me, some of the studio brass, the writer—invited to attend as a courtesy, nobody gives a shit about the writer—some of the promotional people, and most of the actors, including a very reluctant Chance Hardwick. God how he didn't want to be there! I told him he had to come, he had no choice in the matter. He accepted it, but he wasn't happy. And as I've indicated, when Chance wasn't happy you weren't in any doubt about it.

Well, here's the thing. As soon as Chance's name came up on the screen in the opening credits, a bunch of girls in the audience started screaming. I'm not joking now. A fairly sizable number of girls. A quarter of the house? Wouldn't surprise me. And later, after we left—I was a little suspicious—I asked the studio PR guy about it and he swore to me it hadn't been his doing, he said they'd passed the word that a Chance Hardwick picture was going to be screened to help ensure people would show up, but that was all. No deliberate busing in of teenaged girls or anything like that. The screaming had happened spontaneously. The girls might have come as a group, he didn't have any information in that regard, but he'd had nothing to do with it.

It was like what'd been happening with Elvis Presley. But Christ, they were screaming at Chance's *name*. By itself! And after that there was screaming intermittently throughout the picture, whenever Chance was onscreen doing something especially romantic or soulful, or when we gave him a close-up. The execs and I kept exchanging glances during the film. This was obviously a big deal. I tried to catch Chance's eye—he was sitting to my immediate right— because I thought he might be amused or surprised. I thought we could share a moment of sorts. But he had his head down, buried in his hands. It was clearly a nightmare for him, the whole experience. He slipped out of the theater before the movie was over. Probably as much to avoid being recognized by the screamers as anything else. I don't think he disliked the movie—he later told me he thought I'd done a good job—I just think he was spooked.

When we looked at the cards later that night in Dore's office, we were thrilled. I mean, of course there were a lot of "Chance Hardwick is a dreamboat!" kind of comments. There was even one, and I'm not making this up, that said "I want to suck Chance Hardwick's hard wick." Can you believe it? From, presumably, one of the teenagers! Call me naïve, but that was shocking to me. I had no idea girls so young could be so sexually blunt, or even so knowledgeable. Oral sex was something we didn't talk about in those days. It was a closely held secret. But anyway, after all that screaming, we weren't surprised to get fan-type comments about Chance. But in addition, and just as importantly, there were serious evaluations of the picture from people who seemed to be grown-ups, and those were positive as well. Very. It was the first time the studio, not counting Dore now, but lots of the others in the executive building, they realized they might have a huge hit on their hands. And potentially a mega-star under contract. And of course they all pretended they'd known it all along.

Dore asked me to stay behind after the others had left. He clapped me on the back and said, "Great work, Dave. Irving would have been proud of this picture. It's going to make us a mint."

FROM THE HERALD TRIBUNE REVIEW OF LIGHTNING BOLT:

"...CHANCE HARDWICK DOESN'T MERELY fulfill his much-heralded potential, he lays claim to having become the best American actor to achieve prominence since war's end. There are moments in Lightning Bolt where the line between performance and naked human emotion ceases to exist. When Hardwick's character becomes aware that the woman he has always regarded as his sister is in fact his mother and that the man who has played a mentoring role in his life is in fact his father, the viewer doesn't merely witness the character's shock and pain and jolt of sudden illumination but experiences it physically and emotionally. This is screen acting on the highest artistic level."

Briel Charpentier

CHANCE SEEMED TO RELAX somewhat after Lightning Bolt was finished. His agent, Irma, was looking at scripts for his next picture, and the studio was eager to get him into another film as soon as possible, but some of the pressure was now off. The pressure from doubting himself, and also the pressure of expectations. Because of course *Lightning Bolt* was a very big success, both in the sense of prestige and also financially, so that took some of those worries away. He no longer had reason to doubt himself.

Those worries were immediately replaced by others, to be sure. He was now a very big movie star. He had some trouble accepting that, you know. So did I, for my own reasons. I found it amusing that this sweet boy I'd come to like so much was suddenly one of the most famous people in the world. I don't think my head was turned; I was merely surprised that this odd thing had happened. I was a simple girl from Paris. I never thought I'd even know a Hollywood movie actor, let alone…you know…have an intimate relationship with a star. It was confusing!

But Chance was…he was disturbed. He didn't know how to cope with his new status. For one thing, fans—he had many fans now—they found out where he lived and hung around outside his house hoping to see him, or get an autograph, or maybe just say hello. He didn't like that at all, although he tried to be nice. And his neighbors were upset. Woodrow Wilson Drive is a quiet, rather narrow street where regular people live. Not show business people. Crowds assembling there at all hours was inconvenient for everybody.

And it wasn't only practical things. Being famous…of course I think he always wanted it. But he was a very private person, and now he had very little privacy. It was hard for him even just to leave his house. If he went down the hill to Ralph's to buy a quart of milk or Thrifty to buy a tube of toothpaste, he would be assaulted. It's one of the reasons he decided to buy that house in the Malibu Colony. Someplace more remote, you know. Someplace protected, with built-in security. Where many of his neighbors would be as famous as him, which provided a measure of security in itself. But even before that, even for the last few months he still lived in the hills, he began spending less time at his house and more time at my studio in West Hollywood. He was safe there. Fans did not know about me—the studio saw to that—so they did not know where to look for him.

I look back on those days very fondly. They may have been our happiest time in fact, and you can believe me, that had nothing to do with his success. The opposite, I think you might say. It was the only time where we did not have to even *think* about his success. I would paint and he would put his jazz records on my gramophone and listen to the music and read, scripts or books or magazines, and sometimes he'd get up and look at what I was working on and offer some praise or encouragement, and it was all very peaceful and sweet. And *domestic*. The closest we ever came to domesticity. The world outside couldn't touch us.

But what I was trying to express is…you see, what really bothered him, bothered him even more than the attention and the publicity and maybe even the loss of privacy, was losing touch with *himself*, if I can put it that way. Not understanding what had happened to his life, not knowing how he had somehow got from there to here, and not being able to control the events rolling over him like those big waves out there in Malibu that finally took him away from me. From all of us.

Alison McAllister (actress)

I'D SIGNED WITH METRO back in '56, and I guess they were sort of grooming me. For stardom, ha ha. It was quite exciting for a while; they seemed to think I was going to be a big star, and they more or less convinced me that was the case. As it happened, that never quite took, I worked a bit but whatever chemistry is supposed to happen between an actor and an audience never happened. I went from being the second female lead, the ingénue, managed that in a couple of pictures, then it was smaller parts, and then finally horror movies and TV guest shots. I was a good screamer; that kept me employed for a time. But it didn't make me a star...which may have been a blessing in disguise. I really don't have any regrets, although it killed me a little back when I still had big dreams. But anyway, in those days publicity departments wielded a lot of power, more than you can imagine. They arranged camouflage weddings for gay guys and gals and covered up pregnancies and turned commies into Eisenhower supporters. If you had a contract with the studio and the studio expected big things of you, they took you apart and reassembled you in the image they figured would go over well with the public.

They even changed my name. I don't imagine you'd remember me unless you're a fanatic about either black-and-white horror movies or second-rate weepies from the fifties, the ones with that garish Technicolor palette, but the studio thought my real name was ridiculous and that no one would believe it anyhow, so they christened me Deborah Hunt. What's funny is, they thought my real name sounded made up, so they made up a name for me they thought sounded real. My family was kind of offended by this. My dad, who was pretty old-school in his attitudes— I don't want to defend this aspect of his character—but he was so pissed about the studio's high-handedness he said, "Why would they change your name? McAllister doesn't sound Jewish." Nice, huh? But there was no point in reprimanding him. He was who he was, a product of his time and place.

And my brother used to...well, let's just say he used to substitute another letter for the first letter of my stage name. Such a clown, my brother.

And then some genius in publicity thought it would be a terrific idea if Chance and I were supposed to be a romantic item. They thought it would boost my profile, get me some ink, intrigue the public. You know, who's this starlet Chance Hardwick is stuck on? We weren't required to shack up or anything, it wasn't totally crazy—it wasn't like poor Rock and Phyllis—we were just supposed to be seen together at a few previews, maybe go to Ciro's or the Moulin Rouge or have dinner at Perino's or Chasen's. Stuff like that. With press alerted, of course. The whole point was to be photographed. And the Hollywood press was incredibly compliant in those days. Maybe they still are, I don't know the scene anymore. So we'd make moony eyes at one another, maybe hold hands, get our pictures taken, show up in the gossip columns and the movie magazines, be a glamor couple.

It didn't have to last long or pretend to be an engagement. They wanted to give me a build-up and figured this sort of publicity would help, but they also wanted Chance's fan base to think he was still available. So it was a narrow line we were walking...fun couple out on the town and enjoying each other's company, but not quite ready for a ring. Something like that.

It made me uncomfortable, to be honest. For one thing, I had a *real* boyfriend back then, and he sure as hell didn't like it. It even made him suspicious, as if all this ridiculous PR nonsense might have some basis in fact. That's the power of publicity right there, even when you're in on the deception you aren't quite positive it isn't true. And after all, Chance was a big star and an incredibly attractive man—obviously—so it wasn't a completely absurd notion. And David wasn't in the business, he was a pediatrician, so this whole thing seemed especially exotic to him. Not just exotic, but downright weird. He kept grilling me about Chance, and no matter how many times I told him there was nothing to it, told him it was just dream factory make-believe, he was never completely sure if he could trust me. Whenever Chance and I went out, I'd have to call David as soon as the date was over to assure him nothing was going on, and sometimes he'd even be waiting for me back at my apartment just to be sure I came in alone.

And it wasn't just David. Who objected, I mean. I had plenty of reservations myself. The whole fake-romance business struck me as crass—you know what I mean? Not like prostitution, of course—I don't want to go overboard here—but not how I'd assumed my dating life would go, either. I was a small-town Southwestern girl, for goodness sake. I still believed the movies, ironically enough. The ideas they sold us about love. Hearts and flowers and a Dimitri Tiompkin score. This other thing was just…you know, kind of icky. Even when it was pretend it was kind of icky.

But I'm kind of making this all about me, aren't I? And it's supposed to be about Chance. You're asking me about Chance. Sorry. [laughs] Once a starlet always a starlet, right?

But the point I wanted to make is, sure, Chance had the reputation of being a rebel, one of the mavericks, one of the new breed. Someone who refused to play the game. But he sure went along with the studio's idea that we go out on some public dates. If he argued with them about it I never heard anything to suggest so. Maybe later, if he'd achieved the absolutely stratospheric level of superstardom everyone expected for him, he might have had enough power to flex his muscles and refuse outright. I don't know. I don't know if that would have been his choice, and I don't know, if it was, whether he would have acted on it.

The truth is, I don't even know which team he played on. There were rumors in both directions. But of course there would be, wouldn't there? He once told me he had a girlfriend—I think that was to reassure me I was safe with him, he didn't have any expectations of a carnal nature—and I've read about that French woman he was supposed to have been involved with. But who knows what's true and what isn't? Hollywood is like Washington,

DC, in that way. Lies are the basic currency. If they lied about him and me, maybe they're lying about the French girl too.

But the other thing I need to say is that he was a perfect gentleman. By which I don't mean he didn't pounce on me. I mean, maybe I mean that too. He could easily have assumed I was there for the plucking, just considering his fame and his looks and all. So it's entirely possible he wasn't attracted to me, or wasn't attracted to girls generally. But it's also possible he understood this was an artificial set-up and he had no right to those *droit de signeur* assumptions. We'll never know.

But when I say he was a perfect gentleman, I mean something else. He must have understood this was an uncomfortable situation for me, with me being fairly new in town and new to the business and him such a big star and me a newbie and our not knowing each other at all but having to behave in public like we were in love or at least fascinated with one another. He could have let me know this was a tiresome chore, for example, either overtly or by acting bored. Or he could have not talked to me at all when we were alone, and then just talked about himself when people were watching or discussed sports and sports cars and whatever private enthusiasms he had without any regard for what might interest me. But instead he was personable and funny, and freely admitted that this was awkward for him too, and he asked me lots of questions about myself and even seemed to be studying me closely. He made the whole transaction human rather than just a piece of drudgery that was an unpleasant professional requirement.

People sometimes ask me if I'm that "woman in black," as they call her, the old lady who lays flowers on his headstone. [laughs] Which just goes to prove that I've become an old lady, I guess. Well, I can't deny *that*. But no, Chance and I never had any kind of serious relationship, romantic or otherwise—those people must have gobbled up movie magazines when they were young and believed whatever they read—and I definitely don't put flowers on his headstone. Ever. I don't even know where it is.

Sir Trevor Bliss

I'D DECIDED TO MOVE back to London. My marriage had ended, in rather ugly fashion as it happens, and the political situation in the States was quite unpleasant, and I'd been feeling homesick in any case...rather, perhaps, like Ben Britten some fifteen or so years earlier, I was feeling increasingly alienated in America, increasingly drawn to home. It's not that I didn't like Los Angeles—I have very happy memories of my time there, and it had certainly been profitable artistically and financially—but my roots were on the other side of the Atlantic.

My house wasn't even listed yet when Chance rung me up. He'd heard I was leaving. That's Hollywood for you. A small town in many ways, with a lively gossip mill. He expressed an interest in buying my house, and said he didn't want to haggle, I should name my price and if it seemed reasonable he would pay it. Which was very refreshing. In Hollywood, everyone wants to haggle about *everything*. Part of the culture, don't you know? The rag trade transferred to another venue.

He'd been over only once or twice, but he said he remembered the house, he liked it, he appreciated the security, he loved the private beach being right out the back door—which in retrospect feels a little macabre, doesn't it? When I mentioned that it was possibly a little large for his needs, he said he thought he could grow into it, by which I assume he meant that someday he might start a family and the spaciousness would come in handy. Anyway, to make a long story short, we quickly came to terms and frankly, that took one large worry off my shoulders. When you're changing your entire life, disposing of a house is one of the more onerous aspects.

Irma Gold

Everyone wonders about *Not My Fault!* It seems like such an unlikely Chance Hardwick vehicle, doesn't it? Even in retrospect. Maybe if he'd lived there would have been more like it and it wouldn't stick out like that.

And I'll tell you...the truth is, I think they sent me the script by mistake. It probably just got slipped into the pile accidentally. But I read it and thought it was hilarious. Usually I know whether a script is any good after about five pages. This one had me laughing out loud on page one. And I kept laughing. Original situations, sparkling dialogue, great love story. So I called Chance and asked him if he thought he could do comedy. And to my surprise he said he'd love it. Said he'd been dying to do something that didn't require him to be a brooding young man, if only for a change of pace, and because, after his last three pictures, and especially after the success of his last two, he was afraid he'd never get the chance to be anything else. Well, as I say, that kind of surprised me, but I figured, "Hey, the boy's so good he can probably do anything he sets his mind to."

The studio wasn't thrilled. He was right to be worried about being typecast. But by now they also wanted to keep him happy, and, you know, they probably figured, just like I did, he might be versatile enough to pull it off. Who knew? The sky could be the limit with someone like Chance.

Gil Fraser

Chance got me my part in *Not My Fault!* He was a pal about it. Not the kind of guy who forgets his friends. Not that he had to overcome a lot of opposition, I don't think—I knew the AD, he was a fan of mine, so it isn't like I was rammed down anyone's throat—but still, Chance went to bat for me. It wasn't exactly an act of charity, he knew I could play the part, but it was generous all the same. I don't know whether I would have been chosen if he hadn't insisted. Maybe yes, maybe no.

It turned out to be a fun shoot, too. The director, Charlie Cox, was a very funny guy, and not only that, but he was a *fun* guy. He liked his set to be a happy place. He welcomed input from anyone. Grips and gaffers could offer suggestions and would be listened to respectfully, and so of course could actors. We had a lot of laughs on that picture.

Benny Ludlow (comedian)

THERE WAS A BUNCH of us guys who used to buddy around together quite a lot. And Chance was one of us. We thought of ourselves as "Young Hollywood," you know? Kind of pretentious or…what's the word…presumptuous? Kind of presumptuous, but we dared to think the future of movies was in our hands. Not that all of us were necessarily going to make it, but that *some* of us would. And that a number of the most important people in the business would be coming from our group. Some had already made it pretty big, including Chance and a couple of the other guys. And they enjoyed a kind of special status among us. As for me, I was already getting some good nightclub gigs—I worked the Crescendo and Ciro's a couple of times, and even played a few lounges in Vegas—and the occasional TV shot. Plus I was studying with Jim Sterling, so I hoped to get work as an actor, not just a stand-up. That's where I first met Chance, in Jim's class.

But the thing is, we were, for all our silliness and self-importance, we were a pretty hip group. That's how it is in show biz. There's a cynicism and a wit and an irreverence that's the common tongue, you might say. It was the language we spoke, or maybe it's more like our local dialect. It wasn't always comprehensible to outsiders. But basically, if you weren't funny, if you couldn't keep up, you didn't belong, you didn't count. The funniest of us was Lenny Bruce; he'd hang with us from time to time. He hadn't hit it big yet, he was working at a few local clubs, but anyone who knew him knew he was like the funniest human being on the planet. It wasn't clear he could ever go mainstream, he was so foul-mouthed and sick we thought that might hold him back, but among friends he was a fucking riot. I mean, your sides would ache, if you didn't pee in your pants you probably weren't human. None of the rest of us could come near his level, of course. Not even me, and I was a pro. But we were all pretty funny, we all had something to contribute.

And a lot of people don't know this, wouldn't even suspect it, but Chance could be very funny too. In his own way. Very dry, very droll, very understated. Almost British in his approach to humor. If you weren't paying close attention you could easily miss how funny he was. He wasn't out there punching, you know, he'd just mutter something caustic and if you heard it you'd make him repeat it so everyone else could hear it too.

And I'm only mentioning any of this because when he got the script for *Not My Fault!* he was unsure whether he should do it. I don't think anybody knows this story, anybody who wasn't there. He loved the script, he liked the part, but he said, "I don't know, I just think, Christ, there are so many good dramatic actors out there, actors whose work I really admire, but they can't do comedy to save their lives. They try and they try hard and it's awful. Not funny at all. It's downright embarrassing the way they seem to be begging for laughs. I'm afraid I'll turn out to be one of those guys."

And it was Lenny who told him he should do it. We were all out on the beach at Chance's place, one of those lazy Saturday afternoons we used to spend out there, we were sprawled on towels on the sand, it was this gorgeous late afternoon, we were smoking pot and drinking beer and looking out at the ocean and talking about Chance's hesitancy, knocking the pros and cons back and forth, and Lenny finally broke in and told him he definitely ought to do it, he definitely had the chops. And when Chance again said he wasn't sure how to approach it, Lenny said, "Listen, *schmendrick*, cut the bullshit. It's not so complicated and I'm sure you know that already. You're a funny guy. The simple secret to good comic acting is that your character doesn't know he's in a comedy. That's all. That's it." He told him to just play it straight, believe in the script, care desperately about the dramatic situation, and maybe show a little more weakness than you normally do. He said, "Trust me, you're gonna kill."

Well, as far as we were concerned, when it came to funny Lenny was the burning bush, the fucking voice of God. So I think that pep talk was the clincher for Chance. And it turned out to be terrific advice. It's a shame he never got to do another comedy after that. He had the chops. He proved it. He could have been like Lemmon or Matthau, great at drama, great at comedy, a sure thing no matter what the project called for. [sighs] Such a loss. And such a great guy.

James Sterling

HE WAS UNDECIDED ABOUT doing a comedy, the movie that became *Not My Fault!* He was very uncertain about his ability to pull it off. One of his friends—I think it was some stand-up comic, actually—told him the secret to playing comedy is to play it completely straight. Odd advice to get from a comedian, although sound as far as it goes. Still, not the whole story. You can't be grim about what you're doing. There's an added element, a kind of lightness to your performance, a buoyancy—it's very hard to describe—that transforms drama into something funny. God knows I'm not known for comedy myself, if anything I fear I'm considered somewhat humorless. Or so my wife tells me. She sometimes calls me a pompous ass. [laughs] But hey, I teach acting, I have to understand all sorts of styles, and I flatter myself I have some insight into all of them.

But what I was getting at with Chance is very hard to explain, and all but impossible to teach. It isn't really a matter of technique as such. It's more a matter of conveying…befuddlement? Confusion? A kind of very human helplessness or klutziness, something the audience can immediately relate to. Or an awareness of the insanity of normal life, maybe? An awareness that doesn't exempt one from being a full participant in it.

So, because my groping for an explanation felt so abstract, and because what I was describing was so hard to achieve based on words alone, I suggested to Chance we do something I've never done with a student before. I said, "Look, clear your schedule for a day and come on over to my place. We're going to screen some movies." I wanted him to watch how some actors who were good solid dramatic actors could also be great at comedy. I didn't want him to watch W. C. Fields or the Marx Brothers or Laurel and Hardy, I wanted him to see *actors*. So we looked at Hank Fonda in *The Lady Eve*, Clark Gable in *It Happened One Night*, Jimmy Stewart and Cary Grant in *The Philadelphia Story*, Bill Powell in *The Thin Man*, Gary Cooper in *Mr. Deeds Goes to Town*. Coop was always a bit of a stiff, but he managed to figure out how to make it work for him, even in comedy.

So that was a very long session for us. I canceled all my classes that day. We broke for lunch, but otherwise we just stared at a screen in the dark. It was great fun for me—I loved all those movies and relished the opportunity to see them again—and my daughter came in at one point and sat down and watched *The Lady Eve* with us to her very evident enjoyment, and then quietly slipped out again. And you know, by then she'd become pretty blasé about meeting movie stars, they were in and out of the house all the time, she might brag about it to her friends but she played it cool herself. Nevertheless, she was pretty thrilled to be sitting in our den watching a movie with Chance Hardwick. I think all her friends had a huge crush on him by then, and so did she. Every once in a while I'd catch her stealing a glance at him, maybe to see if he was laughing at the same things that were making her laugh. But I honestly don't believe he laughed once all day. He just watched intently, nodding from time to time, and occasionally making a note in this little notebook he kept with him. And when I finally turned the lights back on, we looked at each other bleary-eyed for a few seconds, and then he said to me, "Okay, got it. Thanks, Jim."

As I was showing him out, I told him I wasn't going to charge him for the session. But he insisted. He said, "Are you joking? Of course you need to charge me. I'll pay any fee you name."

"But I didn't give you any coaching. We just watched some movies. Which I probably enjoyed a lot more than you did."

And he said, "I can't tell you how helpful this has been. Invaluable."

And that was that. He was off and running.

Charles Cox (director)

I ADMIT I HAD my doubts about Hardwick being in the picture. I'd mostly worked with actors familiar with high-style comedy, many with Broadway backgrounds, guys and gals for whom comedy was second nature. I was always confident they could deliver, they'd know where the laughs were and how to time them. I wasn't so sure about Chance Hardwick. He was a great actor, I never doubted *that*, but I thought of him as a gloomy Gus, a soulful kind of guy, with *angst* his basic stock in trade. Still, the studio wanted him—wanted him? Hell, it was a Chance Hardwick picture—and once filming got underway, he turned out to be a dream to work with.

And he was really funny in the picture. Different style from what I was used to, very understated, never reaching for the laugh, odd line-readings, off-kilter timing. Took some getting used to. The first few days while we were actually on the set, I couldn't tell what the hell he was up to, and I kept shooting and reshooting hoping to get enough coverage so we could stitch together an acceptable performance. But every time I took a look at the dailies, I realized how wrong I'd been, it was obvious he was scoring. And after a few days of that I relaxed. It was clear I could trust his instincts.

And his chemistry with Dolly Murray was great. Now, I never worried about Dolly. She was an excellent comic actress, always sexy and sweet and funny, a pretty rare combination at the best of times, so I knew she'd be fine. But I honestly don't believe she's ever been better than she was in *Not My Fault!* And I'm not claiming any special credit for that. There was a kind of electric current between her and Chance, and it gave her performance an added oomph. Their scenes together are a thing of beauty, both the ones where they're at each other's throats and the ones where they're lovey-dovey. So charming you could *plotz*.

Dolores Murray (actress)

I CAN'T DENY I developed a huge crush on Chance while we were shooting *Not My Fault!* Who would blame me? He was so gorgeous, and so funny, so amazingly sweet. Dreamy. The kind of boy girls swoon over, and their mothers fall in love with too. I cherished his company. We laughed almost nonstop during that shoot. He and Charlie Cox had this funny rat-a-tat going, you could tell they really dug each other, and he usually hung out with his pal Gil, who had a small part in the picture, and he was a really funny guy too, funny and crude and...well, today you'd call him politically incorrect, but he wasn't offensive. *I* didn't think he was, anyway. And they were kind enough to let me join them as a sort of honorary third musketeer.

I don't know if Chance was aware I was carrying a torch for him. Oh, probably. I don't think he missed much of anything. But we didn't talk about it, goodness knows, and he didn't give me the slightest indication of romantic interest. Unlike Gil, who was always sniffing around and making suggestive comments. But like I said, Gil was funny about it, not obnoxious. Of course, today women would probably be quick to cry sexual harassment at the things Gil said, but honestly, it was all manageable and quite amusing. And I knew Chance was involved with that artist, the French girl, and while I don't know how serious they were, they were serious enough, so I didn't have any serious expectations of him. Just...I mean, I wasn't a teenager anymore, but I *felt* like a teenager. I had teenage fantasies. With an admixture of grown-up lust.

What made it complicated, at least a little bit complicated, is that the publicity people wanted to feature us as having a romance of sorts. Now, my image—this was mainly the doing of my own personal publicist at Rogers and Cowan, who was working in tandem with the studio people—my image was of a pure, devout Catholic girl. They even played up the fact that I'd once considered becoming a nun. Of course that was when I was fourteen or so, and it lasted all of maybe two weeks before I realized I didn't have a calling, and besides, I liked boys too much. But it was enough for the PR people to inflate it and run with it. They thought it was an intriguing hook. For reasons I'll never understand, some people find celibacy sexy. If that's not a paradox, nothing is. But anyway, because of that, Chance and I didn't have to pretend to be sleeping together, they just wanted us to be seen going out on dates and to act like we were smitten. Which didn't take any acting on my part! So we went out a few times, for dinner or a show, and Chance was good company, and we had a perfectly fine time—I was delighted to be able to see him out of school, so to speak—and the studio made sure photographers were on hand. And then we'd go our separate ways.

But then...ah, what the heck, it was so long ago, and I haven't been to confession in decades, so maybe telling you this will win me remission. See, when the picture was released, the studio sent us out to do a publicity tour. Some premieres, some local media, stuff like that. And one night we were in Seattle, and we'd gone to the opening. Chance said to me, "If I ever have to watch this movie again, I think I'll kill myself," which seemed funny at the time, but in retrospect maybe not so much—and the big press party afterward, and then we were both exhausted and drained but also really hepped up, the way you are in those circumstances, so we decided to have a drink in the hotel bar to unwind, and we finally dragged ourselves up to our rooms, which were next door to each other, and I...it was probably a combination of fatigue and alcohol and the feeling of being in a foreign setting, plus I'll come clean and admit to all the unruly desire I'd been repressing for all those months, but I said, "So, do you want to come in?" And he said, "Oh yeah, I sure do."

And we had a very passionate night. Very. Like...I don't even have words. And if I did, I'd keep them to myself! [laughs] But that was that. He slipped out the next morning after giving me a little kiss on the forehead, nothing more intimate than that, and although afterward he was as friendly as ever, we never referred to that night again. I was too shy, and he...well, I suppose he preferred to pretend it had never happened. I was a teeny-weeny bit heartbroken, but I knew I had no right to expect anything else. So that's how I consoled myself, by telling myself it was a magic night and that was a lot more than I could ever have realistically hoped for. Some consolation.

Dorothy Goren Mckenzie

MY DAD DIED RIGHT around the time *Not My Fault!* came out. He lived long enough to see it, though. I'm not saying it killed him, mind you, I'm just saying he saw it. Saw it and dumped all over it, naturally. Said it was the stupidest thing he'd ever seen. He offered that opinion a lot, so I guess those stupid things just kept topping each other. [laughs] What he really hated, what really irked the heck out of him, was the fact that when we saw it the audience loved it and my mom and I were laughing all the way through. We thought it was hysterical. We had no idea Chance could be so funny. We knew he could be funny in a dry, wry way, but not out-and-out hysterical like that. There's that scene where he has one girl hiding in his bedroom and one girl obliviously puttering away in his kitchen and neither knows the other is there and he's kind of going nuts, afraid they'll discover each other, and he has that cross-eyed crazy look of terror on his face—I mean, he's so scared, but also so aware how much he's screwed up and how insane the situation is—it was such a hoot everybody in the audience was laughing so loud we couldn't even hear the dialogue for close to a minute. But Dad just sat there glumly, robotically eating his popcorn and slurping his Coke and grunting his disapproval every once in a while.

It was interesting—this is just by the way—it was interesting the first time Gil appeared onscreen. I wasn't expecting it at all, I didn't know he had a part in the picture. Gave me a little...you know, it gave me that feeling you get. Down in your...in your nether regions. Sometimes your body remembers things you thought you'd forgot.

Anyhow, Daddy died suddenly—heart, which might have been the first definitive proof he actually had one—and Mom called Chance to tell him. And she wanted him to come home for the funeral. He refused. She was practically begging. I only heard her side of the conversation, but after they hung up and she stopped crying, she told me he said, "You know how I feel about Steve, Mom. It would be pure hypocrisy to pay my respects when I didn't *have* any respect. I'm sorry if you're hurting or you feel you have to pretend you're hurting, but *I* don't feel a goddamned thing." And then he told her, "I'll come home for your funeral, but I'll be damned if I'd even travel around the block for his." It didn't occur to him, or to any of us, that he'd never get a chance to attend her funeral, that he'd pass years before she did.

Gil Fraser

CHANCE STARTED HOSTING THESE all-day parties on weekends. All-day parties that sometimes stretched out into all-night parties. Not every weekend, of course, but maybe once or twice a month. The whole deal seemed out of character for him—he was never much of a social animal in the years we were closest. Sure, he liked going out every once in a while, but he always valued his solitude too, and he always seemed relieved when he got back home and could withdraw into his room. But, well, he had this big luxurious Malibu pad now and he had his fame and he had lots of money and he was moving in pretty elevated circles, so he started entertaining.

I went a couple of times and then I stopped. No, no, I was always invited. He didn't drop me. Like I told you, he was a good pal. Chance not only invited me but used to argue with me when I made up some excuse, when I said I had other plans or I wasn't feeling so good. He'd tell me who was going to be there and how it might be helpful for my career and what a good time I'd have. But

I didn't find it to be such a good time. Those things were always packed with stars and heavy hitters, with his Malibu neighbors and this new group of friends of his, and I never felt comfortable in that setting. I try not to be too conscious of status in my life, even in a town and a business as status-conscious as this one, but in that setting status was impossible to ignore. And in my case, to ignore my *lesser* status. I mean, Natalie and R. J. were often around, Steve McQueen, Russ Tamblyn, Roddy McDowell, Rock Hudson, Elizabeth Taylor one time, Gore Vidal, Paul and Joanne...it was like the footprints at Grauman's had grown bodies and sprung to life. Wall-to-wall fame and fortune, except there usually weren't walls, the action was mostly out by the pool or down on the beach.

There's a sort of freemasonry of fame, you know? A social club off limits to non-celebrities. Chance had had the secret handshake revealed to him, so to speak. He'd become a legitimate peer of such people. I definitely wasn't. I was a steadily working actor, I had respectable status in the industry, but I wasn't anything like Hollywood royalty, and being there made me feel like a hanger-on. Like part of Chance's entourage, picking up scraps dropped from his table. A yes-man or a stooge. A younger, thinner Jilly Rizzo. I didn't think of myself in those terms, and I didn't like it. Plus, I didn't like being ignored or just tolerated. So I stopped going pretty quickly.

But please don't think it was Chance's fault or Chance's doing. He was always a good friend. He wanted me there, he treated me great, he never failed to introduce me around and tell people who I was and what I'd done. But the others...I mean, it isn't like people were deliberately rude or anything. They just weren't especially interested. I wasn't on their level. If, say, I attached myself to a little conversational knot and offered a contribution, no one would tell me to butt out or say something dismissive. They usually just wouldn't respond at all, they would pick up the conversation as if

I hadn't spoken. No matter whether what I'd said was interesting or valid or smart. And hey, I don't even blame them. If I'd been one of them, I'd probably have acted the same way. You're a star and you're at a party with other stars, you want to hang out with your fellow stars, right? Measure yourself against them. You don't want to waste your time with some *zhlub* off the street.

So there was a lot of sitting around the pool or lying out on the beach, and it was pretty delicious from one point of view, but if you were like me you'd just be sitting or lying there on your own for several hours with no one to talk to or flirt with, and that can get boring. And you can start to feel like a pariah. You might say hello to one or two people and there was usually a barbecue and the food and drink was always good, it just wasn't enough to keep me there. There was a lot of drinking and often a lot of pot, and I had no objection to either of those— I think heavier drugs came along later, although that wouldn't have been Chance's scene, it might have been some of his friends' though—but I decided I preferred to see Chance one-on-one, or as a threesome with Briel, or on a double-date if I was seeing someone. It was much easier to be natural in that kind of situation. We'd all grab a bite someplace where we knew he wouldn't be hassled, or go to a club to hear some music, and it was just amigos, none of that Hollywood crap.

Speaking of which, I don't think Briel showed up at those Malibu marathons very often either. Maybe for reasons similar to mine, I don't know. It was Chance's new crowd, young up-and-comers. They were at the core of those parties. You know who I mean? They were like an earlier version of the eighties Brat Pack. They expected to inherit the whole world of showbiz soon. They had that kind of cockiness. And hey, some of them succeeded. They weren't completely full of shit. But whether they were full of shit or not, they'd already established their own arrogant little clique, and if you weren't part of it you didn't feel welcome.

Also…well, you probably won't be surprised to hear that sometimes these parties got a little rambunctious. I mean, think of it, the guests are lying out there in the sun wearing practically nothing, all these fabulous-looking people, and there's alcohol and marijuana wherever you look, and you're rich and you're free and normal rules don't seem to apply to you…so you can probably imagine that there were days when those parties more or less spontaneously turned into fuck-fests. And that wouldn't have been Briel's scene at all. Might have been mine, to be honest, but what could be worse than being the odd-man-out at an orgy?

Irma Gold

NOT MY FAULT! PUT Chance in a whole other league. It was a huge hit, far and away the most profitable comedy of the year, which meant he'd had two boffo starring vehicles in a row. And he'd demonstrated a versatility no one suspected he had. Including me. He did that "oh my God what have I gotten myself into?" attitude with such panache I don't think anyone besides maybe Cary Grant could have pulled it off nearly so well. And the physical stuff! Dodging around all that furniture in the warehouse scene, it was like he was made of rubber.

So we were able to renegotiate his contract as soon as the smoke from that picture cleared. Metro barely squawked. I got very good terms. *Very*. He was sitting pretty.

And it's so sad, but his next film turned out to be his last. Also his best, I think most people would agree. *The Judas Kiss* was a beautiful, poetic script, and he fell in love with it right away. As soon as he read it, he called me at home—it was almost midnight!—and didn't even apologize for waking me. He said, "This is it. This is my next one." The studio wouldn't have balked no matter what he wanted to do, he had that kind of power now, but they were thrilled with the choice.

They assigned a first-class director, went A-list with the cast. They knew it was going to be their big prestige picture. Their likely Oscar contender for the year.

Bruce Powers (actor)

CHANCE SAW ME IN a production of *The Emperor Jones* at a small theater in West Hollywood, this little hole-in-the-wall on Santa Monica Boulevard. The show didn't get a lot of press attention, so I'm not sure how he heard about it or what brought him into the theater. Maybe one of his jazz friends…he was passionate about jazz, a knowledgeable fan too, not a finger-snapping phony, he used to go to clubs pretty regularly, he had a gigantic record collection. And after he became famous the players were of course thrilled he was in the audience—not too many white dudes went to those places, at least not *some* of those places, the ones located in iffy neighborhoods, and having a movie star in the club would have been a really big deal—and naturally they were delighted to sit at his table during breaks and have a drink and shoot the shit. I'm guessing it could have been one of them who told him to check me out.

He came backstage after the show and was full of praise for my performance. Which of course is the direct route to any actor's heart. [laughs] But he also just seemed like a good guy. That whole backstage thing can be so bullshitty, you know—*kiss-kiss-you-were-just-mahvelous-dahling*—but he made it comfortable in a way that that stuff often isn't. And he seemed sincere.

And he must have been sincere, because a few days later my agent got a call. Chance wanted to meet with me. He said he might have a part for me in his next picture. So they sent over the script, and I read it through twice, and I was totally flummoxed. I didn't see any parts for a Negro actor. We were called Negroes in those days; it was the polite term back then. So when he and I met a few days later, in his office at Metro, I said, "Listen, I think you must have sent me the wrong draft. There aren't any Negroes in the script you sent me."

And first he laughed, like he thought I might have been pulling his leg, but when he realized I was serious he said, "Well, I thought you could play George. You'd be great in the role."

So I said, "But the script doesn't say George is colored."

And he said, "Doesn't say he's white, either."

Mark Cernovic (producer)

So WE WERE IN a pickle. Chance wanted Bruce Powers in the picture. He was pretty adamant about it. Now, Bruce wasn't a well-known actor yet. Nobody at Metro had heard of him, and there was a lot of resistance. Mostly, although nobody would admit it, because he was black. So at first the studio went through that whole "but the character isn't a Negro" thing, which Chance batted away easily. And then they said it would cost us business in the South, it would cost us a *lot* of business. Like there might be boycotts and things. And that that could hurt Chance's career down the line too. He might acquire a reputation that would hurt him in certain markets, is how they delicately put it.

Well, Chance was still being insistent, he said he was willing to take the risk, he thought it was ideal casting as well as a great gesture in an important cause. And I have to say...I mean, Chance took me to see Bruce in *The Emperor Jones*, and he *was* awfully good. I could see this wasn't *just* a political gesture. Chance had become much more politically conscious around this time, but that wasn't his sole motivation here. I could sympathize with the studio's concerns—for them, the business side of show business was paramount, it's called show *business* for a reason, so I thought that was a legitimate point of view—but if Chance was willing to stick his neck out for this, I was willing to go along. It was a worthy cause and Bruce was a worthy actor. So I backed him up. A small risk on my own part. The brass weren't happy with me. They expected me to be an ally.

Then Sol Siegel raised a new objection, and this one *was* political. He told us that Bruce Powers had been graylisted. It wasn't quite as bad as being blacklisted, he'd never been called to testify in front of HUAC—too small a fish, I guess—and as far as I know he'd never officially been a member of the Communist Party. But his name had come up in testimony a few times, he'd palled around with those people and been to some meetings and signed some petitions. Sol told me Powers—who I'd swear he'd never even heard of till Chance recommended him—he told me Powers was absolute poison. He said the American Legion and the VFW and the DAR and a bunch of other groups would organize all sorts of protests. Ironic, considering that Bruce did his stint in the army and no one raised any objection to him back when he was dodging bullets in Korea. But Sol said this one was nonnegotiable.

When Chance started to protest, Sol asked him if he'd be equally willing to work with a Nazi. I got the impression he thought this argument was a clincher. And Chance said, "Maybe not, but that would be *my* decision, not a decision imposed on me by some cultural commissar. I refuse to be bullied that way. And I despise this industry-wide effort to destroy people's careers. Bruce Powers is a terrific actor and he's right for the part and his politics don't concern me and shouldn't concern anyone else."

Notice that Sol never mentioned race at all. But I'll go to my grave believing it was a factor. Not that Sol was racist himself, but he was worried the issue would kill box office in the South and in

South Africa and Southern Rhodesia, which back then were pretty important foreign markets. And combined with the graylisting, I think he anticipated double trouble.

But—and I'm unbelievably proud of Chance for doing this, and proud of myself for backing him up, since, honestly, I'm no hero and it could have gone either way—Chance told Irma Gold, who was his agent, he told her to tell the front office that either Bruce was in the picture or he himself wouldn't be. She tried to talk him out of it, she told him this was a fight he couldn't win, and he might hurt himself badly in the process, but he was rock solid. "Just tell them to consider us a package," he said. And fuck me if they didn't fold.

Now, the world gives a lot of credit to Kirk Douglas and to Otto Preminger for ending the blacklist a couple of years later by hiring Dalton Trumbo for *Spartacus* and *Exodus*, and maybe to Frank Perry for hiring Howard Da Silva a year or two after that for *David and Lisa*. And they all certainly deserve that credit. But Chance put an early crack in the wall, and I don't think anybody who wasn't directly involved knows about it.

Bruce Powers

THE JUDAS KISS MADE me. The movie was a huge success, and audiences accepted my character without any fuss. All that fear turned out to be based on nothing. People might not have wanted me in their living rooms or dating their daughter, but they seemed to be fine with me as Chance's pal. The reviews for the movie itself, for Chance, for me, were outstanding. There was no boycott from any of those right-wing groups the studio was so scared of, we did good business in the South, it all went incredibly smoothly. And I was launched. Never looked back. For a while there I was the busiest African American actor in show business besides Sid Poitier.

I owe my entire career to Chance Hardwick. He was, as we say in Hollywood, a *mensch*.

Briel Charpentier

AROUND THE TIME HE was making *The Judas Kiss*, we started seeing less of each other. Not a break-up, just a leveling off. It was partly practical…he was busy on that movie and all sorts of other projects, and he was living out in Malibu, which felt quite remote to me. And he had this whole new life based on his being a big star, and most of the time he said he hated it, and I believed him, but still, it came with the territory. Famous friends, a different kind of social life. Glamorous doings. He would have let me be part of it, but I was not comfortable with those people, I did not feel I belonged, and I also had a little feeling that sooner or later he might not like having me around at those times. I was from a separate part of his life. He might not want his two worlds to collide. This could have been my imagination, but I felt it and did not want to put it to the test.

And he had become very nervous about going out anywhere. Anywhere he couldn't control, that is. Restaurants, movie theaters, shops. Public places where fans might recognize him. Might mob him. The prospect of that really made him anxious. For example, we were at Pickwick Books one evening, just browsing before dinner, you know, and a crowd suddenly appeared, seemingly from out of nowhere. They surrounded him, and if you could have seen the look on his face…he was terrified. Terrified and angry. He tried to be a good fellow, he braced himself and forced a smile and signed some autographs and shook hands and thanked everybody, but he pulled me out of there as fast as he possibly could. We had planned to walk down the street to have dinner at Musso's, but he was too shaken. He said "No, let's just go back to your apartment, we can scramble some eggs or eat some cold cuts."

And also, I was starting to sell my pictures, and I was getting some commissions, so I was quite busy too. I could no longer just drop everything if he wanted to see me. He still used to come over to my studio while I painted when he had some free time, but it was rarer than it once was. I think he liked it when it happened, though. He could just be Chance Hardwick, not [holds up hands to indicate a marquee] *Chance Hardwick,* and he valued that. And he said he loved my work. He bought one of my canvases. It was one of my first big sales, and it was the first picture he bought for his new house. "Don't give me a discount on it," he said. "I mean to pay full price." And he did!

Things were different between us, though. I still loved him and I think he still loved me, but his life had changed so drastically. We couldn't pretend things were still the same. He was famous, he was rich, he was a star. That changes you in ways you can't imagine. He used to talk to me about it. Not happily. It was the opposite of bragging. He often sounded despairing. I think the last couple of years of his life were very unhappy, I'm sad to say. He had got what he wanted and he discovered he did not want it after all. He didn't like it. But there was no giving it back.

I will tell you one happy memory, though. It's a little embarrassing, perhaps, a little intimate, but I think I am too old to allow myself to feel embarrassed about such things anymore. He once suggested we go to a drive-in movie. We could sometimes go to regular theaters, we would call the theater and make arrangements to be slipped in and seated in the back after the theater was already dark. But that still made him nervous. He was afraid he might somehow be recognized, and it was also something of a bother to arrange. So he suggested we go to this drive-in instead, where no one would see us. It was a thing I had never done, watch a movie in a car, and it sounded like fun. A typical American experience. And after we parked and put the loud speaker in the window, he suggested we sit in the back seat, he said it would be more comfortable. And after a while…well, okay, what happened was, we actually made love in his car while the movie was playing. "This is how American teenagers first have sex," he told me. Is that true, do you think?

Well, true or not, I have to say it was really fun.

From Proteus—The Films of Chance Hardwick by Gordon Frost

"…IN THE JUDAS KISS, his swan song and by general consensus his greatest performance, Hardwick plays Lucas Penny, an investigative reporter who has gone undercover, infiltrating a fascistic terrorist group as research for a magazine exposé. But as he develops relationships within the group, forming unexpected friendships and one love passionate affair, his loyalties begin to divide in ways he has not anticipated. No one ever played ambivalence better than Chance Hardwick; every pained emotion and agonized spasm of guilt can be read in the actor's eyes. And when his character ultimately finds himself in a position where he must kill or reveal his true identity and thus be killed himself, Hardwick wordlessly conveys the essence of a divided, mortified soul. His work here has remained a touchstone for serious actors of every succeeding generation, a legendary cinematic performance."

Mark Cernovic

ONE AFTERNOON I WAS in Chance's office on the Metro lot, we were discussing possible future projects, and his telephone rang. And he picked up and listened for a minute, and he looked very surprised, even shocked, and then he said, in that menacing low growl he used when he was really angry—either when he was acting angry or when he was angry for real—he said, "Tell him to go to hell," and hung up.

And then muttered something like "fuck" or "shit" or "Christ." He looked…I don't want to say shaken, but…put out. More than put out.

Well, it's rude to ask people about their phone calls, and especially when it's a person as private and reserved as Chance, so I exercised some self-control and didn't say anything. But the look on my face must have said plenty, because he shrugged and laughed a little self-consciously—revealing any genuine emotion in front of anyone else always made him uncomfortable, is my impression; he reserved displays of feeling for his work, so he must have felt he'd permitted me a glimpse of something he didn't want anyone to see—and he said, in this amazingly off-hand, casual way, which I assume he must have struggled to achieve, he said, "My father's at the studio gate. My biological father. Wendell Hardwick Sr. I've never even met the motherfucker, but now it seems his paternal feelings have awoken."

I didn't know whether I should respond at all. There were so many ways any answer might be the wrong answer. But saying nothing obviously wouldn't do either. So I said, "You aren't curious?"

And he said, "Not in the slightest."

And that was apparently that. Now, looking back, it's hard for me to believe the guy gave up after one shot. If I had to guess, I'd guess that he kept pestering Chance, and Chance finally had to buy him off to get him to go away and stay away. Probably gave him some money and at the same time threatened him with a restraining order. But that's just speculation on my part. It's not something I would have asked Chance about, not in a million years.

Letter from Jerome Goldhagen, MD (psychiatrist)

DEAR PROFESSOR FROST:

I am in receipt of your letter of 5th September.

It is with sincere regret that I must decline your invitation to be interviewed on the subject of Chance Hardwick. Not only would the contents of our sessions together be privileged, if he in fact had ever been a client of mine, but I regard it as ethically impermissible to either confirm or deny that Mr. Hardwick or anyone else ever consulted me professionally. Clients need to feel their therapy is and will remain a matter exclusively between themselves and their therapists.

This should in no way be interpreted as confirmation that I ever met with, or indeed ever even met, Mr. Hardwick. It is simply a statement of general professional principle to which I unfailingly adhere.

I trust you will understand my position. I do, however, wish you every success with your book and indeed I look forward to reading it.

Sincerely yours,

Jerome Goldhagen

Briel Charpentier

AFTER THE JUDAS KISS came out and was a big success, Chance was one of the biggest stars in the world, and the studio PR Department all of a sudden changed its mind and decided it might be good for Chance and me to be known as a couple. I think that might have had as much to do with my becoming somewhat better known as an artist as anything to do with Chance. I was beginning to make a name for myself, and they might have thought it would add to Chance's prestige if he had this exotic girlfriend who painted. And who had an accent! So even though we were seeing less of each other at this point, we were instructed to be public with our relationship. I didn't mind—lying low had always bothered me a bit, like there was something dirty about it, something we had to keep hidden—and I guess Chance didn't mind either, or didn't mind so much as to refuse.

So that's how that *Life Magazine* spread came to be. They came to my studio, which I guess they thought was the most photogenic location, or maybe Chance wouldn't let them into his house on the beach. He came over and hung out the way he sometimes did—that wasn't fake—and they took pictures of him lounging around on the sofa watching me work and of me pretending to paint, and of the two of us eating lunch on a blanket on the floor of the studio, picnic style. Then, later, they took us down to Beverly Park, that dinky amusement park on Beverly Boulevard right near La Cienega, to pretend to go on some of the rides. Very cheesy!

Chance and I were embarrassed about it all, but I guess it must have looked cute. My mother, with whom I was having practically no contact, somehow saw it in Paris and wrote to tell me how adorable the two of us looked. She was thrilled to discover I was dating Chance Hardwick, something I had not shared with her. But she knew who he was, which told me something about how famous he had become. Many of my friends saw it and were excited for me, for all the wrong reasons, and I would sometimes now get stopped in supermarkets and places like that. People would ask if I was the girl who was dating Chance Hardwick. Sometimes they even asked for *my* autograph. [laughs] But in addition, I started selling more paintings. That this might be the result of our affair becoming known did not even occur to me, but I now could see why people were willing to pay money for public relations consultants. Publicity can make a big difference. It validates, no? Confers…legitimacy.

Irma Gold

THE JUDAS KISS WAS such a monster hit that when Chance told me he wanted to take a long break before his next picture, I didn't feel I could argue with him. Or needed to. Not this time. He could afford to take some time off. He was an established star now. More than that. He was a superstar. Plus, I didn't think there was much doubt that he, and the picture, would get plenty of recognition when awards season rolled around. People weren't going to forget him.

He seemed very drained when we had this conversation. Depressed, tired, maybe even a little fed-up. Which was odd, since he'd just done this great movie, he'd been great in it and was garnering all sorts of raves from the critics, he was rich, he was famous, he was widely respected by his peers in the industry. I mean, what more could a guy want? Well, genius is mysterious, isn't it? Geniuses are wired differently, maybe, their emotions work differently from other people's. Temperament is a mysterious thing, and it can enable great work and also take you down deep, deep rabbit holes. I just wish I'd realized at the time that he was going through a real crisis. I wish I'd known how serious this depression of his was. I'm not sure I could have done anything to help him, but at least I would have tried. Instead, I had this cavalier attitude, like he was being something of a self-indulgent child but he'd been such a good boy up to now I was willing to allow him to brood.

The one bright spot in this conversation was when he said he thought he might want to do a play. Refresh his theater chops. It was the only time he seemed even slightly animated, when he told me that. So I thought to myself, "Fine, go ahead and do it if you think it will make you happy." [sighs]

Mark Cernovic

I INVITED CHANCE TO meet me for lunch at this Cuban place I liked in Culver City. Funky, noisy, crowded, but the food was good, and it had the additional benefit that we wouldn't be surrounded by industry types. For the conversation I had in mind, I thought it would be better for us to meet away from the Executive Office Building and far from our colleagues.

See, I had a proposal for him. We'd worked so well together on *The Judas Kiss*, and we'd gotten along so great on a personal level—I'd go so far as to say we'd become good friends, although it wasn't always easy to be sure where you stood with Chance—and we seemed to see eye-to-eye on creative issues, so I suggested to him we ought to consider forming our own independent production company, maybe under the Metro umbrella. It would give us more artistic control and also guarantee we'd see a lot more money if our pictures were successful. We could develop our own projects, projects that interested us, working with writers and directors we trusted. I was picturing something along the lines of Hecht-Hill-Lancaster. That was my model. It just seemed like a great idea. More autonomy, more profits. I thought he'd jump at it.

But he didn't. He said he wasn't sure what his future plans were, he wasn't sure where he'd be in the next year or what he wanted to do with himself. He was nice about it, he said he thought under other circumstances it would have been a great plan and he thought I'd make a great partner, but he was rethinking everything about his life and career, so it wasn't the right time for that kind of commitment.

Of course in retrospect this all seems pretty ominous. Was he already contemplating ending his life? Was that what he was talking about, however indirectly? I've pondered that question for decades now. Tortured myself with it. Wondered if there were warning signs I was too obtuse to notice. Wondered if there was anything I might have done to prevent what happened.

Gil Fraser

EVER SINCE HE STARTED work on *The Judas Kiss*, we'd barely seen each other at all. Whenever I called him he kept the conversation brief, and whenever I proposed going out and grabbing a bite or bowling a couple of frames, he said no, he just didn't feel up to it. I got the feeling that...well, I wasn't taking it personally. I thought he must be going through a bad spell. It happens. It can happen even when to the outside world it looks like you're riding high.

But then he called me out of the blue and after a few preliminaries he asked me a very unexpected question: Had I read much Shakespeare? So I said I'd read some in college but not since. And he asked me if I thought I could play Shakespeare. And even though I figured he was asking for a reason, and it might even involve a potential job, I thought I should answer honestly since we'd always been straight with one another. So I told him no, while I thought I could probably play the attitudes all right, I had a notion the diction was outside my skill set. It's important to know your strengths and weaknesses, you know? And while it's good to challenge yourself creatively, it's not so good to bang your head against a wall in order to prove how game you are.

And he said, "Yeah, I'm afraid you're right. Good call, Gil. I'm disappointed, but thanks for being upfront."

It was a few weeks later that I heard about *Richard III*. No regrets, though. I mean, aside from how things turned out, that surely wouldn't have played to my forehand.

Benny Ludlow

I HAD A GIG at this little club in the valley, and one Friday night Chance came in to see me. Didn't tell me he was coming—I woulda been happy to get him comped, but he just showed up unannounced. I had a great set that night, thank God. Good sized crowd, the act clicked. Sometimes it does, sometimes not so much. And I could hear Chance laughing out there in the dark, which was nice.

Afterward, we went out for a drink. And he started quizzing me about stand-up. About what it was like physically, about how I prepared emotionally, about what it felt like to score, what it felt like to bomb. What did I do with my hands? Did I ever ad lib? How did I time the laughs? Some personally probing questions, some mainly technical questions. And I tried to answer, and the questions kept coming, and I finally said, "Christ, you're not thinking of becoming a comic, are you? 'Cause I don't recommend it."

And he said, "No, no, this is just research, Benny."

I never did find out what that meant.

James Sterling

CHANCE HADN'T SEEMED EXCITED or enthusiastic about much of anything in months. We didn't see a lot of each other during the time he was filming *The Judas Kiss* or in the immediate aftermath, and those rare times we did, he seemed dour and down. But when he came to see me this particular day, he seemed pretty upbeat for a change. A nice change.

He said he wanted to run an idea past me. He'd been thinking about *Richard III*, he said. And he thought, while the play itself is of course terribly dark, Richard himself needn't be, at least not till the end. Things are going great for Richard and he's having fun. In fact, according to Chance, he's almost a comedian. He's dealing with the audience like a stand-up, taking them into his confidence, relating to them on this personal, amusing level. He's amusing himself *and* us. And Chance thought it would be interesting to play it that way, inviting the audience in to laugh along with him at the chaos he's wreaking and the way he's outmaneuvering everybody and the way all his nefarious schemes seem to be working out. So I listened, and then told him I thought it was a valid idea, and an interesting one.

"Great," he said. "Would you be willing to direct?"

I was taken aback. I thought he'd simply been trying out an interesting notion on me. But he made it clear he was thinking of mounting a stage production locally. And I have to admit I was intrigued. I started in the theater, back in New York. I always felt it was my natural home. And directing a play—it was something I hadn't done in decades. Since my student days. And to direct an actor as gifted as Chance Hardwick! My God, what an opportunity.

So that's how that production got going.

Bruce Powers

No ONE USED THE expression "non-traditional casting" back then. There was no need to, since no one had thought of the concept. It simply didn't happen. You might do an all-black production, although that would be a novelty unless you were doing something like that Marc Connelly play, what's it called, *The Green Pastures*. But to cast an African American actor in what was traditionally a white role in the middle of a largely white cast, that just wasn't done. I don't mean frowned upon, I mean completely unheard of. Nobody thought of the concept even in order to reject it. But as usual, Chance was ahead of his time.

When he phoned me and asked how I felt about Shakespeare, did I have much experience with him, had I read much of him, I said yeah, I had taken a Shakespeare class in college and had done several Shakespeare scenes in acting classes. So then he asked me if I might be interested in playing Clarence in *Richard III*. At first I thought he was joking. I said, "First you have to tell me how a colored guy might get to fifteenth-century England. And find himself at court." And he said, "You let me worry about that. Do you think you can do it?"

Hell, I *knew* I could do it.

James Sterling

WE ASSEMBLED A STRONG cast. People were thrilled to do live theater, especially Shakespeare, and they were thrilled to be working with Chance. Also, I'd like to think they were pleased at the prospect of working with me. We did find a lot of our people from among my former students, which no doubt helped. But I only recommended the best of the best.

The only one to turn us down flat was Dolores Murray. I don't know why. We wanted her for Lady Anne. She would have been terrific, I believe. And you'd think any actor worth his or her salt would have walked on hot coals for a chance like this. But Dolly, without giving a reason, said she wasn't interested. Chance was powerfully disappointed, that I can tell you. Well, *c'est la vie.*

I guess a lot of people with twenty-twenty hindsight would say she was prescient.

Bruce Powers

REHEARSALS WENT WELL. THEY were lots of fun. Jim and Chance generally agreed on what the production was supposed to be— Jim was inventive with the staging and especially attentive to the lighting, which proved to be an interesting factor. He spotlit Chance during the soliloquies. It was almost as if Chance was performing a solo set in a nightclub. And Chance was really laugh-out-loud funny in some of his scenes. Full of mischief, you know. Eyebrows raised in delight at his own deviltry. It was almost enough to make you forget how evil the character is as you laughed along with him. And then it would suddenly be brought home to you, so you'd feel almost like you'd had a hand in the awful things the character does. You felt dirty for enjoying it, which is, I think, part of what Shakespeare was aiming at.

I loved doing it. They can't take that away from me. Despite everything, I'll go to my grave thinking it was a terrific production and a terrific piece of theater, and I'm proud to have been associated with it.

George Berlin

IT WAS AFTER CHANCE had become a really major star, after *The Judas Kiss*, that I got a note from him. I was shocked. I hadn't heard from him since he'd left college. Of course I'd been following his career from afar, but we'd had no contact. Zero. Nada.

It was a short note. But hand-written, so it really did come from him, not some assistant. He just said he was going to produce and star in a production of *Richard III* at a theater in LA, and that immersing himself in the play made him think of me. He said he wanted to thank me for giving him time and attention and encouragement during a period of his life when he needed all of those. So that was a huge surprise—it would never have occurred to me to think he even remembered who I was—and it was also the sort of thing that makes teaching seem like a worthwhile enterprise.

James Sterling

WE GOT BUTCHERED.

They called the production pretentious, inane, sophomoric. One critic even called it flatulent, whatever that means in this context. They said Chance was mannered, ridiculous, clueless, totally out of his depth. They made fun of the casting of Bruce, saying it was a cheap stunt, which I think offended Bruce deeply. Hell, it offended all of us, reducing that fine actor to his race and nothing else. Oh, they were vicious.

Part of it was just that usual thing, that journalistic thing of building someone up and then feeling the need to take him down a peg. It was Chance's turn. "We can kiss you, but that doesn't mean we can't kick you when we feel like it." He'd received nothing but raves for years, he was riding about as high as an actor can ride—deservedly so—and maybe there was a general sense in the industry that it had gone far enough for the time being, he might be in need of a good whupping.

And doing Shakespeare—I mean, that's just flat-out asking for it, right? An actor known for his performances in the demotic, as you might say, playing ordinary Americans, country boys, roughs, suddenly having the gall to assay a classical role. One of the great classical roles, with a tradition going straight back to Burbage. And a royal! So their judgment was clouded by their prejudice. They simply couldn't see how good he was. They probably didn't care in any case, but I'm willing to bet they weren't able to even notice. They went in with an attitude and they came out with the same attitude. Nothing they saw in between was going to have any effect. They'd been lying in wait. They could have written their reviews in the afternoon before they went to the theater.

But I don't think it was only that. Pardon me if this sounds paranoid, but I'm 100 percent sure politics played a role too. *The Times* and *The Examiner* were both right-wing papers in those days. *The Examiner* was a Hearst paper, need I say more? And although *The Times* mellowed a bit after young Otis took over, back then both papers were red-baiting, reactionary rags. So they treated the casting of Bruce Powers like it was a deliberate thumb in their eye. They were still fuming about his being cast in *The Judas Kiss*, of course—and of course their reviews of that picture criticized him just for being him, if in a roundabout, oblique way. But Chance's casting him again, and in Shakespeare, no less—hiring a black man who was also a known lefty to play a

British peer who speaks in blank verse—this gave them a golden opportunity to unload for both transgressions, and they took it. Boy did they take it. And then there was me, a blacklisted actor directing. And of course by now Chance was known to have liberal politics, so he was a ripe target for them too, even though he'd never been much of a radical. In retrospect, I can see we were basically asking for it. And they went about their task with glee. *Variety* and *The Hollywood Reporter* followed the lead. It was as if they'd all got the same memo.

So listen. You could question things about the production. You could take issue with the concept behind it, you could say it was too cute or too clever or too extrinsic, too imposed upon the text, if that was your honest feeling. And my direction no doubt had its weak spots. I'm not claiming I did a perfect job, although I flatter myself it was damned good. But regardless, any objective observer would have to agree that the performances were all terrific, and Chance—once you grant him his basic choice—was about as brilliant as anyone I've ever been privileged to witness on the stage. But none of that helped. Those reviews doomed us. We closed after five performances.

Bruce Powers

WE HAD A CLOSING night party in the theater. It was a pretty down affair, as you might imagine. The only moment I really remember— we all had a lot to drink that night, so the whole thing is a bit hazy— but when Chance entered from his dressing room, having cleaned off his make-up and changed back into street clothes, we all rose up to give him a rousing ovation. There were quite a few tears, too. Everybody felt it had been a great show. We felt we'd been fucked over by the local critics. They did a hit job on us. And we were just in awe of Chance's talent. Not to mention his guts.

Gil Fraser

I HAD LUNCH WITH Chance a couple of weeks after *Richard III* closed. At the Polo Room. Fancy-schmancy, right? Well, he could afford it now—he insisted on paying, of course—and it was one of the few places in town where he could be pretty confident about not being mobbed. People are cool about celebrities there, deferential and discreet. That's part of what you're paying for.

I had to wash my best pair of jeans to look semirespectable, so that was a pain. I would've been just as happy at the Hamlet. You should have seen the way the staff fawned over him! It was quite a display. Seriously. I half-expected the waitress to give him a blowjob while he examined his menu. I said to him, "So *this* is what it's like to be a star." He just gave me his notorious twisted smile.

But for all that, it turned out to be a very somber meal. I'd seen him down before, but never quite like this. I tried to cheer him up, I told him to ignore the *Richard* reviews, everybody gets bad reviews, plus there was all that extraneous political shit, and besides, critics hate it when an artist steps out of the pigeon hole they've stuck him in so they take it out on the artist. I told him I admired his *Richard III*—I'd already told him the same thing opening night, and I meant it both times, but it seemed to need repeating here—and I praised his movies and told him I thought he was a lock on the Oscar that year and...you know, I tried to be a good friend and a supportive colleague.

But he said, "Nah, thanks for saying all that, but it isn't the show. The reviews pissed me off, but, shit, like you say, bad reviews come with the territory. Critics love to build you up and then knock you down, I'm aware of that. And besides, there have been times I deserved bad notices and got raves, so that side of things more or less balances out. I might feel bad for the cast and for Jimmy, but for myself, I just chalk the whole thing up to experience."

"Then what *is* eating you?"

He sighed. Big involuntary sigh. "I don't know, Gil. I honestly don't know. It feels like...*I* feel like I've...like I've disappeared. Do you know what I mean? With all the stardom nonsense and the publicity and the reviews and overwork and the strategic socializing and my picture in the papers and in the magazines, and Hedda and Louella making up shit about me...it's like I don't even know who I am anymore. I don't even know *if* I am anymore. It's like there's this Chance Hardwick out there everyone thinks they know, and he's a total stranger to me, and then there's me, this little homunculus denuded of his soul, cowering on a moth-eaten sofa in a bare room watching the hoopla through a crack in the window and wondering who this guy is that they're talking about."

"I'm sure everybody feels that way from time to time," I told him. Still trying to cheer him up.

"Maybe. But I feel that way *all* the time. It's like some essential part of myself has been cannibalized. They've chewed it up, they've swallowed every part of me except this shell of a body that goes where it's told and smiles when it doesn't feel like it. The only times I feel real is when I'm playing a part." And then he said, "I honestly can't take much more of this, Gil. I just want to disappear."

"Isn't it what you always wanted?"

He trotted out a very good Bogie impression. He said, "I was misinformed."

Briel Charpentier

I DIDN'T UNDERSTAND MUCH about American politics at the time. I wasn't a citizen yet, and after what my country had been through, politics in any form was something I preferred to avoid. If the government would just leave me and my friends alone, I didn't care too much. Besides, American politics reminded me more of a football match than a contest about government. It seemed like you rooted for your team, you wanted your team to win, that that was the main thing.

But this was the summer the Democratic Party was having its convention in Los Angeles, you know, so suddenly politics was everywhere. It was all anyone was talking about. Most of the people I knew were Democrats, and even though I couldn't see much difference between the two parties myself, it was obvious there was a lot of excitement about the Democrats coming here.

Chance really liked Adlai Stevenson. He wanted Stevenson to run again, he thought he could win this time, could defeat Nixon. He told me Stevenson was the most intelligent and the most civilized of all the politicians. When Kennedy was nominated instead, Chance was disappointed. He was suspicious of Kennedy, you know, because he was so rich, and because of his father. But he finally changed his mind. Frank Sinatra invited Chance to a party to meet Kennedy—those kinds of people, people like Frank Sinatra, they now regarded Chance as being one of them, so he was on their lists for such events—and Chance went and was impressed. By Kennedy, I mean. And he became enthusiastic. He gave money, he made some personal appearances, he even filmed a TV ad for the campaign, mostly talking about Kennedy's heroism in the war. That was the script they gave him. He told me, "Of all the reasons I'm for Kennedy, what he did in the war is very far down the list." But he did what they asked.

And he made me watch the debates with him. And I must say, I liked Kennedy more after watching those debates. I became enthusiastic too. He seemed...in French we say *sympathique*. I would have been very unhappy if Nixon became president. He was not *sympathique*. I was very unhappy when he *did* become president, but of course that was years later, a very different time, and by then I was an American myself, you know, and was able to vote. I cannot say I loved the choices I was offered that year, but I did vote.

But that's all by the way. I am telling you this information about Chance and Kennedy, which in truth is not so interesting in itself, only because of one rather macabre detail. Sometime that autumn, in fact it was Halloween night—which I remember because we were out at Malibu on Halloween and all these kids came to his door, rich kids I guess, because for one thing they were inside the Colony gate, and also because they were wearing very elaborate costumes, like professional-type costumes, and Chance gave them all candy even though some of them demanded money, they said Jack Benny gave out money at his house, and Chance was offended, both by their rudeness and by their being so entitled, and he said, "Then by all means go there, all you're going to get from me is candy"—but anyway, this night, Chance mentioned to me something he had recently read. He said he had read that the number of people who die in the weeks before a presidential election is much smaller than other times. People, even very ill people, even terminal people, are so curious to see how the election will turn out that they somehow *hold off dying*. And considering that Chance died less than a fortnight after the election...well, you can see why this might have stayed in my memory.

Martha Davis (reporter, Variety)

THE CORONER RULED IT an accident by drowning. I don't think too many people were convinced, but it's how they handle deaths that aren't clear-cut suicides, calling them accidents, especially when the decedents are celebrities. To spare the immediate family, no doubt, and to protect the dead person's reputation. And it *could* have been an accident, I suppose. It's remotely possible. He didn't leave a note. That was considered significant. The presence of a note would have made a suicide verdict unavoidable of course, and its absence allowed them to fudge the business and call it an accident. And listen, the undertow around Malibu can be treacherous, that's well known around here. Especially in the cold months and when the tide's going out. People in Southern California warn their kids about the undertow the way folks in other places warn their kids about talking to strangers. But still, let's be real...

Heather Brooke (neighbor)

OF COURSE THE POLICE came around and asked a lot of questions. I didn't have much to tell them. When you have a famous neighbor—and here in Malibu a lot of your neighbors are famous—when that's the case, you don't crowd them. Dan and I would wave to Chance if we saw him on the beach or whatever, he'd wave back. He might say "Good morning" if we were getting into our cars to go to work at the same time, that sort of thing. We had perfectly friendly, neighborly relations. But we weren't close at all. We didn't socialize. Dan and I had never even seen the inside of his house.

So as to whether it was suicide...I don't know more than anyone else. No particular insight. On the one hand you might say, "Who goes into the ocean in November?" I mean, people do, I suppose, and it was pretty warm that day. But the ocean is damned cold in November even on warm days. And the man had a swimming pool. A *heated* swimming pool. If he just wanted to take a dip, he didn't have to come down to the beach.

On the other hand, the cops found a beach towel out there, and a movie script he was apparently reading, and a pencil for making notes, and his glasses. So that sure doesn't sound like...I mean, if you're planning to end it all, you don't need a towel, and you don't bring unfinished work along. Why bother? It's going to stay unfinished forever, right?

So I can argue it either way. I guess we'll never know for sure.

Bernice Franklin (secretary)

I USED TO WORK for an accountant, Lester Strong. He was one of the partners in the firm. Garten, Moscow, & Strong. They had a lot of show business clients, and Chance Hardwick was one of them. When Lester was alive, he instructed me to never tell anybody what I'm about to tell you, and I never have. Up till now. Of course, I was never asked before. Nobody thought to ask. Not until you, Mr. Frost. And at this point, I just can't see the harm in it.

I was Lester's personal assistant—you understand that, right? That's all. Not a colleague or anything. He didn't share a lot of information with me. Men didn't treat their secretaries as equals in those days, we were just...we were "the girls," that's how the partners referred to me and the other secretaries in the firm. "I'll ask the girl to bring us some coffee," like that. It seems really obnoxious now, but at the time we just took it for granted. It was like the smog we all breathed back then, so much a part of our lives we didn't even think about it. But the thing is, when you work in an office, you pick up all sorts of info whether you want to or not, and whether people intend to share it with you or not. So I do know Chance must have had a lot of money, because if you didn't have a lot of money the firm wouldn't even accept you as a client, and I know...see, here's the thing, the thing Lester didn't want me to talk about...[lowers voice] In the days before he died, Chance Hardwick made some very generous gifts to people. I don't know the exact sums, but Lester sort of hinted that they were substantial. Hardwick died intestate, but he sent these checks to his mother, and to his aunt, and to his sister. And to that artist, the French woman he was supposedly dating. And there was some clinic in Pennsylvania, in the Appalachian region, I think the name of the guy who ran it was Dr. Denny. One of the checks Hardwick sent was to that guy's clinic. Maybe he was like a cousin or something.

And because I handled Lester's incoming and outgoing, I was aware of this. And the day after Hardwick's death, Lester pulled me into his office and shut the door behind him and told me I absolutely must keep my mouth shut about those checks. I think…I think Lester believed those checks, especially considering their timing, could be construed as evidence that Chance Hardwick had committed suicide. Had planned it out in advance and taken care of personal business and then done it. And Lester felt his relationship with his clients was privileged and that there was no reason to share such information with anyone else. Hardwick was just as dead whether it was an accident or a suicide. What difference could it make what the coroner said?

Gil Fraser

YOU KNOW WHAT STILL gets me after all these years? All the things Chance didn't live to see. The Kennedy assassination. Vietnam. The Beatles. I mean, he used to sneer at rock music, he loved jazz and dismissed rock as jejune and brainless. But what would he have made of *Sgt. Pepper*? Of Bob Dylan? Or of the other great music from that period? What about Harold Pinter and Tom Stoppard? *The Sopranos* and *The Wire*? Barack Obama, for fuck's sake? You see what I mean? All that stuff would have fascinated him, would have thrilled him, would have horrified him. And it just kills me that he never got to see any of it, and I never got to hear how he felt about it all.

Dorothy Goren Mckenzie

IT WAS GIL WHO called with the news. Which I realize in retrospect was sweet of him, or maybe brave of him. He didn't have to. Breaking something like that to next of kin isn't a pleasant task.

He was sobbing, which surprised me, since I could never have pictured a tough guy like Gil crying. [begins to cry] And then I was sobbing too. And for a while we couldn't even talk, we just wept at each other over the phone. And then we hung up. There was nothing more to say.

And I told my mom and Aunt Mary and all three of us started crying like it was one of those Arab funerals, with the women keening and ululating. I don't think we ever got over it, any of us. My mom died pretty soon after, and though grief is never an official cause of death, nor heartbreak, I think in some fundamental way my mom died of grief. I think her heart broke. She never really knew Chance—none of us did, he was unknowable, even Gil said something like that—but it was still a colossal loss. Just realizing he wasn't there anymore. And coming to realize she hadn't been much of a mother to him. When all the tributes started, well, that was almost unbearable. It was like the world was appropriating him. Appropriating our Chance. But I guess that's how it works when great people die. It's the world's loss every bit as much as his loved ones'.

Briel Charpentier

I HAD NOT TALKED to Gil in several months. Without Chance as our connection, we lost touch a little bit, you know. I saw him at the memorial, and we were both invited to the unveiling of the headstone and we embraced there. But other than that, there had not been any contact. And then, to my surprise, he phoned me in March and suggested we watch the Oscars together. That was sweet of him. He's much more thoughtful than he sometimes appears.

So we were watching at his place. He'd moved out of the apartment on Holloway after Chance left, he now was renting a little house in the Silver Lake. So I went over there. He'd ordered pizza, so we were eating pizza and drinking wine—I'd brought a bottle of wine even though I knew Gil was more of a beer person—and we were watching the Oscars, and we became tenser and tenser as they got closer to the best actor category. Neither of us could eat by then or say anything, we were too nervous, the pizza was getting cold in its box on the coffee table and we were both leaning forward, watching the television intently. And then they announced that Chance had won, and the audience erupted, and Mark Cernovic went up to accept the award for Chance, and Gil and I looked at each other and we both just burst into tears. It's funny...I didn't cry when I first heard about his death, maybe it was too much of a shock, I just went numb. And I didn't cry at his memorial, maybe at most a tear in the corner of my eye. But I cried a lot when he won the Academy Award. I couldn't stop for the longest time.

Ward Paulsen (Memorial Park groundskeeper)

PEOPLE TALK ABOUT CHANCE Hardwick's grave, they come here sometimes and ask me to direct them to it. But they've got it wrong, of course. The body was never recovered. That often happens with these drowning incidents, I'm told. The victims are washed out to sea, and that's what I heard happened with Mr. Hardwick. His mother and aunt and sister flew out here and erected a memorial to him. With a really nice headstone. They didn't count pennies. There was a pretty big service at a church in Hollywood first, a lot of people went to that, big stars and just regular people, and then a few invited guests came out here for the unveiling of the memorial.

It's interesting they picked LA. I guess he never really cared for his hometown, he liked it better out here. This was the place where he settled. And now he's settled here permanently, hasn't he? [laughs briefly] Sorry. You start to have a kind of sick sense of humor when you work long enough at a place like this. It's the only way not to become nutty.

Yeah, people still come out here to leave flowers and notes and things. Even videocassettes of his movies. I guess those aren't much use for anything else anymore. [laughs] But it's been what? Sixty years? Something along those lines. And they still show up. The woman in black, of course, she's famous, a legend. We see her pretty often, and not, by the way, only on the anniversary of the drowning. That's the visit everyone talks about, but she shows up at other times too. Usually late at night, when no one's around. No one but me. I see her walking up the path in the dark, just a shadow, black on black. On the actual anniversary, people sometimes come and wait around for her, like they're whale-watching or something, but she keeps out of sight until the place has mostly emptied out. I run interference for her sometimes, let her know when the coast is on the clear side, flash her a signal. She sometimes gives me a little tip, slips me a century every once in a while. She doesn't have to do that, I'd be happy to help out for free, but I guess she appreciates being able to pay her respects without an audience watching, so she gives me a little thank-you present. It might be a sort of insurance policy too.

That's why the photos of her are always from a distance. She avoids the crowds and the photographers. The, whatchamacallem, the paparazzi. But seriously, even if they waited around till midnight or whenever she chose to show up, what would they see? An old lady in black, wearing a hat and a veil, kneeling down by a headstone, leaving a little bouquet? What's so exciting about that? It's not like she talks to anybody. You get too close, she disappears.

But I tell you, folks are lunatics when it comes to celebrities. They want to see stars' homes, stars' costumes, stars' graves. Judy Garland's shoes, for Christ's sake! They even pay to see wax models of stars at that cheesy Madame Tussaud's place over the hill there on Hollywood Boulevard. I don't get that at all. I was born in LA, I've lived here all my life, and that kind of thing puzzles the hell out of me.

But anyway, the woman in black isn't the only one. Other people come too. Just regular folk. Lotta teenage girls, and women who *used* to be teenage girls. But not only them. All types, from all over. Fewer than used to, but we get a few a week maybe. And they show up in shorts and tee shirts and sandals, I mean no respect at all. They ask me where Hardwick's grave is. I don't bother correcting 'em anymore, I just point 'em down the path over there. The first ten years or so after he died, we were a major tourist destination— it was like we were on one of those maps of the stars' homes they sell out on the street. I swear I don't get it, but people wanted to visit the site. I guess they figure Hardwick's buried here, they make that mistake, they think they'll be near his body, but even still, I just don't get it at all. Let's say he *was* buried here, what does visiting the site do for you that just looking at a photo or watching one of his old movies or just thinking about the guy doesn't do? But they come. It's dwindled down to just a few now, a few every week like I said, but come they do. If you go look—it's along that path to your right—you'll see the stuff they leave: flowers and poems and drawings and even candy. Candy! That's *really* wacko. Not only is he not here, but even if he was, it's been a damned long time since he ate any fucking candy.

Afterword

Gordon Frost

THIS IS THE PART I didn't expect to write. I planned to keep myself out of it. But I was in California, having just wrapped up all my scheduled interviews there, and I was due to fly back to New York the following day, when it suddenly struck me that we were approaching the date of Chance Hardwick's drowning. If I extended my stay by five days I could be around for that anniversary. Under the circumstances, it seemed worthwhile to change my plans. I called New York and cancelled my classes for the week. I negotiated a longer stay with my hotel and for my rental car.

Keeping busy in Southern California for several days, especially for a student of film like myself, was not a daunting challenge. Using my writings and my own brief producing career as an entrée, I was able to secure access to a number of studio lots, production offices, film archives, and even the Motion Picture Home. Which last named is how I discovered Benny Ludlow, incidentally. The comedian. It was pure serendipity. I wasn't looking for him and wasn't even aware he lived there. I just stumbled on him playing gin rummy in one of the lounges. And although it's true his contributions to these pages aren't terribly large, I do believe they're interesting in themselves and do fill a gap.

When the anniversary day rolled around, or rather the night, since I waited till dusk, I drove over to Memorial Park, walked up the serpentine path, and found Ward Paulsen in his little office.

"Oh, hello, Professor," he said, when I stuck my head in. "What can I do you for?"

"I have a rather large favor to ask of you," I said to him.

His face darkened. "The woman in black?"

It's an important lesson I have to keep relearning: The fact that someone may not have a first-rate education, may not speak especially eloquently, may not be enormously erudite or possess a broad, encompassing world view, doesn't necessarily mean they're stupid. Ward Paulsen was obviously aware of the date; he had seen right through me and cut straight to the chase.

Which was a gift, in a way. I had anticipated having to perform a rather delicate quadrille, a slow, indirect, oh-so-coy dance of seduction. "Well, yes, in point of fact," I said. "I don't want to put you in an awkward position—"

"No can do, Professor. I promised her privacy. I gave my word."

"But listen, Ward. I won't expect to take much more than a minute or two of her time."

"But still—"

"And look, I understand you feel an obligation to her and that this causes you some discomfort, so I'm prepared to make it worth your while." To which he didn't say anything. For the first time in this brief exchange, he didn't immediately demur. I thought that might suggest a ray of hope. "A thousand dollars?" I said. "Could you see your way clear for a thousand dollars?" This represented a not insubstantial percentage of my publisher's advance, but I wanted to make a preemptive bid that would forestall any negotiation; I was prepared—no, prepared is the wrong word, none of this had been anticipated, I was simply, suddenly, impulsively willing—to be extravagant. And because I was traveling, I was carrying a large amount of cash.

"You're not gonna take up much of her time? You promise?"

"Word of honor. A few minutes maximum."

He sighed. "And you aren't gonna tell her about this conversation, right?"

"As far as she's concerned, I snuck past you when your back was turned."

He nodded. He didn't look happy, but on the other hand, he grabbed at the cash I handed him. "Okay," he said. "You know where the marker is?" I nodded. "Just wait in the shadow so you don't spook her. If she spots you, she'll disappear on you faster than you can say 'Jack Robinson.'"

"Right."

I wandered along the path till I got to the spot. I didn't want to cower behind someone else's tombstone—that seemed too creepy, too much like what it actually was, maybe. I don't want to sugarcoat this experience or make it seem nobler than it was. I was going to ambush her. No putting lipstick on that particular pig. So I sat myself down behind a tree and waited.

And waited. It was several hours—I almost dozed off once or twice—before, in the full, bright moonlight, I saw a figure approaching up the deserted path. Dressed all in black. Wearing a black hat. A dark veil. Walking very slowly, even haltingly, dignified and stately if a little unsteady. Holding a spray of flowers in a gloved hand. The figure got closer and closer, and when it finally reached the headstone, kneeled and placed the flowers on the ground.

My cue to pounce. I sprung up and approached, crossing the distance in three long strides. "Excuse me," I said, "I hate to bother you, but—"

He looked up. Shocked. Startled. Apparently terrified. That familiar handsome face was older now, the eyes somewhat sunken, with fine lines around the mouth and the forehead deeply creased, but there was no mistaking it.

"Oh my God," I heard myself saying. There was no volition involved; the words simply burst out of me. "It's *you!*"